'So many perfect romantic moments that made me melt. Just gorgeous'
Jules Wake

'A wonderful ray of reading sunshine'
Heidi Swain

'I fell completely and utterly in love . . . it had me glued to the pages'
Holly Martin

'A total hands-down treat. A book you'll want to
cancel plans and stay in with'
Pernille Hughes

'Sizzlingly romantic and utterly compelling, I couldn't put it down'
Alex Brown

'Bursting with warmth and wit'
Kirsty Greenwood

'Funny, sexy and sweep-you-off-your-feet-romantic'
Zara Stoneley

'Perfectly pitched between funny, sexy, tender and
downright heartbreaking. I loved it'
Jane Casey

'As hot & steamy as a freshly made hot chocolate, and as sweet
& comforting as the whipped cream & sprinkles that go on top'
Helen Fields

'Just brilliant. Sweet, sexy and sizzzzling. It was a pure joy to read'
Lisa Hall

'A little slice of a Cornish cream tea but without the calories'
Bella Osborne

'Perfect escapism, deliciously romantic. I was utterly transported'
Emily Kerr

'Utter perfection . . . a total gem'
Katy Colins

'Sexy, sweet and simmering with sunshine'
Lynsey James

A Cornish Love Story

Cressy grew up in South-East London surrounded by books and with a cat named after Lawrence of Arabia. She studied English at the University of East Anglia and now lives in Norwich with her husband David. *A Cornish Love Story* is her seventeenth novel and her books have sold a million copies worldwide. When she isn't writing, Cressy spends her spare time reading, returning to London, or exploring the beautiful Norfolk coastline.

If you'd like to find out more about Cressy, visit her on her social media channels. She'd love to hear from you!

📷 @cressmclaughlin
f /CressidaMcLaughlinAuthor

Also by Cressida McLaughlin

A Christmas Tail
The Canal Boat Café
The Canal Boat Café Christmas
The Once in a Blue Moon Guesthouse
The House of Birds and Butterflies
The Staycation
The Happy Hour

The Cornish Cream Tea series
The Cornish Cream Tea Bus
The Cornish Cream Tea Summer
The Cornish Cream Tea Christmas
The Cornish Cream Tea Wedding
Christmas Carols and a Cornish Cream Tea
The Cornish Cream Tea Holiday
The Cornish Cream Tea Bookshop
From Cornwall With Love

The Secret Bookshop series
The Secret Christmas Bookshop

Cressida McLaughlin

A Cornish Love Story

HarperCollins*Publishers*

HarperCollins*Publishers* Ltd
1 London Bridge Street,
London SE1 9GF

www.harpercollins.co.uk

HarperCollins*Publishers*
Macken House, 39/40 Mayor Street Upper
Dublin 1, D01 C9W8, Ireland

First published by HarperCollins*Publishers* Ltd 2025
1

Typeset in Birka by Palimpsest Book Production Limited, Falkirk, Stirlingshire

Printed and bound in the UK using 100% Renewable Electricity by CPI Group (UK) Ltd

For Mum and Dad

Prologue

Dear Connor,

Being apart from you is harder than I dreamed it could be, and I've done a lot of dreaming since I met you. Mostly, it's been about a future together, how we can navigate the differences between our families, which matter to them more than they do to us. From the moment I saw you, I believed that love was the strongest thing of all – that with it, we could survive anything. Love conquers all. *It's a schmaltzy phrase that I used to roll my eyes at, but with us it felt true. Now you're thousands of miles away, in New York, and neither of us are stupid enough to misunderstand your father: he wants you there, focusing on the business. My faith in us is like the stars that shine over Tyller Klos at night, sometimes obscured by the clouds that roll in, damp and doom-laden, and sometimes burning with a fierce intensity. But it's always there. I don't know about* conquering *anything, but we can hold strong together, can't we? I need you in my future.*

I love you and I miss you.
Yours always, Amelie xx

I let out a deep, satisfied sigh. I had known Ethan Sparks for only a month, and here I was, facing him cross-legged on my bed, reading him passages from my favourite book series, out loud. I flicked my eyes up to his face, then down to the book I held open in my lap.

'It's . . .' I had been about to dismiss it, which was pointless considering I'd just *read it out loud to him*, so it was obvious I cared about it, but Ethan spoke over me, as if he had known what I was about to do.

'It's very romantic,' he said. 'Amelie and Connor, they're your favourite love story?' He gestured behind me, to where the entire Cornish Sands series by S. E. Artemis was lined up in a neat row of tatty, well-read paperbacks – ten altogether – on the bookshelf above my white MDF desk. My carefully laid-out revision book and highlighters whispered at me – I had arranged the highlighters in rainbow order, because I needed a lot of small wins in my exam prep – but I turned away from them: I was allowed to take a break.

2

'Yes,' I said. 'It's a love story, but not a romance.'

He frowned, idly playing with the frayed hem of his jeans. His socks were wide stripes of blue, green and gold. It was March, and the coastal wind was raw and biting; we were still rugged up in hoodies after our walk on the beach. Ethan's was forest green, and highlighted the red tinge in his mess of auburn hair. 'What's the difference between a love story and a romance?' he asked.

I narrowed my eyes, pondering. Would he be grateful to have this valuable knowledge? Did eighteen-year-old boys need to know the difference? Would it help him at university? My stomach tightened with unease. We'd had one month and a few stolen kisses, but I didn't know exactly what we were, or whether I could start thinking about what would happen after the summer, when we went our separate ways. But already, I knew I wanted him in my life. Could he tell that, so quickly, I felt the same way about him as Amelie felt about Connor?

'A love story doesn't have to have a happy ending,' I told him, 'but a romance does. You read a book that's been sold as a romance and the characters don't end up together, it's basically literary treason.'

'I can't believe Amelie and Connor don't get their happy-ever-after.' He shook his head. I looked for traces of mockery, and found none. But then Ethan hadn't once mocked me. We teased each other, and it was like the sun breaking through clouds when he did, because he was serious and focused so much of the time.

3

I placed the book reverently on the duvet between us and folded my arms. 'All the other books in the series have happy endings, and then this – the last one, the *most* romantic one, it just . . . it doesn't.' I was still indignant about it. *The Whispers of the Sands* had come out a couple of years after I was born, so it wasn't as if a sequel was imminent, and a part of me felt silly for caring so deeply about something that was already over a decade old when I discovered it.

S. E. Artemis was a local author, but she hadn't published anything since Amelie and Connor's dramatic finale, and I often wondered if her move from Alperwick House on top of the cliffs to some-where smaller in the village had tied in with her putting away her typewriter. Could she no longer bear to live in the place that had inspired the grand house in her series?

'Connor *does* go off to America,' I told Ethan. 'They write all these wonderful letters to each other – they're sprinkled throughout the book, because they keep getting torn apart – and the story leads you towards this breathtakingly romantic reconciliation, but then he chooses his dad's business over Amelie.'

Ethan frowned. 'That is a pretty bleak ending.'

'It's the worst.' There must have been something in my tone – some of my heartbreak over a *book* – because Ethan's chuckle was a low, warming rumble, then he was on his knees on my bed, drawing me into his arms and kissing the top of my head. The gentle brush of his lips sent a tingle right through me.

'Maybe one day you'll write the right one,' he said into my hair, and I leaned back to look at him.

'I don't mean for Amelie and Connor,' he explained. 'You're a great writer, Georgie. I can't wait until you publish your own book. When you're in control, you can write *your own* stories with the endings *you* want.'

I hoped my smile was nonchalant, but thought I was probably a long way off. Ethan and I were still so new, but he already believed in my writing, and the way he spoke – about looking forward to me publishing a book one day – suggested he wanted to be in my future, too. I buried my head in his neck, hugged him tightly and hoped that, unlike Amelie and Connor, our story would have the ending I always wanted; the one that, for me – in books and in life – was non-negotiable. A happy one.

Chapter One

Now

'Where the flip is my flipping . . .?' I scrabbled around on the too-small table, looking for the notebook I was sure I'd had a moment ago.

'Georgie,' Spence chided from her armchair, the scratches of her fountain pen rhythmic across the writing paper, her head bent towards the leather laptop writing desk she used when she was replying to her fan mail. Her steel-grey hair was cut in an elegant bob, the plum armchair sagging in a way that Spence, even at eighty-two, was not. Afternoon sun flooded into the room, glaringly intense. June was turning out to be warmer than predicted, and Spence's west-facing window caught it all and turned her lounge into a fiery spotlit stage as the hours ticked on towards sunset. 'Do you *have* to?'

'What? I said *flip. Flipping*. Not fu— aha!' I found the notepad under a pile of other papers that were spreading themselves liberally across the table. 'You're not bothered by swearing, anyway.'

'Swearing is beside the point.' Spence looked up. 'Some of us are trying to concentrate, and are you my PA, or are you a journalist for the *North Cornwall Star*?'

'Right this moment I'm a journalist for the *North Cornwall Star,* screeching towards my deadline, and I'm trying to find my notes from the interview I did with Alperwick's most successful fisherman, Geraint Trevellan, who brought in a record haul last week. A good news story, at last.'

Spence scoffed. 'Not for the fish.'

'There are two sides to every story.' I flipped through the notepad to the right page. 'I am not writing this one from the perspective of the fish.'

'I suppose it's good news for Rick at the Sailor's Rest.'

I could tell, without checking, that Spence was watching me, because I had gone out with Rick for almost three years, and she loved prodding me to provoke a reaction. But Rick and I were still on friendly terms, no lingering animosity between us, which – I had always thought – only served to confirm that our feelings had never run that deep. I still felt mildly guilty for breaking up with him, and for my commitment levels while we'd been dating. 'He does love making his fish pie,' I said breezily. 'And selling it. And talking

8

about it endlessly, and putting it on his daily specials blackboard every single day, which technically means it's not a special at all.'

'You would know,' Spence said.

'Not for nearly two years.' I looked up. 'I mean, I've had his pie, but I haven't—'

'Haven't you?' Spence raised an eyebrow.

'That was barely innuendo,' I said, irritation prickling at me. 'Come on, Spence.'

'The longer you backchat me, the longer you will have to spend sorting out your late article instead of fulfilling your duties as my PA, which is why I thought you were here this afternoon, and what I'm paying you for.'

'You're still writing letters.' I wafted a hand towards her. 'I'll pop them all in the envelopes and sort out the postage once you're done. It's much easier that way.'

'You never used to be like this.' Spence tutted and went back to her latest note, and it took me a moment of blinking to remind myself that I was here, that Spence had fan letters because she was Spencer Artemis, as in S. E. Artemis who had written the Cornish Sands series. For the last couple of years, one of my two jobs had been working as her PA, and three weeks ago she had dangled such a juicy, tempting carrot in front of me that I was finding it hard to focus on anything else, let alone the biggest catch of turbot seen in local waters for years.

'I'm just stressed,' I said. 'I have too many things on

my mind, and when I do everything turns to . . .' I looked forlornly at the clutter on the table, '. . . chaos.'

'Friday?' Spence put her pen down.

I fumbled my laptop open, pushing papers aside so I could at least get it down flat. Friday was five days away, and it was already taking up too much space in my brain. 'Friday is an important occasion,' I said. 'Of course I'm thinking about it. I need to do a good job for the *Star*, because the open house for your old place is going to be a big deal in the village.'

'My old place.' I knew she was aiming for dismissive, but I picked up the wistfulness in Spence's tone. That beautiful old house was something of a talisman in Alperwick, and I didn't know anyone locally who wasn't acutely aware of it. But for Spence, it had been home.

She had made all her money writing heart-pounding love stories set on the north Cornwall coast and, growing up, I had been enthralled by their tangled plots full of tragedy and redemption, forbidden kisses and whispered secrets. I'd felt a thrill every time I walked up the hill, past the grand house where Spence had lived, and which everyone knew was the inspiration for Tyller Klos – which meant 'Secluded Place' in Cornish – the stone mansion at the centre of her Cornish Sands series. The house was a fifteen-minute walk from the terrace I'd lived in with Mum, and S. E. Artemis had always been our village's enigmatic but adored celebrity.

She had moved into this cosy bungalow when I was

still a child, while the house on the hill, always known simply as Alperwick House, had been bought by a developer, who had left it standing empty. When I was a teenager I'd made pilgrimages there with my friends, sneaking in through a back window we'd managed to jimmy open. We made it our secret hideaway, and it had an extra layer of meaning for me because I'd been so hooked on the books.

Those were memories I didn't want to think about, but for Spence, it was just one more layer of drama around the mansion she'd called home. And now there was even more drama, because Alperwick House had been completely refurbished. The building we'd sought sanctuary in still had the same silhouette; it still sat on the clifftop with its familiar imprint against the sky, but now every part of it was glossy and modern. The exterior walls had been knocked out and replaced with acres of glass, making the most of the views over the wild coastline; the stone had been polished so it was close to silver in colour; and the interior might as well have been a different building altogether.

According to village gossip, it was a souped-up Smart house, Alexa on steroids, everything controlled by an app and voice activation. There had been questions and furtive investigation into who had bought it, who was renovating it, ever since work had started a couple of years ago, but the answers had remained elusive. And here I was, coming full circle, because now the rumbling lorries and men in hard hats had gone, now that the cement dust was no longer thickening the air, I was having to go back.

I was going to the open house because it would be a good story for the *Star*, one that my editor, Wynn, was keen for me to cover, and I was going because Spence had told me it was crucial for our project. The one where . . .

'Once you've had a tour, we'll be able to create Amelie and Connor's sequel much more vividly,' Spence said. 'The house's new life will reflect their second chance: their love will be revitalized, just as the walls of my *old place* have been. But you have to be thorough. The house is the centre of everything, so you need to go inside, get what we need to inspire our fresh start. The building has changed, and Amelie and Connor will have, too.'

'Right.' I typed my title: 'Turbot-Charged on the North Cornwall Coast', then stared at the words until they blurred, new emails sliding into the top right of my screen, the little red notification number climbing as I imagined being involved in the resurrection of the Cornish Sands series, bringing Amelie Rosevar and Connor Bligh the happy ending I'd always wanted for them. This was the carrot Spence was dangling in front of me. A collaboration. My chance to write words that were destined for a book rather than the local paper. If I went to the open house, I could make my editor happy, make Spence happy and – though it was only a small first step – perhaps get a bit closer to fulfilling my lifelong dream.

Because, before Mum's illness took over, before my future plans got derailed in so many unexpected ways, I had always believed I would be a writer. Not just a journalist for a local paper, but a writer who created magical stories and worlds, with a dedicated group of readers who loved them. Just like I had felt – *still* felt – about S. E. Artemis. Now, when I'd mostly given up on that dream, the author who had inspired me wanted me to help her resurrect her famous series.

'We need tea, I think.' I got up and almost knocked my laptop onto the floor.

'Tush, Georgie,' Spence said. 'Why so clumsy?'

'I'm not, I'm . . .' Giddy? Nervous? Apprehensive? This was a huge opportunity, and one my teenage self couldn't have dreamt up: being involved in my very favourite series and helping to right fictional wrongs. It was the stuff of fantasy, closer to tales of the Alperwick Mermaid than my life. But maybe this was my chance to do something that mattered: to do more than write news stories that didn't get close to ground-breaking while I lived in the village I'd grown up in, saw the same people I'd always seen, regretted the same things I'd been regretting for over a decade; while I stayed in the house that Mum and I had shared until not so long ago. Ignoring the ache in my chest, I switched on the kettle and found the green tea bags that I thought tasted like dust but that Spence swore by.

'What are you wearing?' she called as the kettle picked up steam.

I glanced down. 'A red T-shirt and denim shorts.'

'Not *now*, Georgie Monroe, honestly! On Friday.'

'Oh. I don't know. A dress? Something nice and professional.'

'Do you have anything chiffon?'

I rolled my eyes as I poured hot water into the mugs. 'This is not the Nineteen Fifties, and I'm not going to the house *as* Amelie Rosevar. It isn't role play.'

'You play at being a successful journalist often enough,' she said, and I stopped in front of her armchair. She smirked up at me, and I resisted the urge to cover her neatly written letters in hot tea – mostly because she would just make me write them all out again. Instead, I placed the mug carefully on her side table.

'My pieces are always well received,' I said primly. 'And that's partly because I have a friendly and professional approach, which means I get good interviews. Wynn isn't going to be happy if I turn up on Friday night in a floaty dress and lounge around on the beds pretending I'm a character from a romance novel. I'm going to ask polite questions and show an interest in the house.' I had imagined all the beds . . . all the rooms, really. I had only ever visited the house when it was a damp, deserted shell, full of spiders' webs, unknowable corners and creeping mould, and I couldn't wait to see the transformation.

'Maybe I'll get a car and come with you. I can get my legs to be useful when I really want them to be.'

Spence sounded blasé, but I knew how much her

lack of mobility frustrated her. A condition called sarcopenia had weakened her legs decades before, which was part of the reason – she'd told me when I started working for her – that she'd been forced to move from her clifftop mansion to the comfortable bungalow in the village. It was also why she'd hired me, so I could do the administrative jobs that were outside her carers' remit.

'Really?' I said. '*You're* going to pose on the furniture in a chiffon dress and pretend to be Amelie?'

I hid my panic at the very real possibility she might decide to do exactly that. If she came, she would completely derail our plan, not just because she was getting more mischievous as she got older, but because her appearance would change the whole nature of the event. It would thrust her back into the limelight, and she might get a better offer than resurrecting old characters with the help of her inexperienced PA. I knew I was being selfish, but I didn't want to watch something else I cared about slip through my fingers.

'I'm just worried you won't make the most of the opportunity.' Spence smiled up at me. 'It's not every day you get to explore a house of such extravagant proportions.'

'If there's a swimming pool, I'm not jumping in it.'

'Drink the champagne, at the very least. And take as many photos as you can. I want to see every nook and cranny.'

'I'll take all the photos, because Wynn will want

pictures anyway, and I promise I'll try and find out who owns it now.'

Spence waved a hand, looking out at the view – rooftops rolling down towards Alperwick Bay and the shimmering sea. 'It'll be some faceless developer. They're only doing this fancy open house for publicity, so they can draw the attention of fat-cat millionaires and make a sizeable profit. All that glass and chrome doesn't come cheap.'

'You don't like what they've done with it?' Spence had gone up there on her mobility scooter, though only as far as the high, redbrick wall and towering gates. They had only offered her a hint of the gleaming clifftop palace beyond, but it was enough to see the scale of the transformation.

'I *love* what they've done with it,' Spence said. 'It's better than even *my* imagination could have conjured. I just don't want it to be bought by someone who'll only live in it for three weeks every summer. That house deserves a family.'

'It does.' I slumped into my chair and stared at the blank space where my fishing article should have been. 'It deserves the very best family.' Because it had had the Rosevars, in the Cornish Sands series, and in real life it had been lived in by Spence and her ex-husband, and then, even when it was deserted, my friends and I had shown it love and attention. It deserved owners who would appreciate it. 'I'll find out,' I said, with more confidence than I felt. 'I'll track down the developer or the architect or whatever –

they're bound to be there, aren't they, at a swanky, showy-off event like that? I'll grill them on their vetting process, find out how they're going to choose who buys it.'

Spence smiled at me over the top of her mug, but it wasn't her usual impish grin. 'Oh Georgie,' she said sadly, 'they'll sell it to the person who offers the most money. There's no room for romance in the property market. That's why we have to give it a second life in our new book, because that way it won't be lost to us completely.'

I phoned my best friend Kira as I walked down the hill into the village later that afternoon, as the blazing orb of the sun hovered above the mellowing sea, the sand of Alperwick Bay like a pool of molten gold.

'You're really going back to the house?' she asked, then I heard her shushing her young son, Barnaby, while she waited for my answer. Kira had been my friend since primary school, had married her childhood sweetheart Freddy, and now the three of them lived in Greenwich in southeast London. It was so different from our tiny coastal village in Cornwall, and I sometimes envied their escape while I was still languishing here, but all that mattered was that we were still close.

'I have to cover it for Wynn.' My footsteps echoed as I turned onto a road of neat terraces with front doors that opened straight onto the street, window boxes blossoming with summery begonias. 'It's a major

17

event in Alperwick. I'm honoured to be the one reporting on it.'

'But did Wynn pick you, or did you ask for it because we spent so much time up there, drinking vodka and eating Pringles, telling each other ghost stories?'

'Well . . .' I hadn't told Kira about Spence's offer yet, because in some ways it still seemed too good to be true. Once I'd been inside Alperwick House I would be less apprehensive, not because I really believed that seeing the upgraded version would make a huge difference to the book we were going to write, but because it felt like a test that Spence was setting me: prove how much you care about this by enduring a stuffy, schmoozy sales-pitch event inside your childhood haunt, a place overflowing with complicated memories. Spence loved challenging me, and I only minded about 70 per cent of the time. 'I might have mentioned it to Wynn,' I said. 'And of course I'm curious about what's happened to it. Getting inside without trespassing will be a novel feeling, too.'

Kira laughed, the sound bubbly and luminous, and Barnaby squealed excitedly. 'No dusty fireplaces with cat corpses shoved up them.'

'God, Orwell had such a twisted mind.'

'The ghost stories were fun, though. You know, when you and—'

'They were,' I cut in, because I didn't want to follow the path she was leading me down. 'And it'll force me to do some actual investigating: find out who's behind the renovation, which I've had no luck with so far online. Give Spence peace of mind that it's not being bought by some hotelier or corporate company who are going to run team-building retreats there.'

'Shit, yeah,' Kira said. 'It must be hard for her, looking on from her sunny little bungalow while the grand house she used to love gets pimped up and passed on.'

'She's more curious than anything, but I think she really cares what happens to it – in a rare case of her giving a crap about something other than how she can amuse herself.'

'You love her really,' Kira said indulgently. 'You're PA to your favourite author, even if she is a cantankerous old lady now. And . . . you know,' she added slowly, pointedly, 'with your work for the *Star*, and the generous rate you get for stuffing envelopes, you could think about writing something – for yourself, I mean. You could take a break; get an idea started, then make the time to keep going. Just a few hundred words a day. It soon builds up.'

'It does,' I said, my throat thick. I would tell her about Spence's offer soon, and she was right – I *did* have time, because beyond Spence and my work for the paper, my life in Alperwick was small. There hadn't been anyone serious since my break-up with Rick a couple of years ago; a guy from Mousehole, Corran, who I'd seen a few times before it had petered out, the occasional night in the pub with friends from the paper, long cliff walks by myself, vague notions about getting a dog that I hadn't followed through with because it seemed like a lot of effort. I didn't want to think about how many books I could have written in all the time I'd used idly.

I reached home, took my keys out of my rucksack and opened my red front door. 'I could write something,' I said, and then asked how Barnaby was getting on, which was a subject Kira would never sidestep. As she told me (moaned) about the other women at the mum's group she'd found, and I asked about Freddy's recent promotion at the tech firm he worked for, I promised myself I would tell her everything soon. Once I'd been to the open house and grabbed the carrot that Spence was dangling with both hands, I would feel comfortable telling Kira the whole story. Four more days to go, and I would be on much firmer ground.

Chapter Two

Now

When I woke up on Friday morning, there were a few hazy seconds when I knew I had something important to do, where I could feel excitement and apprehension mingling together, but I couldn't remember why. Then my sleep fug cleared, and the open house event at Tyller Klos slid to the front of my consciousness.

I had kicked the thin summer duvet off in the night, and – as I picked it off the floor – I saw Connor, the cuddly turtle that still sat on my teenage desk, staring at me. I ignored him, went into the bathroom and set the shower on a cooler setting than usual, letting my thoughts flow with the water. I had to frame tonight as a job, a piece I was writing for the *Star*, nothing more. That way it would lose some of its significance and I wouldn't be so nervous. I just hoped that spending the morning with Spence wouldn't completely ruin my approach. She had a tendency to turn everything upside down with a casual aside or pointed comment, and that was something I could really do without today.

'Here you go.'

I put Spence's coffee on her table and sat in my usual chair, the large window to my left, the view of Alperwick village sloping down towards the sea always distracting, but especially when it was dusted with morning gold like it was right now.

'I have something for you.' Spence sipped her drink and tipped her head towards a glossy magazine lying on her footstool. The cover was a photograph of a quaint Cotswold cottage swamped by wisteria, below the title *Home Style* written in a cheery yellow font.

'What's this?' I picked it up and flicked idly through it.

'Research,' Spence said. 'Try page fifty-two.'

'I don't need to be an expert in architectural design to go to one open-house event,' I said. 'I'm the ignorant journalist, asking all the questions with a bland smile on my face. They'll want to impress me with their boundless skills and knowledge.'

Spence didn't reply, so I sighed and turned to page fifty-two, pressing the magazine open on my lap. My first thought was familiarity – I knew that house and had seen it recently – and my second thought was . . . nothing. My mind was wiped clean, replaced by a whooshing sound between my ears and the distinct sensation that I was tipping sideways.

'It seems tonight's event isn't just important for Alperwick,' Spence said, her words reaching me through my brain fog, 'if the house is featuring in magazines like this.'

'How is . . . how is this happening?' I wasn't sure if I'd spoken out loud, and if I had, I didn't expect an answer. I started reading, the truth thudding into me with every new, horrifying sentence. I gripped the magazine, which felt tacky beneath my fingertips.

'A Spark of Heaven on the North Cornwall Coast' read the headline, and for a moment I had to stop, because of course. Of *course*. I should have realized.

The first photograph was a wide shot of Alperwick House, showing off the huge stretches of glass that had replaced the smaller, older windows. The elegant path was made up of large, biscuit-coloured paving stones running up to the wide front step, the generous open porch embedded with spotlights that lit it from every angle. Everything was sharp lines and soft tones, stylish but in keeping with the original shape of the house; its sloped roof and its sturdy, been-here-for-hundreds-of-years demeanour.

The word 'sustainable' jumped out at me, but that wasn't too specific – everyone was building sustainable houses now: you couldn't really say you were going back to the olden days, putting in coal fires and F-rated appliances just to be quirky. The pull quote, on the other hand, was like a punch in the stomach.

It mentioned Sparks, the Smart System that ran the house. Everything about the article was a shock, and yet it was also completely, thoroughly inevitable.

'Why?' I ran my finger over that one word: *Sparks*.

'This doesn't change anything,' Spence said, the glint in her eye unmistakable. 'Just follow the plan. Go to the open house, take photos of the rooms and ask polite, probing questions. Have a proper nosy; absorb all the ways the house is different, find what you need and get out.'

'It changes everything.' I shook my head. 'Did you know about this?'

'The magazine only came this morning. A friend sent it to me, said I might like to see one of the articles.' She waggled an A4 Jiffy bag, as if to prove she wasn't responsible for bringing this world-altering publication into our lives.

'At least now we know who's behind the project.' I glanced at my rucksack, desperate to take out my phone and call Kira.

'We know who the *architect* is,' Spence corrected.

Beneath my flood of panic, irritation bloomed like Japanese cherry trees in springtime because, one, I really could have done without her pedantry right then and, two, she wasn't going to let me use this as an excuse not to go.

'You'll be all right,' Spence said, confirming it. 'Even if he's there, with that gorgeous thick hair and his familiar smile, the one that promises you'll have his undivided attention when you're alone together.'

24

'I should never have told you about him.' I pressed my fingers to my lips, as if the memories might slip out of my mouth. They had started as soon as I'd seen his name in print, his eyes staring out at me, slightly wide as if it was a two-way thing – as if he was experiencing shock like I was, and the camera hadn't captured him weeks ago. Thick, conker-coloured hair, the reddish hue more obvious in the sunshine, and lips that were so often pressed together, pensive or thoughtful. His laughter was hard won, but wholly precious because of that, and his brown eyes had always been warm, especially when they met mine.

It was over a decade since things had ended badly, and I had hoarded those memories, thinking that they were all I would have – apart from my stalking sessions on Instagram, which never made me feel better. Thirteen long years of not seeing him, of not having my resentment or anger to sustain me in his absence because they had lasted a laughingly short time.

Spence tutted. 'Of course you should have. You think I'd be full steam ahead with writing Amelie and Connor a new chapter if you hadn't told me about him? Not your recent ex Rick, but the one who got away, who's the definition of unfinished business.'

'This isn't for me, though,' I rushed out. 'This book, it's—'

'It's fired me up,' Spence cut in. 'All the things you've told me. You're a natural storyteller, Georgie. It's a good thing.' Her soft smile sharpened into a grin. 'You know, in all their decades apart, Amelie and Connor must have written some beautiful letters.'

I rolled my eyes, hoping that would hide the effect her words were having on me.

The Cornish Sands series was full of letters: love letters between star-crossed lovers declaring their intentions, between members of the Rosevar family discussing secrets that really shouldn't have been written down, except that the plots would have been thin without them; notes passed between children sitting at school desks, and dropped through unsuspecting letterboxes in the fictional Cornish village Spence had created. There was something about having the stories partly told in those scribbled monologues, when the characters had nobody to interrupt them, and no immediate judgement on what they were saying. It meant they could be more honest. The letters between Amelie and Connor in *The Whispers of the Sands* had been my favourites, and I'd been gearing myself up for their perfect happy-ever-after, then completely blindsided when it didn't happen.

'I can't wait for the letters,' I admitted.

Spence laughed. 'My dear, you're going to be writing them with me. A true collaboration. Your name on the cover alongside mine. And all you need to do, before we start, is get inside and see the house.'

I folded over the corner of the magazine's cover, pressing it hard so the crease was permanent. 'Not every architect would bother attending the sales event of their project, would they?' I so badly wanted this to be true.

'What utter piffle,' Spence scolded. 'Have you *seen* the photos, Georgie? Read the piece? It's a feat of sheer magnificence. A modern marvel. Of course he's going to be there.'

I wanted to open a window to let the breeze banish the close air in the bungalow. I needed to help Spence with her correspondence, and make a list of all the things I had to get done at the open house, so that I could get enough information to satisfy Spence and to write my piece for Wynn. Then I could leave it all firmly behind me.

'It is beautiful,' I said grudgingly, and looked at the magazine again, a master of my own punishment.

There he was, in all his handsome, stern deliciousness. That conker hair, long on top and untamed as it always would be, every single day of his life. His arms were folded across his chest, the action pressing the simple blue shirt tight against defined biceps, and showing off the strong shape of his shoulders, as if his body was a walking advert for his architectural prowess.

The photo had a plain black background, and there was something stark about the way he was looking straight at the lens. His face was impassive unless you knew him well, and I had done. I knew, for example, that there was a spray of freckles over his nose that the harsh light had bleached out – I couldn't imagine him caring enough to ask them to be airbrushed away, and why would the editor bother? The freckles had softened him, a dot-to-dot that I'd once completed with a biro while he'd protested weakly, a corner of his mouth lifting. I'd known him well, and I'd tried to forget him, after everything that had happened.

But now, here he was, in black and white and glossy colour: the person who had converted Tyller Klos from a deserted shell into a modern masterpiece.

I forced myself to read the paragraph, written in bold, the one the editor was drawing every reader's eye to, the one they wanted you to notice even if you skipped over the rest.

Alperwick House has been reimagined by up-and-coming architect Ethan Sparks, who has returned to the village where he spent some of his formative years to give the house on the cliffs a second chance. This isolated, luxury mansion has a long history, an association with the famous writer S. E. Artemis, whose fictional family pile Tyller Klos was undoubtedly inspired by it. Now it has been renamed Sterenlenn, which in Cornish means 'blanket of stars', imbuing it with the romance of the remote, clifftop setting. 'The house is a part of the land-scape,' Ethan says, leaning forward, his focus sharpening. 'It's a landmark along the coastline, a building seen and admired from land, sea and sky, and I wanted to keep that sense of it being organic alive in my redesign. The name, well . . .' He pauses, nodding to himself. 'It was never going to be called anything else.'

I stared out of the window, at the view of Spence's manicured garden, then a tight cluster of rooftops down to the blue of the Atlantic, a soft haze over everything as the June sun rose steadily in the sky, banishing the dew. It was almost the longest day of the year, the light would be slow to fade, and I knew the evening – this *specific* evening – would be never-ending.

A shiver ran up my spine as the full realization hit me: everything I had to pull off, now that I knew the truth; the fundamental fact that, after so many years without him, I would be in the same room as Ethan. Because those words printed in the magazine, definite and un-smudgeable, confirmed that not only was he behind Tyller Klos's transformation and would, in all probability, be at the event, but also that – even if he'd been trying as hard as I had – he hadn't been able to forget about me, either.

Chapter Three

Now

The day was agonizingly quiet. I pottered through the tasks Spence had given me and kept an eye on the clock, which seemed to have ceased moving at its normal speed. Eventually it was time for me to change into my work outfit, collect my bag and leave.

I already felt like I was walking towards a doom-laden fate, and Spence came to wave me off at the door, which was a big deal for her and somehow made it all worse. I thought my best course of action was to minimize the whole thing, turn it into the list of simple actions she'd given me: take photos; ask polite, probing questions; have a nosy in all the rooms; find what you need to and get out.

I had memorized them while I was folding up Spence's correspondence, sliding letters into envelopes, writing addresses on the front. *One: take photos.* Spence always replied to her fans using a fountain pen filled with navy ink, on pure cotton writing paper she got me to order online from L'Ecritoire. *Two: ask polite, probing questions.* Her handwriting was elegantly slanted, like something out of the earlier Cornish Sands books, when children had to practise their upstrokes and compound curves in school instead of learning how to turn on a computer. *Three: have a nosy in all the rooms.* I felt a sharp spike of adrenaline at the thought of slipping through the house unnoticed, seeing Ethan's attention to detail embodied in every square foot. *Four: find what you need to and get out.* Spence hadn't clarified exactly what I needed to find so we could resurrect Amelie and Connor, so I assumed it was that flash of creative inspiration at seeing the old mansion revitalized, a mental lightbulb flaring on.

Now, Spence pressed her palm into the door frame, her other hand clutching her stick. 'Don't sweat it,' she said, when she saw me looking at her with concern.

'*You* are,' I replied. 'Can't I help you back to your chair?'

'That would completely negate me coming to the door to see you off.'

'It was a struggle, though.'

'Life is full of them. If it wasn't, nobody would bother writing books. We'd all just sail through our days on a cloud of easy contentment, and where would the fun be in that?'

I thought of the last few days before Mum had gone, the mix of anger and loss mingled with guilt-tinged relief; of Ethan in my bedroom doorway all those years ago, a blink that took his expression from pleading to shuttered, before he turned and walked away from me; of the scattered beginnings of stories and ideas on my laptop and in various notebooks, none of them even close to 'the end'. I would prefer easy contentment: it seemed a whole lot more fun than the alternative.

'The struggles elevate the good parts,' Spence went on, as if she could see the thoughts spinning through my head. 'When I get back to my chair, I'll be relieved and grateful, and I'll have earned the Cornish pasty Denise is bringing me for my tea. It'll be sweeter.'

Denise was Spence's evening carer, a broad woman with dyed-scarlet hair, talons for nails and a voice so soft I sometimes wondered if I'd accidentally muted my surroundings. 'And if tonight is so hideous I run screaming from Sterenlenn?' I asked. It was the first time I'd said the name aloud, and I wanted to know how it sounded. Verdict? It sounded beautiful, as if music had been captured in those three syllables, and it was the perfect name for the house on the cliffs. I swallowed.

'Then you'll have felt everything out loud, and that can sometimes be a blessing.' Spence patted my arm. 'Off you trot. You don't want to be late and draw even more attention to yourself. You're far too pretty to be a journalist. Wynn could never send you undercover.'

I smiled at the compliment, and at the thought of

the *North Cornwall Star* covering something so serious and newsworthy that they needed a reporter on the inside. 'I'm surprised you didn't get me to wear a bodycam so you could see tonight play out in real time.'

She gave me her wickedest grin. 'I might win awards for my nosiness – the burden of every writer – but there are some things that simply aren't for my eyes.'

I narrowed mine. 'What does that mean?'

'The *time*, Georgie.' She tapped her bony wrist where a watch would be if she still wore one.

'Fine. I'm going.' It felt like the hardest thing to turn away and trudge down her front path, with its bright marigolds and sweet williams, hot pink poppy anemones dancing in the breeze. The afternoon sun shone mercilessly, a little too intense for June. It felt like a storm was brewing.

'Spine straight!' Spence called, and I jerked upright, then cursed myself for being her obedient little marionette. She had come into my life when I was lost and lonely, with nobody to talk to besides an overworked editor and a best friend in London who was navigating being a new mum. I was just Spence's employee, I told myself for the millionth time, and she was offering me an opportunity I couldn't turn down. It was one night: one uncomfortable, awkward evening – a few hours at most – and then it would be done. I could close the door on the feelings still lingering from that part of my life, and move onto the next, hopefully brighter one.

* * *

33

Alperwick village hugged the Cornish coastline, the houses clustered low in the valley, getting sparser the further you got from the sea, a mishmash of town houses, terraces and bungalows. The mid-terrace I had lived in with Mum, which I now had to myself, was one road back from the beachfront, tiny but so close to the white sandy expanse and aquamarine water of Alperwick Bay that I never felt hemmed in.

Spence's bungalow was a little way up the hill, set back from the wide road and with breathtaking views of the sea over the rooftops. She had a front and back garden, space around her slice of land, but it was nothing like what she'd once owned. Her old house, now Sterenlenn, was on the top of the hill, at the south end of the village. It looked down on Alperwick and the coastline from its clifftop perch, as if it was a castle.

The main through road rose steeply on either side of the village, and was especially winding at the southern end. Minutes into my walk I was breathing heavily, and could feel the sweat slipping down my spine and between my boobs, already slightly uncomfortable in the bra I'd chosen.

I hadn't known about Ethan when I'd picked my outfit that morning, and I congratulated myself on not having rushed back home to reconsider my options. I'd chosen one of my favourite sundresses, rich blue with sprays of yellow flowers that clustered more tightly towards the hem. It had tiny buttons down the front and finished at the knee, and I had worn it to cover stories in the past, so it felt appropriate. It also matched my naturally blonde hair and blue eyes, and now all those things felt like an added defence, a flimsy wall of confidence that would help me make it through this.

But, halfway there, my bare shins brushing the sprays of tufted vetch and oxeye daisies along the verge, I knew I was going to turn up a hot, sweaty mess. The straps of my rucksack, heavy with my notebook and camera inside, were digging into my shoulders, and I chided myself for leaving my twelve-year-old Polo at home, because I had decided it was too short a journey to drive. My rucksack was a tatty thing that had followed me around for the last decade, worn patches in the tan suede like points on a map, the zip on the front pocket broken, so I could only put tissues in there and often ended up losing them.

I had forgotten my spare camera battery, and hoped that I could take enough photos for Wynn and Spence before I ran out of charge. It wasn't going to be the most groundbreaking article, unless the house caught fire or someone kicked up a fuss about the building practices, but then Ethan was a master at tidying away problems. He'd done it when we were together, and . . . there it was, a faint flare of bitterness. Honestly, I was relieved. I needed to stay as far away from him as possible, and thinking bad thoughts was preferable to remembering his tenderness; how he was mostly self-contained but had always been tactile with me;

how safe he'd made me feel. I swallowed and tripped on absolutely nothing, then jumped when a voice bellowed 'Georgie!'

I spun to find Barry Mulligan standing in his front garden, the handle of his lawnmower resting against his paunch.

'Hey, Barry.' His bungalow was one of the closest properties to Sterenlenn, and he'd been the main source of news about the Big House while the changes were happening. 'How are you?'

'Off to cover the event for the paper?' he asked, ignoring my question. 'Caterers' trucks coming in and out all day today, so it should be a good spread.'

'Right.' Barry couldn't see Sterenlenn's gates from his garden because the hill was too steep, but he had a telescope set up on a tripod in his roof conversion. Supposedly it was for spotting dolphins during the day and constellations at night, but none of the locals believed that. 'Anything else?' I asked, hating myself for fishing. Would Ethan come with the caterers? Would he have a sleek Audi or Porsche with a person-alized numberplate? I thought of the images I'd seen on Instagram, of him with various tousle-haired women, one after the other, often against European, city-break backdrops. His captions were always annoy-ingly brief and superficial, but the photos told me enough about how much he'd changed.

'A couple of Range Rovers with blacked-out windows.' Barry scratched his scalp through his thick brown hair. 'All a bit over-the-top, if you ask me.'

'Not surprising though, is it? Have you seen the photos in that magazine? It's getting national coverage.'

'I'd like a proper gander,' Barry said dreamily, and I almost offered to swap places with him. Then I thought about Spence's reaction if I failed to get inside, and the idea drifted away like an outgoing tide.

'I'll be sure to take lots of photos.' I patted my rucksack strap. 'And if I can manage it, I'll bring you a doggy bag of tiny exotic canapés.'

This seemed to delight Barry, and he gave me a cheery goodbye and started up his lawnmower again.

I heaved myself further up the hill, flapping the collar of my dress as if that would allow some air to circulate beneath it. The sky had a yellowy tinge, the humidity too high for late June, the wind sluggish rather than crisp. There were two boys playing with a football in one of the gardens, kicking it up high with wild abandon, oblivious to their position close to the road, where a wayward kick could land on a car or passer-by.

Panic was a whirlpool in my chest, and I paused, wondering if my heaving lungs were due to lack of fitness or anxiety. I slipped my rucksack off one shoulder and unzipped it, reaching into the interior pocket and feeling for the black velvet bag. Inside was my silver mermaid, and even without taking it out I could picture the flow of her long hair, carved to give her buoyant waves, her scales turquoise glass and mother-of-pearl. It was a gift I'd received after writing a piece about the legend of the Alperwick Mermaid for the paper, a reminder that what I produced could really make a difference to people, however small. I squeezed it, then zipped up the rucksack and hauled it back on my shoulder, my breath calmer.

I kept going, thinking of my list of actions, and it wasn't long before I was cresting the hill and could see the smart, redbrick wall that surrounded the property, with cream pointing between the bricks, everything elegant but understated. Then there were the sage green gates, tall and curved and, right now, flung open. Someone was standing in front of the opening. He had dark, close-cropped hair and was dressed like a nightclub bouncer. Did he have an *earpiece*?

'Nothing about this is normal,' I reminded myself, as a silver Mercedes slowed, then stopped in front of me. The bouncer leaned down to the driver's window and there was a short conversation that I couldn't hear, then the car drove smoothly through the gateway. I surreptitiously ran my palms down the back of my dress, expecting a barked 'name?' or immediate, 'You can't come in.' Instead, the bouncer gave me a warm smile, which was somehow even more disconcerting.

'Hello, darlin',' he said in an East London accent. 'You here for the open house?'

'Yes.' I tried for firm but ended up forceful. 'I'm a reporter for the *North Cornwall Star*, covering the event tonight.' I didn't have any kind of pass, which felt like a rookie error, but the bouncer's smile didn't falter.

'You're a few minutes early, but Ethan and Sarah are in there already.'

My next breath got stuck halfway up my windpipe and I coughed, bending over slightly. 'Sorry,' I said, when I had gúlped in enough air. 'That hill is steeper than it looks.'

'One of 'em will get you a glass of water, I'm sure.'

'Right.' I nodded. 'Sarah?' It was a common name. He didn't necessarily mean *that* Sarah, Ethan's younger sister, who had taken up so much of his time when we'd been together. It reminded me how little I knew about him now, and I had to resist the urge to tell this smiling man that I'd made a mistake, that I'd turned up at the wrong open house, then flee back down the hill.

'Like some kind of double act, honestly.' He shook his head fondly. 'Don't tell them I said that, though. I'm supposed to be professional.'

His words put another possibility in my head, and I wasn't sure if I liked the idea of Ethan working with his partner more or less than his sister. 'You haven't been hired for the night?'

'I have, but I'm a mate of theirs. Aldo.' He held out his hand and I shook it, his skin warm and dry. 'They wanted me to provide a bit of *gravitas*, if you know what I mean?' He winked, and I could see how Aldo could charm burglars into not carrying out their crimes – probably by talking their ears off until the police turned up.

'Ethan wanted you to play security guard to up the exclusivity of the event?' I couldn't imagine it, and Aldo frowned, confirming my scepticism was warranted.

'That was actually Sarah's idea. She's got more of a business mind. Ethan's probably in there stroking the marble worktops, checking them for cracks.'

I laughed, because I could picture that easily.

Aldo's gaze narrowed. 'You know them, then?'

'Oh, no. Not for a long time. Do I need to sign in or anything?'

'Nah.' Aldo waved a hand, his attention drawn to a car crawling slowly towards the gates. 'Go on through.' He stepped aside, and I realized his bulk had been blocking the view of the house, and that I had a straight line of sight to it now. It was like a blinding flash of lightning, the big reveal at the end of a film, because the magazine photographs hadn't done it justice.

It looked unreal, the wide pathway a straight line up to the front door, the slabs a creamy beige and so clean they shimmered. The lawns on either side looked like they had been trimmed with nail clippers, and a gravel driveway snaked off to the left, the space for cars set away from the house and the views of the coastline, so they wouldn't ruin the aesthetic. The porch was luxurious, spotlights and gleaming chrome around the sage green front door, a deep enough recess to shelter a whole family from the rain. I felt a glimmer of familiarity at the gabled roof and soft grey stone, but the house was so much lighter, with so many reflective surfaces, that I wondered if this *was* a reinvention, or if they'd knocked down the old building and started again from scratch, creating a modern echo.

Through the window to the right of the door I could see fragments of a spacious kitchen and then, in the next room along, large, pale sofas and a wall the blue of the sky before dusk. They were teasers, tantalizing me, and suddenly I couldn't wait to get inside.

But then the front door slid open, and my fingers began to tingle, a buzz working its way up my arm. If I was going to have a panic attack, now would absolutely be the right moment.

'You can go on up, darlin',' Aldo called from behind me, but I was rooted to the spot.

Two figures had come out to stand on the porch, and I was glad that I couldn't see their expressions clearly from where I stood. The woman was slightly shorter than the man, her slender frame poured into a burnt orange dress that straddled the line between business and cocktail party, with a cinched-in waist, tight skirt and swooping neckline. Her patent heels were gleaming, her dark hair pulled up in a high ponytail. I had known her as a chaotic, sullen teenager, but it was undoubtedly Ethan's sister. She looked as if she'd had as much of a transformation as the house.

The man was wearing a slim-fitting, cobalt blue suit, the jacket done up over a crisp white shirt despite the weather, and a tie in a shade of sage that matched the door and gates. He had always looked good in green, because it brought out the autumn tones in his hair, the conker and amber, the gold flecks in his brown irises.

His arms were motionless at his sides, everything

about him immaculate, but then he took a small step forward, and faltered. I saw the moment he realized who I was, because he lifted his hand, rubbed his forehead and then slid his fingers through that chaos of hair, the one thing about him that was never tamed because he treated it as his personal stress toy.

Ethan Sparks was standing on the porch of his beautiful house, the culmination of all his dreams, and I was about to bring disorder back into his world. 'Sorry, Ethan,' I murmured, and, remembering Spence's words, straightened my spine and walked towards him and his sister.

Dear Connor,

The house feels so empty without you.

When I came back to the village the last time and discovered you had gone, it was as if someone was playing a cruel joke on me, someone who had decided we were too good together, that something so bright and sparkling couldn't be allowed. Everything was better when I was with you – whether we were with other people, our hands brushing, linking our fingers at our sides, or when we were in our own little bubble, walking on the beach and planning our future.

Now I've returned and you're still not here, and so I have to face these stretching, endless days without you. The pen sounds loud, scratching across the paper in this room where only the clock is ticking. But if I listen carefully, if I close my eyes, I can hear the waves breaking against the sand. It's a different rhythm to the clock, and the two of them overlapping make me dizzy, as if I'm not solid enough to stay tethered to the ground.

I'm starting to realize how many things I took for granted. Every time you smiled at me; all the times I made you laugh that felt like a victory. Whenever you touched me, and all those hours I spent wrapped up in you. I was such an idiot, because I thought that, whatever happened, we would make it. But now, all I can see are the places where you're missing; on the beach and the cliff path, the wind chilling my neck where you used to shelter me from it. There's a dent in the sofa cushion beside me, the mug you used to use left dusty in the cupboard when I make tea. Our hands should be linked, your fingers locking perfectly into the spaces between mine, but they're not.

I hope you're well, and that you're happy. I wish you were here, but I never want you to be anything other than happy. Tyller Klos is a shell, all those big rooms empty, and that's how I feel too. This notepaper isn't giving me a whole lot of answers, any ways to escape how I'm feeling, but at least I can get it all out of my head, and maybe things will start to feel easier.

I love you and I miss you.
Yours always, Amelie xx

Chapter Four

February 2012

'Have you seen this new guy, Georgie?' Kira slid her tanned arms along the table in front of me, lounging like a jellyfish, and I looked up from the lame notes I'd been scribbling for my Media Studies class. My teacher, Mr Carson, never checked the homework, because he always got distracted and launched into a discussion about some moral or ethical dilemma at the beginning of each lesson, which was useful for my critical thinking, but not so much for the approaching exams.

'*This new guy.*' I smiled at Kira. 'I have no idea who you're talking about.'

'He got introduced by Mrs Couch today in Maths. Ethan something. Smart or Spartacus or Spunk.'

'His name is Ethan *Spunk*?' I laughed. 'Oh dear.'

Kira's giggle was a bubbling sound that made me feel like I was floating. My funny, kind, smart, beautiful best friend. 'Probably not Spunk. He's handsome, in a cruel kind of way.'

I closed my notebook, intrigued. 'Why do you think he's cruel?'

Kira swapped positions, putting her legs on the desk, her DMs clunking into the Formica. 'He stared us all down, even Daggers Dave at the back, who was looking as scary as ever. He managed a deep *hey* when Mrs Couch told him to introduce himself.'

'That doesn't mean he's cruel. He's probably just shy.' I turned back to my notes. 'Anyway, what about Freddy?'

'I'm not replacing Freddy with Spunk boy.' They'd been dating since the beginning of year twelve, which already felt like a lifetime to me. 'There's not a lot of excitement here, that's all. The new guy is the most interesting thing that's happened all week.'

'I'll have to look out for him.' I was about to throw my biro across the common room, towards the aloe vera plant that had been dying long before we started using it for target practice, when my phone buzzed. It was a clunky Nokia with buttons that kept sticking, and I envied Freddy with his newfangled iPhone, but I didn't have a dad who was high up in the tech industry in London. I had no dad and a mum who worked as a dentist's receptionist when she wasn't laid low by MS. I read the message.

'What is it?' Kira asked, her petulance gone. 'Your mum OK?'

'Yeah.' I sighed. 'She's been given an appointment at the hospital tomorrow, so I'm going to have to miss English and take her.'

Kira frowned. 'Can't she get someone else to take her? I know you're *only* doing English and Media Studies and—'

'Hey!' I whacked her on the arm.

'You still need to pass the exams if you want to go to uni. You work hard enough as it is.'

I nodded, doodling a flower in my notebook. Mum was part of a new MS trial at the hospital, which had the potential to reduce her symptoms and improve her general condition, but it meant lots of trips to Truro, forty-five minutes away, and then periods afterwards when, because of the side effects, she needed a lot more care. She preferred me to look after her rather than strangers, which I understood, but it was putting pressure on other parts of my life, and I was eighteen now, months away from university, so everything – my friendships, my schoolwork – really mattered.

'It's just A levels, G,' she'd say with a soft, coaxing smile. 'You can pick it up so easily. You're clever and you apply yourself. No need to worry, my girl.'

'Tell me about Ethan Spunk.' I slid my notebook into my rucksack, done with Media Studies and thoughts about Mum and everything except some gossip with my friend.

Kira stared at the ceiling and I waited, anticipation building, knowing that whatever she said would be good. 'Ethan Spunk is . . . like the most expensive Easter egg.'

I laughed. 'In what way?'

'He's really hard to crack open, but you know that, when you finally prise him apart, you'll be generously rewarded with the contents.'

I swallowed. I hadn't even seen this guy and already I wanted to know how accurate that was. 'What kind of contents?'

She shrugged, her brown eyes twinkling. 'They could be anything. Something sharp and fruity, like the candied oranges you get at Christmas, or bitter, like 80 per cent chocolate drops. He looks like he'd have a dry sense of humour.' She tapped her lips. 'Or they might be sweet: I can see that about him, too. He seemed wary, but also as if he might warm up, like chocolate truffles with coffee cream inside.'

'Right.' It was my turn to slump over the desk. 'Thanks, Kira. Now I won't have anything to say in Media Studies.'

'Because you're thinking about a guy you've never seen whose surname might be Spunk?'

'You started this,' I pointed out. 'I *am* thinking about him, but now I also want some chocolate truffles.' My stomach rumbled, and Kira laughed and slumped over me, two girls heaped over a desk like we'd completely given up. When the laughter faded, I pushed my blonde fringe out of my eyes and said, 'When's your next Maths class?'

'Why?' Kira took an apple out of her bag. 'You're practically allergic to Maths.'

'I might need to come and give you a crucial message, sometime very soon.' I watched the smile spread slowly over her face, matching mine.

I met Ethan, the most expensive Easter egg, two days later, in inauspicious circumstances. I was walking across the courtyard in front of the sixth-form block, replying to a message from Mum, when something thumped into the middle of my back with a heavy *thwack*, pushing all the air out of me. My mobile flew out of my hands, and I followed it onto the hard concrete, my knees and palms taking the brunt.

'Fuck,' I gasped, tears springing to my eyes at the shock.

'Hey.' The voice came from beside me, and I turned to see a pair of grey trainers, jean-clad knees in a crouching position, fingertips pressing into the ground next to my hand. 'Are you OK?'

'Was that your football?' I sounded shrill, and I swallowed, trying to force the tears away.

'I don't have a football,' the voice said. 'Here, do you want to sit?' Hands cupped my shoulders, gentle but insistent, manoeuvring me until I was sitting on the ground, the pressure off my knees and hands. I looked up into a pair of brown eyes, a furrow between neat brows, his concern aimed at me.

'Thanks,' I mumbled.

Kira's description had been perfect, because I knew immediately that this was Ethan. He looked pensive, and his posture was good even when he was crouching, his shoulders wide and straight in his grey shirt. I couldn't hold his gaze for long – there was something about his expression that made my dizziness linger – so I assessed the damage instead. I brushed at my bare knees, knocking off tiny nuggets of gravel, leaving behind red pockmarks and a couple of grazes where I'd broken the skin. I had on a navy dress and was relieved I hadn't ripped the fabric. I didn't have a whole lot of outfits that I was comfortable about wearing to school. 'Shit.'

'Does it hurt?' Ethan squeezed my shoulder, his hand radiating heat through the cotton of my dress.

'It stings a bit. It's the shock more than anything.'

He glanced over my head. 'We're sitting ducks here. That ball's bouncing around like Lego in a spin dryer.'

'A *spin* dryer?' I laughed. 'How old *are* you?' But when he held his hand out, I took it, and he pulled me easily to my feet.

'I'm eighteen.' He started walking, without letting go of my hand. 'Same as you, I imagine, unless you're still seventeen?'

'I was eighteen in November.' I didn't try to take my hand back.

We walked across the courtyard together, and it was obvious that we were getting stared at. 'Good,' he said, and it took me a beat to remember what he was replying to. My age wasn't something I had control over, but I was still glad that he approved.

'Where are you taking me?' I asked, as he pushed open the door into the sixth-form block. The linoleum squeaked against the soles of our trainers, and the slightly stale scent of lunchtime chips wafted down the corridor. A student shouted from one of the floors above us, the sound echoing down the stairwell.

Ethan kept walking until we were outside the girls' toilets, then he turned to face me, his shoulder skimming the wall. 'You need to get your grazes cleaned up now.'

'I will. Thanks.' I brushed my palms together and he winced. 'What is it?'

'You could be pushing the gravel further in.'

'I don't . . .' I looked at my hands. He was being far too cautious, considering it was just a standard playground fall. 'I'm Georgie, by the way.'

He nodded. 'Ethan.'

'I know that,' I said with a grin.

'Right.' He sighed. 'The new boy.'

'You can't escape it in a school this small.'

His gaze flickered behind me, down the corridor then towards the common room. 'Come on.' He pushed open the door into the girls' toilets.

'You can't . . .' I started, as he pulled me inside.

He elbowed the doors of each of the three stalls, and they flung inwards one by one, slamming against the walls. 'Empty,' he announced needlessly.

'Anyone could come in at any moment.'

'I'll tell them it's an emergency.'

'It's not though, is it?'

He dipped into a stall and pulled off a long roll of toilet paper that was, thankfully, a lot softer than the stuff in the main building. Ages eleven to sixteen you were apparently adept at coping with tracing paper, but once you got to sixth form you were allowed the dignity of something better.

'You need to clean your cuts, and something tells me you wouldn't do a great job yourself.'

'What *something*?' I crossed my arms, but he gently prised them apart, then ran the paper under the cold tap and dabbed it against my left palm, which had fared worst. I winced at the cold and the sting, and then his warm fingers, gently pressing.

He shrugged. 'You just seemed like you weren't that bothered.'

'I was, I . . .' I remembered what I'd been distracted by: Mum, who that morning hadn't got out of bed, who had told me she was fine and that I didn't need to worry. I'd left feeling guilty, knowing she had really wanted me to stay, every step on the walk here cementing my status as Worst Daughter Ever. 'My phone,' I said forlornly.

'It's in my back pocket,' Ethan told me. 'I don't know if it's OK.'

'Oh.' Dread mingled with relief, because that Nokia was like a brick and I was sure it had survived the fall, and if I didn't reply soon then Mum would call me. A couple of times when I hadn't picked up, she'd phoned the school office, as if I was the one who needed checking up on. 'Thank you.' Thinking only of stopping that scenario playing out, I reached around Ethan, felt the back pocket of his jeans and slipped my fingers inside, but it was empty and then . . . He'd gone completely still, tissue pressed to my hand, and I realized I was exhaling onto the side of his neck. A tiny muscle was jumping in his jaw. I pulled back quickly. 'God, sorry.'

'It's fine,' he said gruffly, and got on with cleaning my palm. 'I'll get it for you in a second. You OK?'

'Absolutely.' Except it suddenly seemed as if everything was spinning out of control. Mum, waiting for my reply to her message, her patience running down, and me, standing in the girls' toilets while a boy I didn't know took care of me, and I'd just slid my hand into his jeans pocket like I was in *Pretty Little Liars* or something. 'No, actually.'

Ethan looked up at me. For some reason I decided to elaborate.

'It's my mum. She's not very well, and it's . . . been a bit of a juggling act, recently. School and looking after her, I mean.' I hoped I sounded competent, like I was taking it all in my stride.

'I'm sorry,' Ethan said, turning his attention back to my hand. 'That sounds tough. Does your dad help? Brothers or sisters?'

'No dad or siblings. It's fine, really.'

'It sounds like it's not. Though I guess siblings don't always make things easier.'

'Do you have brothers and sisters, then?'

'A sister, Sarah.' His voice tightened. 'She's going through a rough time at the moment.'

'I'm sorry,' I said softly. 'Also, I'm not having to deal

with being the new guy at school, with people speculating about me all over the place.'

'What have you been speculating about me?' Ethan
asked without looking up. His voice had dropped, and
I could feel his breath on my skin. It was as if he was
putting me under some kind of spell, and I wouldn't
be able to lie even if I wanted to.

'That you're an expensive Easter egg,' I said. 'Rich
and bitter, really hard to get into.' I wrinkled my nose,
because that wasn't how I'd meant it to come out. 'Not
that I'm sayi—'

'Might add that to my uni application,' Ethan said
lightly, then he *did* look up. 'Unless I can change your
mind about some of those things? I'm not rich, for
example.'

'I didn't mean—'

'And can you really say I'm hard to get into, when
you haven't tried yet?'

'Yet?' I echoed. I had been expecting him to be
annoyed at my (Kira's) assessment, but he seemed
quietly amused.

'This is the first time we've met. It's natural to be
guarded at the beginning.'

'I didn't even say . . .' I started, but I lost my train
of thought when he lowered my left hand and lifted
my right one, where there was barely a scratch. I felt
a sharp sting and he caught my eye, triumphant, as
he held a minuscule bit of gravel between his thumb
and forefinger. 'There. You would have left that in there
to fester.'

'It would have fallen out by itself,' I said dismissively.

Ethan laughed, a low, rusty sound that I felt in the pit of my stomach, like the swoop of a rollercoaster.

'I knew it,' he said. 'I just *knew*.'

'All right, smarty pants.' I grinned at him, but it faded when he dropped into a crouch and I felt his fingers brush against my knee, his hot breath on my thigh through my dress. My 'Oh' was involuntary, and then it was joined by another chorus of 'ohs' as, inevitably, a group of girls in my year burst into the toilet, all Tommy Girl perfume and bubblegum lip gloss, and came to a crashing halt when they saw Ethan crouching in front of me, leaning his head of tousled, auburn hair towards the lower half of my body.

I should have been mortified, desperate to flee the school grounds and never return, but I felt the opposite, especially when Ethan looked up and gave them such a confident, gorgeous grin that *I* had to lean against the porcelain sink, even though it wasn't directed at me, then went back to cleaning my knee, entirely unruffled.

'Won't be long,' he said loudly into the skirt of my dress, and I was given the kind of gawping, envious looks by my perfumed, shiny-haired peers that I had never dreamed, in a million years, I'd be worthy of.

Chapter Five

Now

'Georgie.' It was Sarah who strode down the front path to greet me. 'It's so lovely to see you.'

She was even more polished close up, with thick, groomed eyebrows and the sort of sheer makeup that looked effortless, a brush of subtle shimmer on her cheekbones. Her dark eyes were twinkling – her colouring was a few shades darker than her brother's – and I was caught off guard by her warm smile and outstretched hand.

'Sarah,' I said. 'I didn't . . . how are you?'

'I'm thriving, actually – thank you. Working for Ethan now, as you can see.' She gestured behind her, her laugh soft and melodic. I'd hardly heard her laugh at all when we were teenagers. 'I'm so proud of everything he's achieved.'

'It's a magnificent house.'

'Wait until you see inside.' There was a moment's pause, then she said, 'How are *you*, Georgie?' Her eyes swept over me, from my gold sandals up over my dress, to my flushed face and my hair, which I knew had lost to hers in the battle of the ponytails.

'I'm great!' I was stuck in perky, fake enthusiasm. 'I'm really, really good. Excited to be covering this for the *North Cornwall Star*, even more so now I know . . .' *That my ex is the architect? That he's here right now? Was that exciting?* 'Now I know Ethan's transformed it. He was always going to achieve his dreams.'

'That was never in doubt,' Sarah agreed.

I blinked. This whole situation was surreal, standing with her on the path of the real life Tyller Klos, exchanging pleasantries. She and the house had both had a huge impact on my life, and both had changed so much. I tried to regain some footing. 'It's going to be a great piece. There's already so much history here – it's like a fairy-tale reinvention, especially as Ethan got to know the house when it was empty.'

'All your trespassing,' Sarah said with a smirk. 'And I thought he was on his best behaviour back then, that I was the only one running amok.'

She said it so nonchalantly, I felt a white-hot flash of anger. Did she really not realize what it had cost everyone? I silently repeated my list of tasks so that I didn't say anything I shouldn't, but then I realized that Ethan was coming to join us.

'Quite a reunion for you two.' Sarah's expression was carefully neutral.

'Yeah.' I couldn't give her anything more, my heart climbing higher in my throat as if Ethan's measured steps towards us were pulling it out of me. He looked good. He had filled out in all the right places, his limbs no longer slightly too long for his body. He was a few inches taller than me, and I remembered that when he used to hug me, my head had fitted perfectly under his chin.

A bead of sweat slid down my temple. I couldn't do this. It was too hard; too much. It was—

'Georgie.' He stopped a couple of feet in front of me. He sounded calm, as if this was exactly what he'd been expecting, but I could see a muscle jumping in his jaw and knew the relaxed persona was an effort. 'It's good to see you.'

'Is it?' I asked, which wasn't the best start.

'It's been a long time.'

He was going for easy-breezy and noncommittal. OK, I could do that. 'Thirteen years. Almost exactly.' Shit. That was *not* easy-breezy. I could feel Sarah staring at the side of my face, and I wondered if she could see right through me.

'Are you here for the open house?' Ethan asked.

'No, I was taking a stroll up the hill and the gates were open, so I thought I'd come and see how much of Tyller Klos was left.' His eyes widened a fraction in shock, then he was back to calm. It was a shitty thing to say. Spence hadn't once bemoaned the renovation, and it was either this restored, glorious building or it

58

would have eventually fallen down, nothing more than rubble on the clifftop, ready to be swept away. 'Sorry,' I said. 'I'm here for the open house.'

I saw a tiny flash of amusement, the smallest quirk of his mouth. 'You're covering it for the *Star*?'

'You know I work for the *Star*?'

'My brother knows everything,' Sarah said with a smile.

'Can you go and check the champagne's cold enough please, Sarah?' Ethan asked, and there was a moment when they glared at each other, but then Sarah nodded and spun on her heels. She strode up to the house, glancing over her shoulder once. I heard a car crunch on the gravel, someone who must have been directed by Aldo round to the side of the house.

'Hey,' Ethan said, when his sister was out of earshot. He shoved his hands in his trouser pockets, and his voice was softer, as if he wanted to start again.

'Hey.' My throat felt thick, and I decided it was the oppressive weather and the pollen in the air. 'You know I work for the *Star*,' I repeated.

'I liked your piece about the dairy cows escaping. "Udder Chaos in Alperwick".'

Shame washed over me. Hard-hitting investigative journalist, I was not. 'I don't know,' I said, 'I'm not sure I milked it enough.' I saw the smile light his eyes, but he didn't give into it. 'I didn't know you had done this.' I gestured past him.

'I wanted to keep it low profile. Until it was done, anyway.'

'And now, glitzy open house with champagne?'

He glanced towards Sterenlenn, and I watched as an elegantly dressed couple, the woman wearing a floral dress and sky-high heels in buttercup yellow, walked from the secluded drive towards the front door. 'That was Sarah's idea.'

'I was surprised to see her here,' I admitted.

'She's an important part of the business.' Ethan's defensive tone took me straight back to being eighteen. 'She's changed so much since you last saw her.'

'Of course,' I said, because what was the point in dredging up old arguments? 'And you're well, are you?'

'I am, thanks. What about you? Are you doing OK?'

'Oh, I'm great!' I tried to picture the most recent woman he'd shown off on Instagram. Did he have a girlfriend here tonight? A wife? I shouldn't care. 'Everything's fine and dandy here in Alperwick.'

Ethan frowned. 'Are you—?'

'The house is beautiful. *Sterenlenn*. A blanket of stars.'

He pressed his lips together. 'Georgie, I—'

'I was saying to Sarah that it's going to be a great piece for the paper. Huge local interest because everyone's so nosy, and a whole lot of history because of the Cornish Sands series, and because you knew it when you were younger. You obviously set your sights on it as a project a while ago. I'm glad it's all working out so well.'

'I don't know about that,' he said. 'We'll have to see how this evening goes first.'

'I'm sure it'll be a success.'

The silence between us was punctuated by the wind picking up, loose bits of gravel skittering over the driveway.

'I didn't know if you'd be here,' Ethan said eventually. 'I thought, maybe, but . . . I also thought you might stay away.'

'I wish,' I muttered, but there was a traitorous part of me that was rejoicing at seeing him again, at my game of spot the difference: what was the same about him, and what had changed. I could play it for hours.

'I need to go inside,' he said, as two men in the hot weather skeletons of business suits strolled past us, one of them jostling against me, as if I was taking up too much space. Ethan wrapped his hand gently around my arm and pulled me to the side of the path. 'I need to greet people.'

'Of course. You're the architect, after all. And congratulations – I should have said that first. It's what you always wanted, and I . . . I'm really happy for you.'

'Thanks.' He nodded. 'And Georgie?' He took a step closer.

'Yes?'

'There he is!' Sarah's singsong cut through the humid air, and Ethan closed his eyes briefly. 'Ethan, Mr Jasper is keen to hear all about Sterenlenn. The champagne's waiting for you, chilled as requested.'

'I have to go.' He looked down at me. 'Come and find me later. I'd love to know what you think.'

'I can't wait to see it.' I let him stride ahead of me,

so he could reach Sarah and all the people he needed to glad-hand. I wondered if he was feeling as shaken by our reunion as I was.

Then I saw him pat the back pocket of his trousers, and I was there again, at our first meeting, when I'd searched for my phone in his jeans. But I knew that gesture meant he was nervous, because at eighteen he'd been a smoker – a small rebellion against his overbearing father, one of the things that had surprised me about him. We were only together for a few months, and I'd quickly convinced him to stop, so then the action – looking for his lighter in his back pocket – became something he did when he was anxious: reaching for the mood calmer that was no longer there. Or maybe he smoked again now? It had been thirteen years, and I didn't know him any more.

One, take photos, two, ask questions, three, have a nosy in all the rooms, four, find what you need to and get out. I repeated it as I walked up to the house, joining the other guests gravitating towards the porch, with its spotlights and glass panels either side of the open door, the scents of vanilla and mandarin wafting out to greet us, a slice of gleaming pine floorboard visible in the entrance.

There was an elaborate-looking panel next to the front door, a digital screen above a keypad, showing the date and time: *Friday 20 June 2025, 4:48 p.m.;* the conditions: *25 degrees Celsius and 60 per cent humidity;* and the status of the house: *Front door unlocked and open.* This must be part of the Sparks automated system, I realised, and I had a sudden, fatalistic urge to press some random buttons and see what would happen; anything to relieve the tension that had crawled inside me.

I squared my shoulders and took a deep breath. I was a reporter, I needed to shake hands and seem interested, drink a glass of champagne and be enthusiastic about taking photographs. I could do this in my sleep, if I put everything else to the back of my mind. I stepped over the threshold, into the most magnificent house I'd ever seen.

Chapter Six

March 2012

I kept bumping into Ethan. It wasn't a big sixth form, so it wasn't exactly unprecedented, but after that first time in the bathroom, the way he'd looked after me even though he didn't know me, I kept thinking about him, and then there he'd be. We'd pass each other in the corridor, and he'd give me a knowing, secret smile; I saw him on the opposite side of the lunch hall, where he usually sat by himself, or occasionally with a couple of boys who Freddy said were in their Art and Design class. One day, I summoned up the courage to ask him to join us, but then a girl with long caramel hair put her hand on his arm and my confidence deserted me.

'His surname is Sparks,' Kira announced, one unusually warm afternoon in March when we were walking from school to Alperwick Bay, dawdling and decompressing from lessons.

'What are you talking about?' I pretended I didn't already know.

'Ethan,' she confirmed. 'He's called Ethan Sparks.'

'It's better than Spunk,' I said, but I felt disloyal bringing up that joke again now that I'd met him.

'I can't believe he took you into the girls' toilets.' Freddy liked to pretend he was an anarchist in training, but he was as sweet as they came, and even his dyed black hair and multiple piercings couldn't disguise it. 'Weren't you worried he was going to push you into a cubicle and ravish you?'

'Hopeful more like,' Kira said with a grin.

'He's going to be an architect.' Orwell kicked a pebble, his sandy hair ruffling in the breeze. 'That's what Dagger Dave said.'

'You can't trust anything Dagger Dave says,' Freddy told him. 'Although admittedly that's not scandalous, so maybe it's true.'

'He's so focused.' Kira sounded accusing. 'He knows what he wants to do already.'

'I'm going to be a journalist and a writer,' I reminded her. 'I know, too.'

'Of course,' Freddy said far too brightly, and my spirits sank.

The concrete turned to sand under our feet, the blue water stretching ahead of us. Aquamarine shifted to indigo on the horizon, the waves large and unruly even though the tide was out, so we had a good ten-minute walk to reach the water. Alperwick Bay was big enough that we didn't feel crowded even when it was busy, the cliffs bookends on either side, the deserted mansion peering down from the clifftop to our left.

It was beautiful, and it was home, but I wanted so badly to leave – at least for a little while – and my friends, as much as they loved me, didn't think I would.

'The MS trial is going to work,' I said. 'Mum will get better, and we can sort out a programme of carers before I leave for any help she needs while I'm away.'

Kira busied herself pulling off her boots and tights.

Freddy was staring at the rocks as if he'd spotted a piskie, so I appealed to Orwell. 'She knows how important it is to me. She'll do everything she can to make sure I go.'

Orwell laughed, but let it die when I didn't join in. 'Yeah,' he said sheepishly. 'Course.'

Kira slung her arm around my shoulders. 'We know she wants what's best for you, but she is constantly on your case. And it's awful for her, *obviously*, having MS, but you didn't give it to her, Georgie. You're not responsible for her.'

'Shouldn't I be, though?' I was the only one who saw her when she was in so much pain she could barely stand, or when her hands were shaking so badly she couldn't pick up her mug. 'We'll sort it out. There are always options, aren't there?' I smiled, able to easily dismiss the horrifying possibility of being stuck here for ever, my journalism dreams, my *writing* dreams, gone. 'Are we going into the water, or not?'

Kira and Orwell were off before I'd finished the sentence, and I followed with Freddy, the wind bellowing around us as we skipped over eddies, our feet sinking into pockets of softer sand. By the time we reached the crashing waves, we were breathless and laughing, and *this* was the power of Cornwall. Right now, it was where I wanted to be.

'Oh,' Kira said. She'd been bent over, resting her hands on her knees and getting her breath back, but now she stood up straight.

'*Oh* what?' Freddy pulled her against him and kissed her neck. 'Exercise made you frisky, has it?'

'No.' Kira pointed. '*That* oh.'

We followed the direction of her outstretched finger, and I got her *oh*. Ethan was walking in the shallows, his jeans rolled up, carrying his trainers. His head was tilted, gaze focused on the floor as he listened to the slender, dark-haired girl at his side, who was talking and gesticulating wildly.

'He just *looks* like an architect, don't you think?' Orwell said, as my insides fizzed with envy.

'He looks like a guy.' Freddy was nonplussed. 'Honestly, what's the fuss? Apart from the whole bathroom thing. That was bold.' He held his fist out to me and I bumped it, as if I had orchestrated that stunt.

'She walks the same way as him.' Kira was standing with her arms folded, studying them. 'Honestly, Georgie, I wouldn't worry.'

'Why would I be worried? I've spoken to him once.'

'You've done a lot more than that, by all accounts.'

I knew Orwell was teasing, but it came out as a sneer, and I took a step away from him just as Ethan raised his head and locked eyes with me. He looked surprised, then he smiled and said something to his companion before striding towards us, and I focused on being nonchalant and unaffected. From the look Kira shot me, I might have failed.

'Hi, Georgie,' Ethan said.

'Hey. How are you?'

'Just giving my little sister a pep talk.' Relief settled inside me, and I hoped it wasn't showing on my face.

'Sod off, Ethan.' The girl scowled at him.

'This is Sarah,' he said, as if she hadn't spoken. 'Sarah, this is Georgie, who's in my year.'

'Hi, Sarah, it's nice to meet you.' I waited for her 'you too', but she just nodded sullenly, so I went on. 'This is Kira, Freddy and Orwell. Guys, this is Ethan – and Sarah.'

There was a round of *heys* and handshakes between the boys, *I've seen you in Design,* and *we're in Maths together* politely exchanged, like we were proper grown-ups.

'I'm going home,' Sarah said, and Ethan frowned.

'I should come.'

She put a hand up in front of his face. 'No offence, *big brother*, but it's a ten-minute walk. I can manage it by myself. I'm really starting to get bored of you being my shadow, for absolutely no reason whatsoever.'

'You know why.' He turned away from us, as if that would stop us from hearing their conversation. 'I can't protect you if I'm not there.'

'I don't want you to.'

'You *know*—'

'I'm going home now.'

He dropped his shoulders, defeated. 'Text me when you get there.'

Sarah rolled her eyes and stomped off across the sand. Ethan stared after her, his arms limp at his sides.

'I'm the youngest of four,' Freddy said, 'so I have experience of being a shithead to my older sisters and brother. Looks like she's taking the job seriously.'

Ethan shook his head. 'She's unhappy. We moved here a couple of months ago and she had to leave her friends behind. But even before that, things weren't great. I'm just trying to look out for her.'

'Seems like it's a losing battle,' Kira said gently.

Ethan rubbed his eyes, then his gaze found mine. 'How are the injuries?'

'Gone,' I said, because it had been two weeks. 'All down to you, of course. Otherwise, the gravel would have burrowed inside me and given me blood poisoning.'

'You shouldn't joke about it,' he said, but he was fighting a smile. 'It could have been serious.'

'It wasn't, because of you. You settling in OK?'

'Not too bad. It's great having the beach so close.'

'It's the best,' Kira said. 'Race you to the rocks?'

It was a standard thing we did to blow off steam, but Ethan looked surprised because the rocks were quite a way out, past some pretty big waves, and it was also March, and freezing.

'You wear costumes under your clothes?' he asked. 'Do you bring towels with you, then?'

'I know it looks a long way, but there are sandbanks – it doesn't get that deep.' Freddy pulled off his beanie.

Kira was already lifting her T-shirt, revealing her sleek black swimsuit underneath. 'You can't live in Alperwick and not give the rocks a go.'

Ethan glanced towards the seafront, as if he regretted not following his sister home, then looked at me. 'Are you doing it?'

I hadn't been planning to stay long. Mum had been in a weird mood that morning, physically OK but staring out of the window a lot, distracted and vacant, and I needed to check on her. But the idea of leaving Ethan to race to the rocks with my friends, without me there, was unbearable.

'I will if you will.' I started unbuttoning my dress.

He watched my fingers move and, despite the temperature, I wished I was wearing a slinky, sexy bikini, low cut and brightly coloured, instead of the modest navy costume I had on. After a moment's hesitation he mirrored my movements, unbuttoning his shirt, exposing his strong shoulders, a lean chest, pale but with clusters of freckles. My gaze snagged on his belly button, the trail of brown hair that ran down his stomach, and I turned away, letting my dress pool at my feet. When I risked a glance, Ethan had taken off his shirt and jeans and was standing in a pair of blue boxers. He didn't seem self-conscious, but my cheeks heated at how much of him was on show.

70

'You do *know* that it's March, don't you?' he said. 'Aren't we heading into hypothermia territory?'

'It's exhilarating,' I said, though I knew it would be almost unbearably cold.

'After you, then.' He gestured to the water, where Kira, Freddy and Orwell were already splashing in the smaller waves.

'OK.' I sprinted into the water, squealing at just how right I'd been, the cold numbing my feet and legs in seconds. Ethan was behind me, a hint of warmth at my back.

'Jesus fuck it's freezing,' he panted out.

'The trick is to not hang about,' Freddy said, wading further out. We followed him, dodging breakers and ducking under swells, bobbing up to wipe water from our eyes.

The sun was already sliding towards the horizon, making diamonds out of the surface that were blinding to look at. I turned to check on Ethan and found him beside me, treading water.

'OK?' I asked, as icy currents drifted around my legs.

'I'm good,' he said, with more conviction than he'd had on the beach. 'This is good.' He laughed. 'I'm swimming in the sea, in my pants. This is not the sort of thing I do.'

'It's inevitable when you live here.' With his wet hair slicked back, his face was all sharp angles, his eyelashes dark and glossy. I risked a step towards him, the water swirling around us, making us weightless. Orwell and

Kira called out from beyond the biggest waves – they were near the rock, we had lost the race – but I ignored them.

Ethan moved closer too, cupping my shoulder like he'd done in the courtyard. But this time my skin was bare, and he was mostly naked, and I felt the pull of him, the way his touch made me ache in other places. Our childish seaside game, our way of letting off steam, changed for me in that moment, and I thought of the way Ethan had said 'Good' so firmly when I'd told him I was eighteen.

'I might have to get used to it then,' he said.

'Which bit?'

'All of it. The sea. Swimming. You.'

Me. 'Glad I could introduce you to this important Alperwick tradition,' I said loftily, daring to flick my eyes down to where he was hazy and indistinct under the water, 'in your pants.'

He grinned, the surface of the sea bouncing sunlight onto his cheeks and making them glow. 'Not to sound like a dickhead, but I'm glad you got hit by that football.'

'Me too. Though you could have just spoken to me whenever, not waited until I needed rescuing.'

'I wasn't . . .' he started, then looked away. 'I was going to. I was working up the courage.'

I was about to ask him why he needed courage to talk to me, and why my words had frustrated him, because he had rescued me, hadn't he? In a very small way. But then Kira shouted over, in a voice I was always surprised could come out of someone so delicate, 'Hello!? The rocks are *this* way! Have you got lost *in the open sea?*'

Freddy joined in, cupping his hands around his mouth. 'This isn't make-out time! Ethan and Georgie, you are not limpets! Get your asses over here!'

I laughed, hoping it would cover up my mortification. 'We'd better go before they get even more creative. Limpets is bad enough.' I waded forward, Ethan alongside me.

'Why are we limpets?' he asked. 'We weren't kissing.'

I was going to tell him that the truth didn't matter when it came to my friends and their insults, but I got distracted by the word *kissing*. And then, although maybe I imagined it, with the waves crashing around us and the shouts of people enjoying the spring afternoon, I was sure he added quietly, 'Not yet, anyway.'

After that, I couldn't think of anything but kissing him, and even when I made it home to Mum's strange mood and a heap of English work I couldn't find the enthusiasm for, my dress sticking to my damp costume, hair in rattails, I felt like I was still floating in the sea, weightless and without limits.

Chapter Seven

Now

The inside of Sterenlenn was like nothing I'd ever seen in real life, and it was a world away from the dark shell I'd known as a teenager.

It was a palace of open spaces and polished textures, marble and chrome and wood that was buffed to a high shine. The entrance was double height, the pale wooden stairs with open risers at the back of the airy foyer, where tall windows showed off the blue-green of the sea and the hazy sky beyond, so it felt as if the landscape was breaching the walls. To the left, a door led into a study where I could see pine bookshelves, each row of paperbacks subtly lit with LED lighting, and a sleek desk in front of the window, the only item on top a brushed chrome uplighter. I hesitated on the threshold, wondering if any of the books were from Spence's Cornish Sands series.

People milled about in the foyer, stopping to look at a large, spangled mosaic that was part decoration part mirror, and the discreet, gunmetal wall panel that I realized, after a few confusing seconds, was a built-in sound system: part of the Sparks set-up that ran the whole house. But most of the guests had gravitated towards the kitchen, which was to the right of the entrance. I'd glimpsed black marble countertops, pearly white cupboards with sage green trim, a room big enough for a squashy sofa in front of the sea-facing window and a double sink at the other end, a hot-water tap probably the most mundane of all the luxurious features.

There were wall panels in every room, with winking lights to represent the status of the underfloor heating and the water pressure, the ambient air and the speaker settings. It was in complete contrast to the peeling paintwork and mouldy carpet the five of us had been greeted with when we sneaked in with torches all those years ago. To a soundtrack of scrabbling rodents, I had told Ethan that I wanted to be a writer, and he had explained how he would bring buildings back from the brink of collapse; that he wanted to be the kind of architect who took what was broken and made it whole again. It had been a statement so entirely Ethan, that my chest constricted just thinking about it. And, standing here, in the realization of his dream, was a stark reminder of how far I was from mine.

'Gorgeous, isn't it?'

I turned to find the woman with the bright yellow heels standing next to me. Her dark hair was a glossy wave down her back, and her eyes were a darker blue than mine: cornflower instead of forget-me-not. I thought I recognized her, and knew it could only be from Ethan's Instagram posts.

'It's a miracle,' I said, because that's what it felt like compared to before. 'Are you . . . a friend of Sarah's? An estate agent?'

She laughed lightly. 'No, I've come with Ethan. We both live in Bristol.' I nodded, because I knew his firm, Sparks Architecture, was based there. I had done my own digging, but had never found anything about this build, and I'd obviously missed Sarah's name on the website, though I presumed it must be there somewhere. It felt like one more thing I'd failed at: no wonder I'd been stuck writing reports about cow elopements and charity bike rides.

'Do you work together?' I asked.

'I'm a friend.' She examined one of the elaborate bouquets that were placed throughout the house. Cream and pink roses nestled alongside baby's breath, deep purple orchids, the soft foliage fitting in perfectly with the green accents in the decor.

'Why are *you* here?' I was sure Ethan's perhaps-girlfriend hadn't meant it to sound so accusing.

'I'm covering this evening for the local paper,' I said. 'Actually, I'd better get started.'

I opened my rucksack and she slunk off, champagne

glass in hand, while I took out my old Nikon and checked it was working. I started taking photographs, distracted by all the ways Ethan had let the sea into the house. There were the large windows, framing the coast as the ever-changing focal point of every room, and I could see chinks of bright blue everywhere: in the foyer mosaic, and round the rim and base of the vases; a thin stripe along the chrome staircase railing, and a bright fissure threaded through the black marble surfaces in the kitchen. The chandeliers were textured crystal, the pieces mostly clear but with a few turquoise and aquamarine, like an exploded sea-glass glitter ball.

Standing on the landing, I got held up trying to get the perfect shot through a distorted-glass porthole – which was positioned between the tall, rectangular windows at the back of the foyer – of the stepped garden that ran down to the cliff's edge, and was halted only by the redbrick wall surrounding the property. My mind drifted to Amelie and Connor, how they had ended *The Whispers of the Sands* on opposite sides of the Atlantic, and how Spence and I could bring them back together in this house. It was the perfect setting: a space so beautiful and elegant, it was as if Ethan's careful fingertips had brushed over every inch.

There was the high 'ting' of cutlery against glass, and Sarah's voice rang out from the kitchen. 'Ladies and gentlemen, I'd like to welcome you all here this evening, to celebrate the feat of modern architecture that is glorious Sterenlenn. Please take yourself through the rooms (there is a lot to explore), sip champagne and eat canapés. But, before we leave you to drink your fill of this shimmering cliffside escape, I'd love to introduce you to the talent behind it, who just happens to be my big brother, Ethan Sparks!' There was a smattering of applause, and I slunk down the stairs to join everyone else.

I leant in the kitchen doorway, one of the Sparks panels on the wall next to me, as Ethan stepped out of a sea of bodies, champagne glass in hand, two pinpoints of colour on his cheekbones as he faced his waiting audience. He had never sought out the lime-light, had always talked about his work speaking for itself, and I could see how uncomfortable he was.

'Thank you all for coming,' he said. 'I know this isn't the easiest place to get to, so I appreciate the trouble you've taken to make the journey and see what we've achieved with this property. It had solid foundations long before we got anywhere near it, so I can't claim the credit for how grounded it feels to be here, and it has a long history that hasn't been celebrated enough. It's been immortalized in fiction, and it's a part of my own backstory, too.' He swallowed, and I wondered if he was focused on any particular memory.

'Now it's Sterenlenn,' he continued, sounding more confident, 'and while I hope my transformation gives it the second chance it deserves, I didn't want to erase its past. I've been sympathetic to the landscape, to the environment and our increasingly urgent quest for sustainability, but I haven't compromised on luxury. The innovative Sparks system lets users manage the house using voice activation, the wall tablets and the accompanying app: temperature and heating options – there is underfloor heating throughout – as well as lighting and air conditioning.

'The sound system, intercom and speakers are embedded, so you can be in touch with every part of the house – but you can also switch rooms off together or in isolation if you need privacy.' Someone caterwauled, and a furrow appeared between Ethan's brows. 'There are security cameras covering the grounds and the outside of the property, and a sophisticated alarm system that connects to the local authorities if you activate Panic Room Mode, or in case of a threat. It's as modern as it comes, but it's subtle, too. Above everything else, I want this to be a home, not a spaceship.'

'No chance of that,' a woman called out. 'The views are magnificent.'

Ethan smiled, back on safer ground, and I remembered that he'd never got over his awe of the Cornish coastline. He'd grown up in London, and his family had moved around before landing in Alperwick, but they'd mostly stuck to cities. He'd been mesmerized by the landscape, and it made so much sense that he'd come back here for his first major project.

'Nothing I create can match this stretch of coast for beauty,' he said, 'but I've tried to work in harmony with it. I've focused on bringing the outside in, and the bifold doors in the lounge,' he gestured to his left, 'open onto the gardens and the sea beyond. You can tint them against the sun's glare without ruining the view, and we've adapted the roof throughout, installing skylights, so each bedroom can be exposed to the sky, the stars at night. That's probably the closest it gets to a spaceship, actually.'

There was a ripple of laughter, then Sarah added, 'Wait until you see how they work. They're one of the most impressive features, and we're starting with a long list. It's a genius touch.'

They sound magical, I thought, then jumped when Sarah's eyes found mine through the crowd and she said, 'You'll love them, Georgie.'

I shrank back. Things were going seriously wrong if I was blurting out my thoughts without realizing.

'Speaking of genius,' Ethan said, ignoring our exchange, 'I have to talk about the experts: builders and craftsmen, electricians, plumbers and structural engineers who turned my vision into reality. It has been such a solid team, and I couldn't be more grateful to have had them on my side. This is Andy – AP.' He gestured to a wide-set man with thinning brown hair and twinkling hazel eyes, who was holding an empty champagne glass, his shirt untucked as he leant against a marble countertop. 'He was our foreman, so he's the one who made this happen.'

Andy raised his glass and grinned at the applause, then exchanged a nod with Ethan that was full of affection. I wondered if they were friends; whether they'd gone for pints together, celebrating the wins, strategizing over beer mats when the build went wrong or they hit a hurdle. I'd seen enough episodes of *Grand Designs* to know a thing like this could break you completely, and Ethan hadn't just been a passive architect, focusing on the maths and physics, every tiny calculation that needed to be spot on to avoid disaster. Despite our years apart, I knew how much of his heart was in this building, how desperate he would have been for his ideas to work. I tried not to imagine a sultry brunette – like Yellow Shoes – giving him a massage at the end of a long day, working out the kinks in his broad back.

'Tell us about the name,' someone said, and my neck prickled, because I recognized the polished voice. It was Jean Durand, field reporter for the local TV news. I had seen him on countless bulletins, all floppy dark hair and smug smile. He'd asked the question that had me freezing, breath held, my eyes back on Ethan in time to see him blanch.

'If you didn't want to answer,' I murmured to myself, 'you should have named it something else.'

'Sterenlenn,' Jean went on, when Ethan didn't respond. 'Literal translation "star blanket", so I guess you're saying this house is under a blanket of stars. Why did this name make the cut, above all the other possibilities?'

The room fell to a hush. The sweet scent of roses suddenly seemed overpowering, and I knew that this was what really mattered: not the nuts and bolts of the build, the materials they'd used and the sustainable features factored in, but why it was so personal – what

81

someone felt about it, and why they'd made certain choices. What was inside someone like Ethan, who seemed so restrained, cut off from everyone, even though he was standing in the middle of them? How had this design come out of his head, and why did he give a fuck?

Would he admit it? I didn't want everyone looking at me, but I also didn't want him to dismiss my role in it. I wanted him to acknowledge that part of the reason he cared about the house was because, once upon a time, he'd cared about me. We could be pleasant with each other tonight, then go our separate ways, but I was desperate for him to admit the real origin of the name he'd chosen.

I realized he was watching me. He swallowed and ran a hand through his hair, then looked away. The few sips of champagne I'd had curdled in my gut.

'I got to learn a little of the Cornish language when I lived here,' he told everyone. 'It's as lyrical as the landscape, and I knew this house needed a Cornish name. Here on the cliffs, away from any light pollution, the stars are almost unbelievable. You won't get a chance to see them tonight, because they won't appear until long after this event is over, but those of you who are local know what I mean. You feel small beneath them, you feel covered, overwhelmed by them and so . . .' He shrugged. 'Blanket of stars.'

A few people cooed, Jean stupid Durand seemed satisfied by his bland answer, but the champagne had fully turned to acid in my stomach. I'd been written out of the story, which would have made sense if I hadn't come tonight – I would never even have known. But I was standing right here, we'd spoken to each other calmly, *warmly* almost, and I'd felt drawn to him, as I'd known I would, the moment I realized he was behind the transformation; the moment I'd known he'd be here.

But he'd left out the important fact that I had given him the name, that it was his and mine, together, woven through the memories of this house before, when we'd been falling in love. I caught his eye, saw his shame, and then quietly turned away from him and his speech, and the crowd of sycophantic onlookers smiling up at him.

I would tour the house like Spence wanted me to, and so I could gather all I needed for my article, then I would get out. I would leave Ethan and Sterenlenn behind, and I wouldn't look back.

Chapter Eight

March 2012

We were sitting in the canteen, talking over the backdrop of scraping cutlery and chattering students when Kira reached into her bag, took out a large cuddly tarantula and plonked it on the table, almost upsetting my water glass.

'What the fuck?' Freddy scooted away from the table, his chair screeching against the floor.

'Look at its eyes,' Ethan said calmly. Ever since that day on the beach, he'd been hanging out with us at lunchtimes, sometimes meeting up after school too. 'They're so red.'

'It's my birthday soon,' Kira announced, 'and Mum won't let me have a party.' Kira's mum was a wedding planner, their house was showroom perfect, and whenever I went there she seemed to follow us around, picking up glasses and bowls the second they were empty. I was surprised she hadn't tidied *me* away. I was not surprised Kira wasn't getting a party.

'So you bought yourself a tarantula as a commiseration present?' I asked.

'He was pleading with me from the window of that trick shop in Truro, and I thought about putting him in Mum's bed in protest. I want to do *something* for my birthday.' She waggled the spider in Freddy's face and he flinched away from it.

'Beach trip?' Orwell suggested.

'Cinema?' I tried.

'We can go to the Sailor's Rest,' Freddy said. 'You're the last of us to turn eighteen, so it would be legit.'

'I want to do something *different*.' Kira threw the cuddly spider to Ethan and he caught it easily.

'Is this our talking piece?' he asked. 'So, now I have it, it's my turn to speak?'

'Exactly,' Kira said smugly, though I was sure she hadn't thought of that.

'OK then.' He frowned at the demonic spider, then looked up, and we were treated to his half-smile, which did funny things to my insides when it was combined with his thigh pressed against mine under the table. 'What about that house on the cliffs?'

'Tyller Klos?' I blurted.

'It's only called that in your romance books.' Kira rolled her eyes. 'What is that? "Secluded Place"?'

'It's not secluded,' Orwell said. 'It's sitting on top of the cliffs like a big sore thumb.'

'Creepy though.' Freddy narrowed his eyes at Ethan. 'What do you have in mind?'

'Maybe we could get inside. It's been abandoned for years, right?'

'S. E. Artemis moved out over fifteen years ago, the same time she stopped writing books. It's a really big house, and it's at the top of that huge hill, so . . .'

'You little fangirl.' Kira squeezed my arm affectionately. 'You really think we can get inside?' she asked Ethan. 'What if it's all boarded up? Padlocked?'

Ethan shrugged. 'We won't know unless we try.'

Kira whooped, drawing looks from the girls further down the table. 'We could take torches so we weren't too terrified. Snacks, some drinks. It would be the best birthday.'

'And Ethan can look at the structural integrity of the building,' Orwell said. 'Right, Ethan?'

Ethan stared steadily back. 'I'm interested in buildings, but I'm not going to ruin Kira's birthday by carrying out a full site survey. I can bring some gin or vodka – whatever you want.'

'Yessssss Ethan,' Kira said. 'I knew there was a reason we let you into our group.'

'Several reasons,' I corrected. Ethan pressed his leg more firmly against mine, and I slid my hand down his thigh, felt his muscles tense beneath my palm. 'He's an expert in crisis situations – especially getting gravel out of cuts – so we definitely need him.'

'Sure your mum will let you have the night off?' Orwell asked me, mock serious.

Freddy whacked him on the arm. 'Not cool, dude. Ignore him, Georgie. He's being a dick.'

Ethan put his arm around my shoulders and threw the spider back to Kira, but she was staring at us, dumbfounded, and so were Freddy and Orwell. I felt a rush as I leaned into Ethan, enjoying the weight of his arm around me.

'Georgie has to come,' he said. 'She's Kira's best friend, and she knows more about the house than the rest of us combined.'

'Agreed.' Kira leaned over the table so she could high-five Ethan.

'Solid,' Freddy said, and I saw Orwell throw Ethan a filthy look before he nodded along with the rest of us, and we started concocting our plan to get into the abandoned house for Kira's birthday.

Later that day, once we'd said goodbye to Freddy, Kira and Orwell in the village, Ethan offered to walk me home. Sarah was silent beside us, hovering like a storm cloud ready to erupt.

'I suppose I'll go back by myself then,' she said sullenly.

'It's five minutes that way,' Ethan gestured patiently. Their house was a double-fronted semi-detached, set back behind a long driveway, so different to the terrace I lived in with Mum.

'I'll see you tomorrow, Sarah,' I said, and got a glare in response.

'Are you enjoying Ethan's attention, Georgie?' she asked, surprising me.

'Sarah.' Ethan's voice was a low warning.

'I like him a lot,' I told her, refusing to be intimidated.

'Don't get used to it,' she said. 'Don't think he'll stick around.'

'I'll be home in ten minutes, OK?' Ethan's tone was sharper than I'd ever heard it, and Sarah strode off without another word. He sighed. 'She doesn't want me to crowd her or walk home with her, but when I try and do something else, she's offended.'

'You're very protective.'

'I want her to be OK. There was . . .' He stopped talking, a muscle pulsing in his jaw.

'What, Ethan?'

'Before we came here, we lived in York. One night, she went to a party and called me around one a.m., asking me to come and get her. She woke me up, and I was angry, and stubborn about it.' His laugh was humourless. 'She sounded frantic, but she'd called me so many times before and it had never been an emergency. Usually she just wanted me to pick her up. So I said I'd come, but I took my time getting dressed, and I walked because she was in the centre of town.' He shook his head. 'When I got there, she was bleeding – she had a cut on her head – and the police were there.'

'Shit.' I brushed my hand against his.

'She'd got into an argument with another girl and her boyfriend, who were both older than her. Sarah had lashed out, the other girl had retaliated, and honestly, I was glad that the police were called – even though Sarah got in trouble. It stopped it escalating.'

'You were there for her, though.'

'I could have got there sooner and been less pissed off about it. I should have protected her better, so now I am, and she resents me for it.'

'Hey.' I squeezed his arm. 'You're doing all you can. I'm sorry it's so difficult.'

'Maybe it'll get easier if we settle here.'

'It's *bound* to get easier.' I nudged his shoulder. 'Also, can I just say, especially now I know how responsible you are, that I would never have expected you to suggest breaking into an abandoned building.'

'We might not be able to. Kira's right, it's likely to be padlocked and boarded up.'

'What if it's not, though?'

He smiled. 'Then we can jimmy open the door and have a look around. You'd like to, right? Considering how important it is in those books you love?'

'I would love to.' I'd told him about the Cornish Sands series a few days ago, and was even toying with sharing some of my favourite passages with him. 'But at *night*?' I shuddered theatrically.

'There's less chance of being caught in the dark.' We had reached the turning onto my road. There was a shop on the corner, Alperwick Watchmaker's, the name written in faded, elegant script above the door, though it had been empty for as long as I could remember. It was glass-fronted and faced the beach, and I thought it would be perfect as an ice-cream parlour or coffee shop, one of those community hubs where regulars got to try all the new specials for free.

'We could practise, if you wanted?' Ethan gestured to the door of the watchmaker's. Its wooden frame was cracked and rotten, possibly infested with woodworm.

'We can't.'

'Why not?'

I held up my index finger. 'One, it's broad daylight.' I held up my middle finger. 'Two, there are people everywhere.'

'But this glass.' He pressed his palm against it, fingers splayed. 'It feels like picture glass to me. I bet I could break it with my elbow.'

'Are you a secret rebel, Ethan?'

He raised an eyebrow and then, as if in answer to my question, took a cigarette out of his pocket. He put it in his mouth and brought a silver Zippo up to light it, cupping his hand around the flame. I was torn, because he looked like a golden age Hollywood film star, with his mess of hair and high cheekbones, a cigarette dangling from his mouth. But I thought about the poison going into his lungs, and after his second drag I plucked it out of his fingers and ran up the road, my rucksack bouncing on my back.

'Hey!' I heard his footsteps behind me and swerved left, across the seafront road and onto the beach.

90

I dipped right, so I was running along the edge, where the cliffs rose up from sea level. Little streams of water ran down the stone, through patches of moss, making trails on the sand. It was damp from an earlier shower, squidgy beneath my feet, the sky still bustling with clouds. I stubbed the cigarette out against the stone.

'Hey!' Ethan called again. His legs were longer, he could have caught up with me already, but for some reason he was holding off. I kept going along the cliff line, the jagged rock rising above me until there was an overhang, a shallow recess that was close to but not quite a cave, and I risked glancing behind me.

He was on me immediately, his hands gripping my hips, lifting me slightly and then placing me back a step, so I was inches from the cliff face. I let my bag slip off my shoulders, heard the scrape as it met rough rock on the way down.

'Hey, Georgie.' Ethan stepped forwards, crowding me, his legs on either side of mine.

My head knocked gently into the overhang as I looked up at him.

'You,' he said through laboured breaths, 'are a little thief.' His eyes blazed, but he brought his hand up behind my head, a soft cushion to shield me from the rock.

'Smoking's bad for you,' I said. 'You're only eighteen. What if it stunts your growth?' I'd meant it as a joke, but it hadn't come out that way.

He raised an eyebrow. 'I don't think . . .'

'I don't want you getting ill,' I blurted, then flushed,

embarrassed. I'd tried so hard to keep my fears about Mum away from this part of my life; it was a personal promise I'd renewed when I met Ethan, and this was only the odd cigarette: I was being ridiculous.

But his gaze softened, and he brushed my hair off my forehead. 'I'm OK,' he said, 'but I will stop, if you want me to?'

His words hung in the air, the crash of the waves punctuating the quiet, and I realized what he was offering me, because how could I make him stop smoking if we were just friends, if we just hung out occasionally? Why would he do that for me?

'I want you to stop,' I said.

His gaze flickered, and then he smiled, wide and bright. When he leaned towards me, the smoke lingering on his breath, I parted my lips and invited him closer, closing my eyes when he brushed his mouth over mine.

I'd kissed a couple of other boys in school, but those encounters had been overeager and desperate, more about getting important milestones out of the way than the people I was with, and I hadn't gone any further than that. Ethan was patient, his lips exploring gently, his hand on my hip again, pulling me against him.

'Is this OK?' he whispered.

I nodded and tried to moan seductively, but it came out more like a squeak.

'Good,' he said. That one word reminded me of the first day we met, and then my mind went blank as he kissed me again, increasing the pressure. I slid my hands around his back, clinging to him like I never wanted to let go.

It felt unreal and reckless, kissing Ethan on the beach, in sight of the cold, raw ocean, the March wind twisting around us.

When he finally pulled away, his cheeks were pink. 'Are you all right?' he asked hoarsely.

I tried to catch my breath. 'I'm . . .' I didn't know what else to say, so I pressed my fingers to my lips and grinned at him.

He puffed out a breath, as if he was relieved, then returned my smile. 'I will stop smoking for you, Georgie.' He picked up my rucksack and shrugged it onto his shoulder, then took my hand. 'Can I walk you home?'

I nodded, helpless to do anything else. My world had changed in those few minutes, and I couldn't wait to go to the clifftop mansion with him, no matter how dark it was, how many spiders or rats or ghosts there might be waiting to terrify us, because I knew he would make me feel safe.

Chapter Nine

Now

I strode up the stairs clutching my camera. I could hear the low timbre of Ethan's voice, laughter echoing up the double-height foyer as I stepped into the first room I came to on the right of the landing. I let out a long, slow breath as I took it all in. This, surely, was the master bedroom.

I had no teenage blueprint to lay this over because, when we'd trespassed, we weren't sure if the stairs were safe, and none of us had been brave enough to try them. So this was completely new to me. It was a huge room, decorated in soft tones of off-white and dove grey, with touches of the blues and greens that I'd seen in the rest of the house. The king-sized bed stood against the far wall, and the window that looked out over the sea was framed by a luxurious window seat in a rich blue fabric, a bank of green and white scatter cushions adding to its plushness. There were no blinds, and I assumed the glass here could be tinted, or blacked out completely at night, like Ethan had mentioned in his speech.

Cushions on the bed matched the ones on the window seat, sitting proudly on a silver bedspread that looked like glistening water. There was a chaise longue at the foot of the bed in emerald green velvet, and I felt a pang, because everything about this house was opulent, but having a seat at the end of the bed – having a bedroom big enough to fit one – had always seemed like the height of luxury to me: so simple but desirable, to be able to sit there and put on your socks. Here, there was so much floor space between the bed and the wardrobe that I was almost tempted to perform an entire dance routine on the plush grey carpet, though I would have to find one on TikTok first.

Anglepoise lamps were built into the walls on either side of the bed, above floating bedside tables, and there was an oil landscape of a windswept coastline above the headboard, the reds and earthy greens of fields running down to the sea, the layers of bold texture a rugged contrast to the room's soft hues and clean lines. It would be a local artist, I thought, and made a note in my notebook to ask Ethan – or Sarah – so I could mention it in my article. At this moment, neither of those prospects was appealing.

I walked into the bathroom and found a claw-foot tub under the window, the view of the grassy, wildflower-strewn clifftop stretching away from Alperwick, towards the next bay along. There was a separate shower, with spotlights recessed in the pearly tiles. I touched the panel next to the door and a rainbow of lights illuminated the floor, cycling from pink to blue, green to yellow, like a steam room in a spa hotel. I pressed the button again and again, watching the lights change from pulsing to a slow fade, to static colours and then off. Who needed disco lights in their shower? Suddenly, it was all I wanted.

I returned to the bedroom, and touched the rose petals in yet another elaborate bouquet. I had a sudden idea that it was fake, and they were pumping the scent through the discreet Sparks vents, but there was nothing plastic about it. Ethan wasn't – or at least *hadn't* been – a dishonest person, unless the lies were to protect someone he loved. I moved some of the cushions aside and sat on the window seat, trying not to think about the choice he'd made all those years ago, and how I'd reacted.

I could hear the murmur of people below, soft voices and the tread of footsteps in the corridor outside. I smiled as a couple paused in the bedroom doorway, eyes wide as they took in the opulence, then I turned away from them, towards the window, and heard them move on. The sun was hovering above the mirrored horizon, but a bank of thick cloud was gathering to the north, obliterating the blue sky. In here, the air was cool, but I could almost feel the heavy humidity outside, and I wondered if the weather would break tonight. I pressed the panel next to the window and watched the glass go from clear to frosted. I pressed it again and it went dark, the room plunged into a thick gloom. Soft lighting immediately took its place, running along the skirting board and from hidden spotlights I hadn't noticed in the ceiling. I pressed it again and the view reappeared, the lights winking out.

'It's Smart glass.'

I jumped, then turned to see Ethan standing in the doorway. He'd discarded his jacket, loosened his tie and rolled up his shirtsleeves. The glass he held only had a dribble of champagne left in the bottom.

'Have you let go now that you've given your speech?' I gestured towards him, and he looked down, as if he hadn't realized he'd started to unravel.

He took a step into the room.

I picked up my rucksack and my camera. 'It was a great speech.'

'I said what I had to.'

He was resolute, as if I'd imagined the moment of shame when he'd written me out of Sterenlenn's origin story. 'And I have all I need, too.' I tried to slide my Nikon into my bag but it got stuck, the wrist loop catching on the broken zip. 'I can go now.'

The carpet was thick and I didn't hear him crossing the room, but then he was crouched in front of me, trying to untangle the camera from the zip. I pulled my hand away.

'I meant what I said outside, about it being good to see you.'

My stomach swooped. 'You too,' I said, though I wasn't sure if I meant it.

'You've really got everything you need?'

'This isn't a long-form piece for the *New York Times*, Ethan.' I yanked the bag back, and the zipper flew off and pinged against the wall.

He huffed out a frustrated, 'Fine.'

'Great.' I jammed the camera into my bag, no longer caring if it broke in the process.

'You seem irritated,' he said, and I resisted the urge to roll my eyes.

'I'm not, I'm just on a schedule.' Sweat prickled down my spine despite the air conditioning, and I felt as if all the composure I'd carefully gathered during the day was deserting me, with his face so close and the sound of his breaths punctuating the spaces between our words.

'You didn't have to come today.'

'I really wish I hadn't.' I stood up and so did he. He was between me and the door. 'I wish I hadn't bothered but Spence—'

'Spencer?' His brows knitted together. 'Who's Spencer?'

I felt a thud of satisfaction. He might have been keeping tabs on me, but he wouldn't have found evidence of a boyfriend, because I didn't have one – not since I broke up with Rick – and S. E. Artemis had been out of the limelight for thirty years. So let him think Spence was Spencer. Considering all the beautiful women he paraded on Instagram, it seemed only fair.

'I have to go,' I said.

'Everyone will be gone soon.'

'Great. Then you can dance around in your perfect house and roll about on the huge bed.' I tried to move past him, and he put his hand on my arm.

'Don't you want to at least have a conversation?'

I turned my head. He was so close, bent slightly so he was on my level, his brown eyes – which seemed to change shade depending on whether he was happy or upset or annoyed – fixed on me.

'There's nothing to say,' I whispered. 'I need to go.'

'I want you to stay.'

'Tough.' I leaned in a millimetre, and my hip brushed his thigh. 'I don't want to be here any more.' My gaze drifted to the hollow at his throat. He'd opened a couple of shirt buttons, and the knot of his tie was tight, as if he'd yanked it. I looked up, and our eyes met. I wondered if he was holding his breath too. I parted my lips, awareness tingling through me, making me lightheaded.

'Wait for me,' he said firmly, breaking the spell, then he was striding out of the room and down the stairs, and as I tried to regain my composure I heard a cacophony of cheery, champagne-oiled goodbyes. 'We'll be in touch,' and 'Perfect house, darling,' and 'I want to know when it's on the market.' I wondered which voice belonged to the brunette, which one of those people were actually considering buying it. It was a prime, luxury property, it would go for several million at least, and then it wouldn't be Ethan's any more, and it wouldn't be Spence's, and it certainly wouldn't be mine . . . though it had never been mine.

I turned in a circle, trying to memorize everything. I had photographs, and I would probably be able to close my eyes and picture these rooms for years to come: I could be convincing about it for Spence's new book. I zipped up my rucksack and strode to the doorway.

'I'm taking Cassie back to the station, Ethan.' Sarah's voice echoed, as if she was standing at the bottom of the staircase, the double-height foyer projecting her voice upwards. 'I can come back and get you afterwards, so you have a little longer here.'

'I can't leave yet anyway,' he said, and I peeked round the doorway and saw the top of his head. He was halfway up the stairs. 'We need to clear up the kitchen, all the glasses and crockery.'

Sarah laughed. 'The catering company is in charge of all that. We should gather up any full bottles, because we've paid for them, but leave the rest. I'll be back in thirty minutes, give you some alone time with the house.'

'You don't need to do that. I'll get a taxi to the station.'

'Are you still heading back to Bristol tonight? We should follow up with everyone in the morning, remind them that this place won't be available for long.'

'Great.' Ethan's voice was flat, and I leaned my forehead against the wall. This was the first day he'd been able to show Sterenlenn off, and it could belong to someone else in hours. That must always have been the endgame, but I knew he would hate letting it go.

And it felt like I was losing it, too: like I'd been given a chance to have more time here, and I'd squandered it by being angry and unfocused.

'OK then,' Sarah called. 'See you later, big bro. You did great, by the way.'

'It was only a speech.'

'And you nailed it. Don't forget, this is the start of all the good things. Now, make sure you take some time.' Her tone softened. 'I know how much this place means to you.'

There were some muffled thumps, then footsteps and the sound of keys jingling, and I heard the quiet, expensive clunk of the front door sliding home. I knew I was imagining it, but the house seemed to let out a breath.

'Georgie?' Ethan called up the stairs. 'We're alone.'

'Right.' My voice was raspy. 'I'm still leaving.'

'Of course.' I heard his slow, measured footsteps as he climbed the stairs again. 'I wouldn't keep you here against your will.'

'Shame,' I whispered, even though I was still – mostly – intent on leaving. I needed to loosen the tension coiling inside me, and realized that, like Sarah had done for him, Ethan was giving me a little more time in the house before it was gone for good.

When he appeared on the landing, looking knack-ered and deliciously dishevelled, a small smile was lighting his eyes, and it felt like, for the first time that day, he had let his mask slip – just a bit. I couldn't help but smile back.

Dear Connor,

Things are not great in the house right now, and as much as I'm trying not to resent being here, sometimes I think I might bubble over with frustration. How have I let it come to this? We all make decisions, and – even if it seemed like I had no choice – I am responsible for everything I've done, every place I've ended up, how much I've let other people sway me.

I know you understand, because the few times we fought, that was what it was about. How much of what you're doing is your decision? How often do you invite other people to dictate what you do with your life?

Yesterday, I saw a woman who lives on the other side of the village, who gave up the job she loved to look after her husband when he got cancer. She'd worked hard as a librarian, spent years dedicated to spreading the joy of books, and had eventually got her dream job managing a little independent bookshop in Porthleven, right by the harbour. Then, when her husband got ill, she gave it up to look after him. His treatment was brutal, and she supported him through all of it, and thankfully he recovered. But what did he do after that? He told her he was in love with someone else, and he left her.

It's a shocking story, which is the only reason I got to hear about it, but it makes you think, doesn't it? You have to look after yourself as much as you look after others; hold onto what's important to you too, because otherwise you'll lose everything that matters.

This story, at least, has a perfect ending. The woman sold the house she'd shared with her husband, went back and bought the independent bookshop and the flat above it. She owned and ran the shop, and six months later she fell in love with a customer – they bonded over their passion for Thomas Hardy novels. While I was there she showed me an anthology of short stories written by local authors, and honestly, the whole thing felt like a lesson: one of those events that doesn't seem real because it's basically someone holding up a huge, allegorical mirror and exposing all your tender bits.

What matters to you, now? Are your plans the same as they were when we were together, or have your priorities changed now you're older? I would give anything to go for a coffee with you, to find out how you are. Sometimes, when I'm lying awake at night, I imagine you're next to me. I imagine your hands tracing pathways on my skin, and I close my eyes tight, but I can never fully lose myself to it. I have never been as completely myself as I was with you, and I'm scared I won't find that again.

If you got this letter, and you were replying to me, what stories would you tell me?

I love you and I miss you
Yours always, Amelie xx

Chapter Ten

March 2012

'We could stay in and watch a film. *Halloween* or *Scream*, a cheesy romcom, whatever you wanted.'

Mum was sitting at the kitchen table, sorting through a Tupperware box full of packets of herbs and spices, most of them probably out of date.

'It's Kira's birthday, so I can't stay in tonight.' I pulled my mascara wand through my eyelashes, peering at myself in the hall mirror.

'It's already dark out. Where are you going?'

'Just around the village.' I couldn't look at her, and knew I should have come up with a more solid lie, but if I said I was going to Kira's, there was a chance she would call Kira's mum and we'd get busted. 'But there's five of us. Freddy will be there, and Orwell and Ethan. We'll be fine, Mum.'

'You've been talking about this Ethan a lot, lately.' She sipped her tea, and I saw the tremor as she lowered her mug to the table. But she was fine, she'd had three good days, and her friend Helen might be coming over later.

'Ethan's been hanging out with us,' I said, not for the first time. I didn't add that since our kiss on the beach, we'd tried to get as much time together as we could, just the two of us – which wasn't actually that much. 'He's nice, and he's new at school, so he needed some friends.'

'I don't know him,' Mum said. 'You should bring him round.'

'Maybe. Not tonight though.' I put on my black jacket and arranged my ponytail artfully over one shoulder. I tried to picture what was waiting for us, the spooky house on top of the cliffs and what it might be like inside.

'Right.' My rucksack was heavier than usual because I had my copy of *The Whispers of the Sands*. I wanted to take one of S. E. Artemis's books, and this was the last one she'd written in that house. 'I'm off.'

'Last chance.' Mum held up a tub of sweet and salty popcorn, her smile wide, as if she was on QVC and trying to sell it to me. 'I bought this from the farm shop. Thought we deserved a treat.'

I winced, because we could barely ever afford anything from the farm shop. 'We could have a film night tomorrow?' I kissed her on the cheek. 'I can't abandon Kira on her birthday.'

'You need to be careful, Georgie.'

'Of course we'll be careful,' I said as the doorbell rang.

Kira was wearing a tiara, her dark hair straightened so it hung in glossy curtains, Freddy had on more eyeliner than I'd ever worn, Orwell was peering past me into our hallway and then there was Ethan, standing at the back, taller than everyone else. His eyes were already on me when I looked at him and smiled.

'Birthday, baby!' Kira shouted. 'Let's go!' She pulled me outside and, laughing, I closed my front door, refusing to glance behind me to confirm that Mum was watching us out of the window.

'Fuck this hill's steep,' Freddy panted as we trudged up the road out of the village, towards the dark hulk I would always think of as Tyller Klos. The sea was the midnight blue of fortune-teller curtains, the white froth of every wave luminous below a star-pricked sky. The moon was high, giving the landscape a frosted glow, and a chill wind slunk around us, cooling the sweat on my palms.

'Are you all right?' Ethan slipped his hand into mine. 'You seem tense.'

I laughed. 'We're about to go into an abandoned house. *Break* in, in fact.'

'That's all it is?'

'Isn't that enough?'

He didn't reply, and my shoulders sagged. 'Sorry, I didn't mean to snap at you. It's Mum stuff.'

'Is she OK?'

'She's good at the moment, health-wise, but she didn't want me to come tonight.'

'Because she knows you're breaking into a dangerous clifftop property that's been left to the elements for over a decade?'

I laughed and squeezed his hand. 'I wouldn't put it past her to have found out somehow. She's so protective of me.'

'You're all she's got,' Ethan said, and I could hear the shrug in his voice. 'But it's not fair of her to stop you doing what you want. You're there for her when she needs you.'

'I try to be,' I said quietly. 'What about you? Did your folks give you a hard time about coming out tonight?'

'They were too busy grounding Sarah.'

'Oh, really? What's she done?'

'The usual. Some light vandalism, skipping school, shouting at her teachers when she does bother to turn up.'

'Wow.' I tried to imagine the slender, petulant girl I'd met doing all that. 'She's still unhappy, then.'

'Yeah. I don't . . . I'm not sure what the answer is, but I'm pretty sure grounding isn't it. She's going to rebel more. I nearly didn't come tonight.'

'Oh.' I thought how much my excitement would have dimmed without him there. 'I'm glad you did.'

'Me too,' he said, as we reached the dilapidated wall than ran around the once-grand property.

'Here we are guys!' Freddy announced it like we were on a tour of tourist hotspots, and this was the pièce de résistance.

We walked along the wall until we found a section that had completely fallen down, and took turns to step over it into the overgrown garden. Twigs and leaves swiped at my arms and legs as we waded through the vegetation, then we angled a trio of torch beams up at the front of the house. It had a dull stone façade and a steep, angular roof, cracked window boxes with any flowers long since gone, the paved pathway sprouting with weeds. Ornate details in the window frames looked like gasping, screaming faces in the stark torchlight.

'That is one spooky building,' Kira murmured, and Freddy grabbed her hand.

'Come on Mr Architect,' Orwell said. 'It was your idea so you're in charge.'

'Right.' Ethan walked up to the front door and rattled the chain. 'This one's secure, and the padlock looks new.'

'Arse.' Freddy sighed. 'Let's do a circuit and see if there's another way in. Call out if you find anything.'

He and Kira headed left, and I followed Ethan right, with Orwell bringing up the rear. We tried each window as we passed, but they were all locked. When we got to the side of the house, Alperwick appeared below us, with lights twinkling and smoke coming from chimneys, the inky sea to our left. It was straight out of a fairy tale, and the witch's house was looming behind us. I shivered, and Ethan took my hand again.

'Come on.' I saw his smile in the glow from his torch. 'Let's check the back door.'

It was Kira who found our way in, a window on the cliff side of the house unlocked, creaking slowly open when she prized it away from the frame. 'I broke a nail,' she announced gleefully, the pane swinging outwards, silently inviting us in.

'You fucking genius.' Freddy picked her up and spun her round and then, one by one, we climbed through the window, into the real-life Tyller Klos.

The air was cloying and smelled of mould, and I covered my mouth with my sleeve, a crunch of debris beneath my feet. The room we were in was small, and there was no furniture left, the place bare besides structural features and fittings.

'How old is it, do you think?' Kira asked.

'Nineteenth century,' Ethan said without a pause. 'The high-pitched roof, the decorative moulding – look.' We peered up, seeing the floral shapes framing the ceiling. Something scuttled to our left and I jumped, leaning into him. He put his arm around my shoulders.

'Let's go to the big room at the front,' Kira said. 'Escape whatever *that* was.'

'The rats will have the run of the place,' Orwell pointed out. 'Hey, do you think that old lady is still here? What if she died in her bed and nobody noticed, and the rats have been snacking on her ever since?'

'She moved into a bungalow in the village,' I said, because I had researched S. E. Artemis's life and career.

Her decision to stop writing in the 1990s had compounded my devastation that the last book had ended the way it had.

'She's still in Alperwick?' Kira asked.

'As far as I know.' There hadn't been any press about her for a long time. 'This place has been empty for almost twenty years.'

'It's well preserved.' Ethan pressed his hand against the ornate door frame as Kira skipped ahead, into the room at the front of the house, and we all followed. 'I don't think we should try the stairs, though.'

'We might fall through?' Freddy sounded thrilled and horrified all at once.

'We might.'

'Here.' Kira pulled a blanket out of her bag, followed by packets of crisps and a bottle of Absolut Vodka.

'It's nuts that nobody's bought it,' Freddy said.

'I think some property developer owns it now. I don't know why they've chosen not to refurbish it.' Ethan's gaze was everywhere, taking in as much detail as he could by the light of his torch.

'Probably waiting until the land increases in value,' Orwell said, taking a four-pack of beer out of his rucksack. 'Loads of developers hold onto old properties or land until the prices go up and they can make a fortune selling it on.'

'How do you know that?' Freddy asked with a laugh.

'My old man.' Orwell shrugged.

Ethan was standing by the huge fireplace, running his hands over the mantelpiece and the decorative plasterwork that framed the hearth. 'This is beautiful,' he murmured, then crouched and shone his torch up into the dark space.

'Careful,' Orwell said. 'You don't know what's been hidden up there. Could be a dead cat, and if you start poking about, a tiny skeleton will rain down on you.'

'Gross,' Kira said. 'Orwell, have you forgotten that it's my birthday?'

'We're in an abandoned house,' he replied. 'You didn't pick a luxury hotel with a six-course meal and champagne for your celebration, so this is what you get.'

'Murdered pets is still a low bar,' Freddy said as he helped Kira spread the blanket on the dusty floor-boards.

I crouched and took my own blanket out of my bag. It was fleecy, one of those ones that rolled up really tightly, navy blue with white stars all over it. I spread it on the floor and looked up to see Ethan watching me.

I sat down and patted the space next to me. 'Come and join me on my blanket of stars.'

He sat beside me and took a bottle of gin and a packet of peanut M&Ms out of his coat pocket, adding them to our haul.

I tried to ignore the creaks and groans from the open doorway behind me, the rustling, scuttling noises that sent goosebumps racing over my skin.

'What now?' Ethan asked, handing me the gin bottle. 'What do you want to do, Kira?'

'Now?' Kira took a swig of vodka and passed the bottle to Freddy, then held her torch under her chin so her face looked surreal, the shadows of her eyelashes like spiders' legs on her cheeks, her eyes black voids of nothing. 'Now, we tell each other ghost stories.'

Chapter Eleven

Now

'How are you really?' Ethan asked.

He had fiddled with the panel on the wall of the master suite, so the window was frosted, blocking out the intense glare of the evening sun. Cool air snaked around me, taking some of the heat out of my cheeks.

'Really, I'm fine.' I had to leave. I couldn't be swayed by this decadent room and the man standing in it. He was a stranger now, anyway. So different to the boy I'd been in love with.

'Are you getting lots of work at the paper?' He had brought up two fresh glasses of champagne, and he held one out to me.

Despite my firm plan, I took the glass. 'Don't you know how much I'm getting, if you've been looking out for my byline?'

His smile flickered out, and he was back to being inscrutable.

'I should go.' I downed half my bubbles in one swallow. 'The open house is over, so—'

'I'm glad you're here.' Ethan leant against the chest of drawers. 'I know it's strange – it feels *really* strange – but I'm still glad you came.'

I shrugged. 'Why?'

He looked surprised. 'I . . . wanted to see you. I've thought about you a lot, while we've been getting this place done.'

'I've been in the village,' I said. 'In the same house. I haven't gone anywhere.' He could have knocked on my door when he'd been visiting the site. Even if he hadn't known I was still there, it would have been a good starting point, because Alperwick was small and most people were eager to pass on gossip.

'I know, but I wasn't sure you'd want to see me. I thought you might slam the door in my face.'

'Thirteen years is a long time, and we were teenagers.' That was the sensible answer, something my mum might have said. I didn't add that I would have let him in the day after our last argument, that by then I was already sorry for the things I'd said, and that I'd wanted him back above everything else.

'Do you want to . . .?' He ran a hand through his hair. 'I don't know where to start.'

'There's too much,' I said. 'And you need to get back to Bristol, don't you? Sell this place to some business executive or hedge fund manager, someone who's only going to live in it for two weeks a year.'

Ethan's shoulders slumped. 'I will have *some* say over who buys it.'

'Is Sarah managing that side of it?'

He held my gaze. 'She's changed a lot. She knows the Sparks system inside and out, but she can also put on a shiny exterior, say all the right things, when I have no patience for it.'

'I'm glad she came through.' I meant it, even though the shock of seeing her hadn't quite faded.

'I'm wondering how much you've changed,' he said quietly.

'I'm surprised you've been wondering about me at all.' I paused to finish my drink. 'Or I would have been, except I saw that interview in *Home Style*, where you talked about the house's name. "It was never going to be called anything else."'

He closed his eyes for a beat. 'I didn't know if . . . in my speech – if you'd want me to talk about us.'

I nodded, then gestured to the frosted glass. Beyond it, the sun was sinking, shifting from soft glow to burning embers as it neared the water. 'I need to go. It's going to be dark soon and I . . .'

'You don't want to stay here with me.'

I swallowed. 'A whole lot of time has passed, and we're such different people, Ethan.'

'You're as beautiful as ever,' he said, his gaze confident and assessing. 'More beautiful, if anything.'

'Wow.' I tried to ignore the flutter in my stomach. 'You must have been working with some shady estate agents if you can say that and not wince at how cringy it sounds.'

He let out a surprised laugh. 'I was just being honest.'

'So was I.' I folded my arms. 'But thank you. You look very . . . dapper.'

He frowned. '*Dapper?*'

'I love how you matched your tie to the furnishings.'

Irritation flickered across his face. 'I wanted today to go well. If I'd known I was coming across as dapper, I would have rethought the whole plan.'

'How did you want to come across, then? The genius, nerdy architect? The mysterious, unknowable man behind the Sparks system? Is dapper too commonplace for you?' I raised my eyebrows. 'Does Sparks really control the whole house? Do you need to be set up as a user so it recognizes you?'

His nod was wary, as if he didn't know whether I was teasing him or not.

'OK.' I took a deep breath. 'Sparks, please turn on the disco lights in the shower.'

'I'm sorry, I don't know who's speaking.' The soothing female voice bounced off the walls. I could barely tell she was electronic.

'Sparks,' Ethan said, 'I want to add a new user.'

'Good evening, Ethan,' the voice replied. 'Who would you like to add?'

'Sparks, please add Georgie to Sterenlenn.'

'Good evening Georgie,' the voice said. 'I will need to learn your voice to add you to Sterenlenn. Please say: *Sparks, what's the weather like today?*'

I glared at Ethan and he gazed back at me, amused. 'Sparks,' I said, 'what's the weather like today?'

'The humidity is high, at 74 per cent, with a chance of thunderstorms overnight. Now please say: *Sparks, turn on the underfloor heating.*'

'Sparks, turn on the underfloor heating.'

'The underfloor heating is activated,' the voice said, then she made me run through a few more questions to get the timbre of my voice. 'Thank you, Georgie,' she said when I'd obeyed all her commands. 'You have been added to Sterenlenn. I am here to help you with anything you need.'

'Very impressive,' I said to Ethan. 'Can she bring you breakfast in bed, too?'

'That's one of the few things I haven't got her to do yet.'

'Shame. What about a back massage?'

He shook his head, smiling at me.

'Fine. Sparks, please turn on the disco lights in the shower.'

'Shower lights activated.'

I glanced behind me and saw the rainbow glow emanating from the bathroom doorway. I thought of one night when we had come up here as teenagers, when the rain had been relentless and our path from the broken wall to the front of the house was a quagmire, the stones slippery and the vegetation slick, the earth turned to sludge. We'd let the mud dry on our jeans while we talked and drank inside, then had to face the same obstacle course on the way out. We'd walked down the hill with our clothes plastered to us, mud mingling with rainwater so we looked like swamp monsters.

'My dad isn't going to be impressed when I turn up like this,' Ethan had said.

'He'll still be awake?'

'Yeah. He always has a beady eye on us when he's home.' He'd sounded defeated, which was so unlike him.

My mum would be sound asleep this late, and sometimes took pills to ensure she slept through. 'Come back to mine. You can have a shower, or . . .'

'OK,' he'd said immediately, then grimaced at how eager he'd been, but I'd laughed and leaned into him. We'd slept together by that point, and he'd sneaked into my room more than once. That night we'd peeled each other's clothes off in my tiny, humid bathroom, and got into the shower together even though it was barely big enough for one person. I remembered urgency and gasping, slippery skin, falling onto my duvet still damp, and Ethan scrambling for a condom in the pocket of his ruined jeans.

It had been this house, in its dark, horror-film incarnation that had led to us being pressed together in my cramped, dated shower all those years ago. Now it was a gleaming masterpiece with an en-suite bigger than my bedroom.

'It was important that the shower had a lot of space,'

Ethan said, and from the gravel in his voice I wondered if he was remembering the same night I was.

'I don't know,' I said lightly, 'we achieved quite a lot with limited room.'

He cleared his throat.

'Who needs disco lights in their shower anyway?' I said, trying to dispel the tension.

'Who needs separate beer and wine fridges, alongside their giant, American-style fridge-freezer?'

'Those are essentials,' I said with a laugh.

'It keeps a record of everything inside and updates your shopping list automatically. And it has a self-filling water dispenser.'

'Seriously?'

'Check this out.' There was a gleam in Ethan's eyes as he walked to the bed, toeing off his polished black shoes without bothering to untie the laces.

'What?'

'Come on.' He held his hand out.

I hesitated. He was tempting me, just like he'd done when I'd fallen for him at eighteen. He had that look of quiet amusement that told me I was about to be let in on a secret, and it was impossible to resist.

'George.' He waggled his fingers.

I reached my hand out and let him pull me onto the bed. Then he crawled up it as if he was going to lie down.

'What are you doing?'

'Come with me,' he said. 'Come up here.' He lay down, his head on the pillows. Frowning but intrigued,

I copied him, and as my head hit the pillow the female voice said, 'Nightlights, activated.' The wall lamps on either side of the bed came on with a slow glide, and I shot up to sitting.

'How did she know?' I looked up at the ceiling. 'Are there cameras in here?'

Ethan sat up beside me. 'The lights are pressure activated. When you lie down in the right place, they turn on. If the main light is on, it turns off at the same time.'

'Does it pull the cover up for you too? Tuck you in at night with a teddy bear and a lullaby?'

He shook his head, but his lips tipped up.

'What if you're not going to sleep?' I asked. 'What if . . . what if there's pressure on the mattress for an entirely different reason? Do you have to say, "Sparks, we're having sex now, don't bother with the nightlights and please avert your eyes"?'

'I'm sorry, I don't understand your request,' the soothing female voice told me.

'You might want the nightlights on if you were having sex,' Ethan said. 'You might want to see every inch of each other.'

I raised my eyebrows, my cheeks flushing despite the air con.

'You can ask her to turn them off,' Ethan said quickly. 'Or change the settings in the app, obviously. You can set it up exactly how you want it.'

'Bit of a mood killer,' I said, then, because I couldn't resist, and I wanted to make that suggestion of a smile bloom fully across his face, I tipped my head back and gasped out, 'Oh, oh Ethan! Oh God! Sparks – please turn off the nightlights! Thank you, *thank you*, Sparks! Yes, *yes*. Finally!'

'Georgie.' Ethan's laugh burst out of him, and it was brighter than any voice-activated light, or even the glowing sun outside.

'Does your house have a sex mode, Ethan?' I was on a roll. 'Is there a hatch in the ceiling that drops rose petals when you say, "Sparks, we are getting it on right now"?'

'No,' he said, at the same time as the voice said, 'I'm sorry, I don't understand your request.'

'But there are the skylights.' He gestured up, and I saw the faint lines in the ceiling, the place where, with a simple command, it would slide back and show off the sky, give us direct access to the heavens. It must have been a feat of engineering brilliance to have redone the roof in a way that incorporated these skylights throughout the top floor.

'A blanket of stars,' I murmured. There wouldn't be any stars yet, but there would be the mesmerizing, ethereal blue of the sky just before dusk, and I couldn't deal with that level of romance while I was here with him.

'You know I named the house for you,' Ethan said. We'd skirted around it, but this was the first time he'd admitted it to me.

I slid to the edge of the bed. 'I can't do this. Nope. No no no.'

'Why not? What's wrong?'

I stumbled off the bed and pulled my sandals back on. 'It's not real, is it?' I gestured around me. 'It's a fantasy.'

'I *made* it real.' Ethan scooted across the duvet. 'I did this.'

'For someone who won't appreciate it,' I finished. 'It's going to be bought by people who don't understand how magical it is, or that it's featured in all Spen . . . S. E. Artemis's books, or how many of our memories are bound up here. They'll love the separate beer and wine fridges and the disco shower and the views of the stars and the sea, but they won't know about its soul.'

Ethan stood up. 'We will, though.' He sounded defeated, as if my words had pushed the reality home. He'd worked so hard and made such a difference for someone else.

I moved closer and, tentatively, dangerously, wrapped my arms around his waist. My head fitted perfectly under his chin as it always had, a favourite jigsaw being pulled out of its box and slotted together again. His chest rose and fell on an exhale, and I let myself hold him for a couple of seconds, nostalgia and contentment rushing over me. Then I stepped away from him.

'Bye, Ethan.' I put my rucksack on and, when I reached the doorway, let myself glance back. He was looking at me, a puzzled expression on his face, as if he couldn't figure me out. I hurried into the hall, heading for the stairs.

'Bye, Sterenlenn,' I murmured, as I trailed my hand

along the chrome handrail with its thread of seaside blue.

'Farewell, Georgie,' the house said, making me jump. A prickle ran down my spine, because I hadn't said 'Sparks', so how had it picked up my voice?

I reached the bottom of the stairs and peered into the kitchen. There were empty glasses and canapé plates strewn about, and one of the bouquets was starting to droop. I could see the living room beyond, and I wavered. Did I have time? But then I heard a bang from upstairs.

'Georgie, wait!' Ethan's footsteps were fast on the stairs.

Panic welled up inside me, because I couldn't spend any more time with him. It was too confusing, we were too far apart, and I didn't know him any more. I had to let him go for good, like the house, so I went on the defensive.

'Your house is fucking creepy, you know that?' I strode towards the front door and pulled the handle, but it was locked.

'It's not creepy,' he said from behind me.

'It just said "farewell, Georgie", even though I didn't say "Sparks".'

'That's not possible.' Ethan cleared the last couple of steps.

'Yes, Georgie?' the house asked innocently. 'What can I help you with?' I ignored it.

'Do you get a kick out of saying your surname over and over? That's a very specific kind of narcissism.

Can you open the door?' I pulled on it, but it wouldn't budge.

'Stay for ten more minutes,' Ethan said. 'Please.'

'Sparks, open the front door!' There was a loud clunk, and the door started to move.

'Sparks, close the door,' Ethan said, and it whooshed shut.

I glared at him.

'Ten minutes,' he said, his hands out in front of him. 'I don't want us to part like this. Not after last time.'

'Sparks, open the front door,' I gritted out.

'Yes, Georgie,' the voice cooed, and I felt a surge of triumph as the door moved towards me.

'Sparks, lock the door,' Ethan said, and I was once again denied exit.

I spun around. 'You told me you wouldn't keep me here against my will!'

He looked pained. 'Please. I'm sorry. I'm so sorry about what I said upstairs, about naming the house for you. This has been . . . obviously it's been a dream, getting this place done, but it's been hard too. And then, you turning up . . . I know I'm not expressing myself well, but I should never have—'

'You have to let me go.' I could feel the burn of tears behind my eyes.

He nodded, holding my gaze. 'Sparks,' he said, 'open the front door.'

'Bye, Ethan.' I turned around and pulled the handle, but it didn't move. I glanced at him, and he frowned.

'Sparks, open the door,' he repeated. I waited for the

click, for the door to slide towards me as I tugged the handle. Nothing happened.

'Sparks, unlock the front door.' He was louder this time, but still nothing shifted. 'Sparks, give me a status update.'

'Sterenlenn is fully functional,' the house said smoothly. 'No bugs or anomalies detected.'

'Great,' Ethan said, and I noted the sarcasm in his voice that, despite everything, made me smile. 'So, Sparks, unlock the front door.'

There was no clunk, but I pulled anyway. The door was still locked. We exchanged a puzzled look.

'I don't know what's wrong with it.' He turned to the wall panel and pressed a few buttons, the cute electronic beeps filling the silence. 'What the actual fuck is it doing?' He jabbed at it angrily.

'I know,' I murmured, losing patience. 'Sparks,' I said loudly, 'open the front door now! This. Is. An. Emergency!'

'No!' Ethan shouted as the last word came out of my mouth. The house made a series of bleeping, whirring noises, and I heard a heavy *thunk* behind me as the front door seemed to settle even further into its metal frame. The panel Ethan had been stabbing at warbled melodically and its lights flashed blue and red, then the tall windows behind the staircase slid from transparent to solid, like blackout blinds, and all the lights in the house flickered on.

'Ethan?' I said. 'What is this?'

He turned to look at me, his eyes wide. 'I-I don't—'

he started, but then the house spoke over him, as calm as ever.

'Emergency procedure activated,' it said. 'Entering Panic Room Mode. Sterenlenn is in lockdown.'

Chapter Twelve

March 2012

'I saw a mermaid once, out on the rocks.' Freddy's voice was sombre in the gloom of the abandoned house.

'*Our* rocks?' Kira said. 'For serious?'

'Yup. I was walking past one evening, and there was this weird light.'

'Were you drunk?' Orwell asked. 'On your way home from the pub?'

Ethan danced his fingers down my jean-clad thigh and leaned into me. We'd been there a couple of hours, Kira had asked for ghost stories on her birthday, and I was slightly miffed that nobody was buying into the spirit of it, questioning everything like they were seasoned paranormal detectives instead of letting themselves get spooked.

'What did you see?' I whispered. 'Did she sing to you?'

Freddy stuttered out a laugh. 'Nah, no singing or anything. But the light was, like, a strange blue-green colour – not like a boat's lamp – and there was this silhouette, someone sitting up there as the sun was fading.'

'That sounds so scary,' I said, and was glad when the others stayed quiet, nobody poo-pooing it. 'It sounds like you definitely saw *something*.'

'And what have you seen?' Orwell turned towards us. 'I bet Ethan doesn't believe in ghosts and ghoulies.'

'I do, actually,' he said calmly. 'I saw one, not that long ago.'

I glanced at him, glad that he was joining in, and saw that he was worrying at his bottom lip with his teeth. 'What did you see?' I threaded my fingers through his.

'Was it in Cornwall?' Kira handed the bottle of vodka to Orwell. Despite all our bluster about being reckless, we'd been sipping slowly, and I got the sense that we all wanted to stay alert, in case unexpected torch beams swung over the windows or the flash of blue lights pulsed outside.

'It was in York,' Ethan said. 'We lived there for a couple of years – we move around a lot for my dad's job.' He swallowed. 'I saw this hunched-over figure in an alleyway. We'd gone out for dinner and Mum and Dad had stopped to look in a shop window on the way back. Sarah was dawdling, and I was ahead.

It wasn't quite dark, but the alley was gloomy, and I got a weird vibe from this guy. He was slouching, dragging his feet, and his clothes were filthy. I noticed that he wasn't wearing any shoes, and I thought he must be homeless. I glanced behind me to check the others were following, and when I looked back he was gone, and so was the oppressive feeling.'

'Woah,' Freddy murmured.

'So he reached the end of the alley.' Kira shrugged, but her voice was wavering.

Ethan shook his head. 'There was no way. He wasn't that far along it, and he couldn't have reached the end in the time I looked away.'

'God.' A tingle ran up my spine. I'd been about to launch into a made-up story about the Knockers that haunted the mines along the coastline, but Ethan's was so much better. 'The alley would have been bad enough on its own, but then . . . *that*.'

'Oh God, yeah,' Kira said. 'You don't like being in small spaces.'

'Who does?' I asked.

'That time Ferris shut you in the stationery cupboard at school.' Orwell snorted. 'You went nuts! He was such a shit.'

'Why are you laughing then?' I crossed my arms.

'Someone shut you in a cupboard?' Ethan's eyes were on mine; I could see the gleam of torchlight in his pupils.

'Just a stupid joke from our year's stupid joker,' I said. 'It was before sixth form.'

'What happened?'

I reached for some crisps, not wanting to tell him.

'She had a panic attack,' Kira said. 'I was trying to get Ferris to open the cupboard – for some reason there was a key, and he'd locked the door and pocketed it.'

'It was pitch-black,' I said hotly. 'Tiny and dusty and . . . when it's that dark, and you can't get out, you imagine all sorts of things are in there with you.'

'It sounds horrible.' Ethan put his arm around me, bringing me close to him. 'Being trapped, no matter where it is, is one of the worst feelings.' He spoke into my hair, his lips brushing my head like feathery kisses. 'Have you had a lot of panic attacks?'

'It was a one-off, thankfully.' I didn't add that I sometimes felt that tightness at home, the slight shadowing at the edges of my vision when things went wrong with Mum, when she seemed really unwell or, conversely, when she was at her brightest and most challenging. The twin pressures of losing her and being stuck with her long after school ended competed for awfulness in my thoughts.

'We can't get trapped in here, at least,' Kira said.

'Unless that window jams,' Orwell pointed out. 'Or something's blocked our exit.'

'A particularly possessive rat with opposable thumbs?' Freddy raised an eyebrow.

'Imagine if there's something lurking in here, waiting to pounce,' Ethan said, and I got the impression he was genuinely worried, not trying to add to the scares.

I squeezed his hand. 'If there's anyone lurking here, it's the characters from the Cornish Sands series, the Rosevar family going about their days – and we just can't see them. Perhaps all the little creaks, the rustling sounds, are them. They're probably wondering what we're doing here.'

'OK, dude, was that supposed to be comforting?' Freddy asked. 'Because you missed the mark.'

'Sorry,' I said, but I wasn't really. I loved imagining the characters existing outside of the books – those gorgeous love stories that were hard won but so worth it, the glamorous parties in the breathtaking clifftop gardens. They weren't real, but they were people I'd come to care about, living and loving and dying in the house we were sitting in. 'It's just . . . if I ever get to be a writer, I want my books to make people feel all the emotions that series makes me feel.'

'You're going to be a writer?' Ethan asked. 'You've never said.'

'Not *going* to be. I want to be.'

'If you want to be one, then you will be. You can do whatever you decide, Georgie.'

'I don't know,' I said, but inside I was unfurling, a flower blooming at his belief in me. I snuggled against him. 'Thank you, though.'

'Who's your favourite?' Kira asked. 'Not that I've read any of them.'

'Amelie and Connor,' I said. 'They're the couple in the last book, and I thought they'd get their happy-ever-after like the other heroines and heroes, but

Connor went to America and left Amelie behind. Sometimes I imagine them reuniting here. Although,' I added with a laugh, 'that's going to be harder now I've seen inside. It's not exactly a luxury mansion any more.'

'It might be again one day,' Ethan said. 'A place this grand can't stand empty for ever.'

I closed my eyes, imagining a future for Tyller Klos, and that's when I heard it: a sound behind me, in the shadows. I must have invented it, but every hair on my body prickled to attention.

'What is it?' Ethan squeezed my shoulder. 'Are you OK?'

'Yeah,' I said shakily. 'I'm fine.'

'You look like you've seen something horrible.' Kira was peering at me.

'Not seen.' I burrowed into Ethan's side, wishing he was between me and the black void of the hall. 'I thought I heard something.'

'Something more than our furry friends?' Orwell asked.

'I don't know, but . . . it sounded like someone laughing. Or sobbing.' I swallowed. 'It was hard to tell.'

'No fucking way.' Freddy sounded horrified.

'It was my ears playing tricks on me,' I said quickly, sensing my fear travel round the room. 'It can't have happened.'

'It can't,' Orwell confirmed.

'But maybe . . .' Ethan glanced at his watch, using

his torch to illuminate the face. 'It's ten to midnight. I think we can safely say we've spent enough time here.'

I expected a protest from Kira, saying her birthday wasn't over, but everyone took Ethan's words as an instruction. We retrieved our empty bottles and cans – because we were hardcore teenagers but we weren't litterers – and shoved full ones into pockets and bags. Then we made our way wordlessly through the house, retracing our steps, my gaze fixed firmly on Freddy's legs in front of me, and not on those dark hollows where I thought the strange sounds had come from.

Once we were back on the solid tarmac of the road, relief pulsed in my veins. The moon was higher now, its silver sheen coating everything, so we didn't need our torches to light the way back into the village.

It was against the steady echoes of our footsteps that a shrill mobile blared. We all stopped, taking out our phones, but it was Ethan who slipped his fingers away from mine to answer.

'Hello?' He frowned. There was a pause and he said, 'No, I haven't seen her all evening.' Another gap, then, 'I'm out with friends. I haven't seen her since after school, and . . .' His jaw clenched as the other person spoke. 'What party? I don't know anything about . . . I'm on my way home now. I'll be there in fifteen minutes.' He hung up and jammed his mobile in his pocket.

'OK?' I said.

He shook his head tightly. 'Sarah's gone AWOL.'

'That was your mum?' Kira asked.

'Dad,' Ethan said miserably. 'He's going apeshit. Sarah was supposed to be grounded, but she snuck out and apparently there's this wild party, so we have to go and get her.'

I squeezed his hand. 'Why you?'

'I'm her big brother.' He shrugged. 'It's my job to keep her out of trouble, and I'm failing.'

'It's not your job.' I was indignant. 'It's theirs, surely? Your mum and dad's.'

'Try telling Dad that,' he said quietly, and the last glimmers of triumph I'd had, from breaking into an abandoned house with my friends, from being so close to Ethan all night, faded as we made our way solemnly into Alperwick. Ethan was tense and silent beside me, his hand gripping mine a little too tightly.

Chapter Thirteen

Now

'What is Panic Room Mode?' I put my hand on the front door handle and gave it another futile tug. But I'd seen the film. Jodie Foster didn't have a particularly great time. 'Why is the whole house in Panic Room Mode?'

Some of Ethan's hair was standing on end, because he'd been worrying at it constantly for the last two minutes, and his cheeks had blanched to the colour of the path I knew was outside, but could no longer see. He peered at the Sparks panel, then his phone.

'What's going on, Ethan?' There was a fluttering in my chest, but I tried to ignore it. This was fine. It was just a weird blip.

'I don't know,' he admitted. 'I mean, I *do* know, some of it.'

'You know *some* of what's happening with the house you built?'

'Shush a minute,' he said distractedly.

I inhaled through my nose, and let it out slowly, like a whoopee cushion deflating. The house was deathly quiet, and the spacious, elegant hall looked strange, with the windows dark and the lights on. The sunset was probably spectacular, but we couldn't see it.

I walked over to the study, as if I might find some kind of answer in there. Ethan was still tapping away, working between the wall panel and his mobile. After an indeterminate amount of time, when I thought I was in danger of fidgeting myself to death, he let out an emphatic 'Fuck!' and the fluttering in my chest intensified.

'What is it?' I went back into the hall.

He looked up at me. 'When you said there was an emergency, you activated the Panic Room feature, which essentially shuts the house down and stops anyone from getting inside.'

'I sort of got that, but there has to be some kind of mechanism, a way the house will open up again. What if there was a fire? What if an intruder had got in and . . . and was coming after us?' I swallowed heavily, and Ethan took a step towards me.

'Ordinarily, the moment Panic Room Mode is activated, the local authorities would be notified. But because nobody has bought this house yet, it's still set up as a show home, so that loop hasn't been closed.'

'Right. So . . . what? Nobody's coming, but there must be some kind of override. Some way of turning off Sparks and unlocking the door. The house can't be so modern that it stops you from turning a key in a lock.'

Ethan ran his hand through his hair again, tugging at the strands, and a little thread of my patience snapped. I gripped his forearm, pulling it away. 'Your hair is too nice for you to yank it all out.'

He gave me a bleak look.

'Your override?' I prompted.

'It seems my override has been . . . overridden,' he said quietly.

'What?'

'Something's not right. Panic Room Mode turns off the Wi-Fi in case of a cyber-attack, so—'

'Of course it does.' I massaged my chest. 'But we can still phone out, can't we? We can get Sarah to come back or the local police to turn up? I know DC Sommer, he can be creative when he needs to be, he could jimmy one of the locks or . . .'

Ethan held his phone up so I could see the screen. In the top right corner, where the Wi-Fi logo should have been, or 4G or 5G, there was that horrible SOS symbol that looked like a sticking plaster.

'This *is* an SOS situation.' I slipped my rucksack off and ferreted inside it for my own phone. My hand brushed against the soft black bag that held my silver mermaid, and I squeezed it as if it might bring us some luck. But when I looked at my phone screen, mine was also showing the SOS logo, alongside a red alert sign. I had less than 10 per cent battery left. 'You idiot, Georgie,' I muttered, and put it back in my bag. 'OK, so what do we do?'

Ethan took a step back, so his head thudded against the wall. 'I don't know.'

I stared at him. 'You don't *know*?'

'No, I . . . You said the system said goodbye to you, even though you hadn't mentioned Sparks?'

'It said *farewell, Georgie*.'

'Something's not quite . . . right.'

'Something not quite right that has trapped us *inside*? We must be able to call out from here. Does it have a landline?'

'It's . . . like I said, those final links haven't been secured, because nobody's bought it yet. The plan is to do that with the new owner, set up all their favourites, their preferred contacts and emergency services.'

'Who else is there other than the police? You think whoever buys this house will have a direct line to MI5? Ethan!' I threw my hands up in despair.

'It's a sophisticated system.'

'A system that's so sophisticated it's managed to lock us inside with no means of escape?' It was my turn to pull at my hair, snagging the elastic tie so my ponytail came loose. 'This cannot be happening.' I tugged the door handle again. It didn't budge. 'Where are the other doors?' I strode towards the back of the house, past the staircase. There was a door here too, wider than my back door at home but a lot less grand than

Sterenlenn's entrance. Hope surged, but I grabbed the handle and yanked it, and got the same, strong resistance.

'Sparks, open the back door,' I tried.

'Panic Room Mode is activated,' the voice said.

I rolled my eyes. 'Sparks, override Panic Room Mode.'

'Panic Room Mode cannot be overridden. Emergency services are on their way.'

'They're *not* though. What other doors are there, Ethan?'

'There are the French doors in the living room, but you won't—'

'I'm going.' I hurried through the kitchen, my arm knocking against an ice bucket that still held a bottle of champagne, condensation beading the glass. I kept going, rubbing my arm, then came to a halt. I hadn't made it in here so far, unable to squeeze through the crowds congregating in the kitchen, and it was sumptuous. Ahead of me were the French windows. Their glass was dark too, which meant I couldn't see the view, but it also meant there was nothing to distract me from the beauty of the room.

The fireplace that Ethan had been so enamoured with when the house was abandoned was the focal point, preserved while the walls either side had been knocked out, so the room stretched the full length of the house. There were large windows that should have been showing off the gardens at the front and the back, with the French windows opening onto the side aspect.

The walls were a dusky grey-blue, and three huge, cream sofas that looked comfy enough to sleep on were arranged, not around a television – though one was mounted on the wall, so thin it was almost flush with it – but around the beautiful fireplace.

Glass and chrome occasional tables were dotted throughout, with more extravagant bouquets, the flowers cream and blue to match the decor, vibrant pink roses adding a pop of colour. The rug in front of the French windows was woven through with the same sea tones I'd seen glimmers of in the other rooms, and chrome uplighters stood sentry in the corners. It was a soft, calming space, and I would have appreciated it a lot more had I not been in panic mode, just like the house.

I strode to the French windows and pushed down on the handles, but they held firm. 'Sparks,' I said, 'please open the French windows.'

'Georgie, we are in Panic Room Mode.' Had she sounded *extra* soothing?

'Sparks, there is no intruder. Please end Panic Room Mode.'

'I need authorization from the emergency services.'

I balled my hands into fists. 'Sparks, nobody is coming to save us.'

'You are safe in Panic Room Mode,' the voice said, and I pressed my hands into my eyes, trying to will away the fear that was crawling up my spine.

'Georgie.' I heard Ethan come up behind me and turned around, dropping my hands so I could see him. 'I'm so sorry.'

'There must be other doors,' I said. 'Or we could . . . have you left that window open in the back, for old times' sake? Some sentimentality would really help us right now.'

He put his hands on my shoulders. 'I'm sorry. I never meant for this to happen.'

'I know.' I said it automatically, but *did* I know that? Was he really as helpless as he was making out? 'Your Sparks system isn't bug-free yet, is it?'

He rubbed his forehead. 'It's gone through thousands of hours of testing, and I don't know what the fuck it's doing.' He glanced at the fireplace. It still had its original moulding, the floral designs that had been there for over two hundred years. 'Do you remember that first night, when Orwell said there might be something dead shoved up the chimney?'

'I think he said there might be a dead cat up there. Thinking back, he could be properly creepy when he wanted to be.' I shook my head. 'But I also remember that you loved this fireplace, and it's so gorgeous, now, the way you've restored it.'

'It was important to me.'

'Did you spend a lot of time here, during the build? Or did you only visit occasionally?'

'I came as often as I could, to see how much progress had been made, see if things were going as planned.'

I nodded. 'Well, they're not going as planned right now. What options do we have left?'

Ethan's hands were still on my shoulders, and I could feel the slow sweep of his index fingers as he rubbed the juncture with my neck. I wasn't sure he knew he was doing it, but it was sending soothing tingles down my spine and I didn't want him to stop. 'I can't get in touch with anyone,' he said. 'Not Sarah or anyone else from the office. Aldo's gone, and I can't seem to call out, either from my mobile or the house's communication system. Your phone's the same?'

'It has the little SOS thingy,' I said, not adding that it was almost out of battery.

'Right. And Sparks is firmly in Panic Room Mode, and—'

'Panic Room Mode is activated,' Sparks confirmed.

'—my override code is doing nothing.'

'OK,' I said, my voice suddenly smaller. 'So then . . . what? We break a window? fiddle the lock on one of the doors? Open a skylight and climb onto the roof?'

'We can't do any of those things,' Ethan said quietly. 'The build is too solid. And for some reason that I don't understand, there are things stopping us getting *out*, as well as anyone getting in.'

'So that means we . . .' I blinked a couple of times as darkness slid into the corners of my vision, blurring the edges of Ethan standing in front of me. 'We're trapped?'

'We might have to wait it out a little.' Ethan's tentative tone told me he was hedging.

'Wait out your automated Smart system until it gets bored and gives up existing? Wait until someone misses us, and traces our movements back here?' I wondered how long it would take Spence to worry. I was supposed to see her tomorrow, to update her on the event, but if I was a no-show, how long would it take her to realize something was wrong?

'Sarah will get concerned.'

'Even though you told her you'd be back later, on the train?'

Ethan glanced away from me.

'She won't start worrying for hours, then.' Dread gnawed at my stomach.

'Eventually, she'll—'

'We're trapped,' I said again. 'We're . . . not going to get out.' I sucked in a breath, then another, wondering why the air wasn't reaching my lungs.

'Georgie, it's OK.' Ethan squeezed my shoulders. 'We're fine. We're safe here. It's not ideal, but it's OK.' He bent his knees, so he was on my eye level. 'You're all right, I promise.'

'It's just that I-I—'

'I know,' he murmured. 'You don't like being shut up anywhere. But we have space here, and—'

'How do you know that?'

His eyes widened in surprise. 'Because you said . . . When we were together, you told me. We were here, and I was worried about the ghosts, and told you that story about the figure in the alleyway in York, and you said you hated the thought of being trapped – you panicked when some dickhead shut you in a stationery cupboard at school.'

'You remember that?'

He brushed his fingers across my forehead, where

there were a few runaway strands of hair. 'Of course I remember.'

'Oh.'

'I haven't forgotten anything,' he said, and his tone was firm, as if he was annoyed that I would have even considered him forgetting a moment of our time together. He'd been distant, closed-off when I got here, but now . . .

'Neither have I,' I admitted, and even though my pulse had started to settle and my breathing was levelling out, I didn't feel a whole lot better, because I was suddenly faced with something a lot more daunting than being trapped in a glamorous house: being trapped with a quickly defrosting Ethan. My sanity-preserving plan of avoiding him as much as possible, of getting in and out as painlessly as I could, was lying, torn and tattered, on the plush rug at my feet.

Dear Connor,

I met someone today, in the village. I was in the shop, buying some biscuits (are you surprised?) and I walked round the end of an aisle and bumped into this man. There was a flurry of apologies, and I dropped my custard creams. I heard them break, and I must have looked forlorn, because the man asked if I was OK. He asked me if I'd broken anything, and when I frowned, he pointed at my biscuits and said, 'These guys.' (I have to admit, I liked that he called the custard creams 'guys'. Is that weird?)

Then he said he had some time to kill, and he asked if I wanted to have a coffee with him. I hadn't seen him before; I thought he might be a visitor, here for work or on holiday, and for a moment I was tempted. But there were several reasons why I didn't say yes. I've thought about it since I got home, so here they are.

One, he had thick shoulders, and I know I'm being judgemental, but I couldn't help wondering how he got them. Does he have difficulty buying T-shirts that fit? If it progressed beyond one coffee, then . . . reason two, is he going to regale me with stories about lifting concrete posts or doing hundreds of press-ups a day? Would that be my future? Three, he wasn't great at eye contact. He would look at me for a second then glance away, as if he wanted to check out who was watching us – as if our little moment was a noteworthy scene — or he was keeping an eye out for someone more interesting. That never makes anyone feel special. Four, he winked at the sales assistant. He was buying a loaf of white bread and a bottle of skimmed milk, and when he paid for them he said, 'Thanks, love' and winked at her. I shuddered. Five, he wasn't you.

OK, so number five could have been number one, and then I wouldn't have needed any of the others. He wasn't you, and he didn't even ask my name. I imagined you winking at the woman serving, and I knew it would have been so much classier. I've seen you do it, seen how you make it work, despite the odds.

It led me down a rabbit hole to the first time we met, and how I was caught off guard by your calm confidence. We shouldn't have been there, but you weren't worried, and you didn't hurry. You were perfectly in control and I think, in that moment, I fell for you . . . hard. I was already on the floor for you, and then somehow, every day, there was further for me to fall.

It's been almost two years since we last saw each other, and I'm not even close to moving on. I wonder what you're doing right this moment. I hope you're happy.

I love you and I miss you.
Yours always, Amelie xx

Chapter Fourteen

Now

Ethan led me to one of the plush sofas and lowered me onto it as if I was fragile. The cushion felt firm beneath me but also soft, the fabric against the backs of my legs slightly velvety.

He strode into the kitchen, his shoulders a tense line, then came back with a bottle of champagne and two glasses, along with a plate of canapés. There were little salmon blinis with what looked like caviar pearls on top, the golden pastry shapes and creamy sauce of what could have been chicken vol-au-vents, and mini quiches.

'These were in the fridge.' He sat next to me and put everything on the glass table in front of us. 'They haven't been sitting out getting warm.'

'That's good,' I said, 'because I have really high

standards even when I've been kidnapped by a *house*.'

He sighed and gestured at the plate, then poured two glasses of champagne, the bubbles reaching the rim but not quite spilling over.

'This sofa is alchemy,' I said as I picked up a blini. 'Is this caviar?'

'Sarah ordered the food.' He handed me a glass. 'I'm not a caviar sort of guy.'

'I know that,' I said with a smile. 'Unless things have changed drastically since we last saw each other. But I think if you were a caviar guy now, then you would also have bought this place for yourself. You would be the sort of person who needed separate wine and beer fridges in their luxury kitchen.'

Ethan sat further back on the sofa and held his glass up.

I clinked it. 'To being trapped together.'

'To getting to spend time together,' Ethan countered, and he gave me a hint of a smile, despite the worry still evident in his tight shoulders. He put his phone on his thigh and swiped and jabbed at the screen. 'I don't understand,' he muttered. 'I don't get why it's doing this.'

'Won't someone at your office get an alert that something's wrong? That the house is in Panic Room Mode?'

'They should,' he said, 'but seeing as nobody's going to be in the office until Sarah gets back – and she probably won't go in until tomorrow morning – I don't think that's going to help us.'

'She won't get an alert on her phone?' I tried a mini

quiche next, and the salty, rich flavours of some expensive cheese, a delicate herb I didn't recognize, burst on my tongue.

'Sarah's committed to the company, and she knows the Sparks system as well as anyone – she was there throughout the testing. My worry is that now she's off the clock, she won't think anything *could* have gone wrong, because she's as convinced as I was that it's glitch-free.'

I sipped my champagne, and there was that niggle again: the one that suggested Ethan might have done this on purpose. 'So the person we really need to get us out of this mess is you?'

'Pretty much.' He scanned the opulent room, as if looking for an escape hatch he'd forgotten about. With the Smart glass set to blackout and all the lights on, it felt slightly suffocating – the lack of natural light made me crave it, and I imagined how, right now, the sunset would be turning the grey stone exterior, the fields and sea and houses nestled in the village, to gold.

But there was no chance of seeing it, so I kicked off my sandals and sat cross-legged on the sofa. I tried not to think about how long this might last – whatever had caused it – and decided to trust that we would be here for an hour or two, max. 'How long have you been planning this?'

'What?' Ethan asked dryly. 'Locking myself up with my ex-girlfriend on what should be the proudest night of my life?'

I wrinkled my nose. There was something so ordinary about *ex-girlfriend*, and I wanted to challenge him on it, but it wasn't exactly the right time. 'It's not the proudest night of your life, then? Being stuck with me has ruined that?'

He glanced at me, his gaze flicking down to my bare legs. He hadn't put his shoes back on after showing me the nightlight trick, and he mirrored my position, shifting so he was angled towards me. His trousers tightened around his thighs and I looked away. 'How can it be,' he asked, 'when the Sparks system – the thing that makes this build stand out from so many others – has gone wrong?'

'It's only the open house.'

'Which is the showcase. The event that's meant to demonstrate how good it is, how sophisticated and smart and idiot-proof.' He closed his eyes for a long blink. 'How can I sell it if the first time that people come to see the finished property, the house shuts itself down – with us *inside*? I can just imagine the headlines: "Architect and ex-lover trapped inside flagship property by overzealous Panic Room feature".'

I liked the sound of ex-lover better than ex-girlfriend, but that wasn't the point. 'That's not punchy enough,' I told him. 'I'd go with: "Spark fizzes out for architect Ethan as house holds warring exes captive". It's not quite polished to perfection, but something like that.'

'Oh God.' Ethan ran a hand over his face. 'You're going to write about this in the *Star*, aren't you? You could syndicate it, get it picked up by other papers. It's the kind of thing they'd love. Fuck.'

'You think you're that important?' I said, but the truth was, this was a *real* story. An actual thing that had happened – was happening – to me. It was already so much better than a bland report about an open house event for an impressive new redevelopment. I could resuscitate my career by damaging his, I realized, the flare of possibility mingling with something sour tasting.

'Architect and design magazines would cover it,' he said. 'Sarah got me interviews with a couple in the run-up to this. She said it would be good publicity.'

'I read one of them,' I said quietly. 'It was how I found out you were the one who had done all this.' I gestured to the ceiling, the original moulding restored around the crystal chandeliers. 'You said, *the house was never going to be called anything else.*' I deepened my voice, trying to mimic him, hoping it would raise a smile.

'I wondered if you had seen any of them. I was half-expecting an Instagram DM or an email via the company's website.'

My desire to make him smile was obliterated in an instant. 'So – hang on. You wanted me to get in touch, but weren't prepared to yourself? You wanted me to do all the running, even though I'm still in the same house and you could have literally knocked on my front door?' I scooted off the sofa, picked up one of the pastry squares and bit into it. Ugh. There was some sort of blue cheese hidden beneath the chicken and I gagged. I turned away from him and forced myself to chew and then swallow it. So much for storming off elegantly.

'I told you.' He sounded equally annoyed. 'I didn't know if you'd speak to me. I haven't exactly forgotten how we left things, how angry you were, and I thought it was best if I left it up to you.'

I walked to the window and tapped the glass, as if that would somehow wake up the house and force it into action. 'You could have been brave and given it a go.'

'And what would you have said? Honestly?'

I turned around. He was still cross-legged on the sofa, but his arms were folded tightly across his chest and I wondered if he'd chosen a tight fit on purpose so his clearly toned body was on show. Eighteen-year-old Ethan wouldn't have cared, but thirty-one-year-old Ethan – the one who had a string of incredibly elegant girlfriends – might. Maybe he *was* a caviar guy now, after all. I walked back over and perched on a cushion.

'I would have spoken to you,' I said. 'I would have let you in and I-I would probably have given you a hug. Even the day after.'

He blinked. 'The day after I came to Alperwick, on this build?'

I shook my head. 'The day after our argument.'

His eyes widened, but the rest of him went still. 'You mean the day after we broke up? The day after prom night, when I turned up at your door after I'd got out of the police station? The *next day* you would have let me in and hugged me and . . . what? Forgiven me?'

I nodded at the cushion. 'I regretted our fight so much. I was angry with you, and frustrated, but after a few hours I understood why you'd done it. I just . . .' I looked up at him, saw how he'd composed his features into his original, impassive mask. 'I spent so much time putting Mum first, skipping classes to take her to appointments, and I was starting to realize – being with you was helping me realize – how important it was to put myself first when it mattered. You were so kind, Ethan. But then you put yourself *last*, you jeopardized everything, and I—'

'You would have forgiven me?' he repeated. 'The next day? But we didn't speak to each other again. I was away that whole summer, thinking you didn't want to see me, then you went off to university, and . . .'

'I came back for Christmas and your family had moved away.'

'We had to. Again.' Ethan rubbed his forehead, the movement hard, as if he was trying to wipe away a Sharpie mark. 'Fuck, Georgie. So they were true, then?'

'What were?'

'I was convinced, for years, and then I found . . .' He sucked in a breath. 'But I didn't really believe that . . .'

'I thought you'd forgotten about me,' I admitted. 'I thought that you'd got over me quickly, and so I tried to forget about *you*, but then there was Instagram.'

153

'What about Instagram?'

'My username is nondescript,' I explained. 'I didn't expect – or want – you to realize that I'd followed you.' He'd posted a photo not that long ago, a shot of the beach at Porthgolow, where there was a vintage double-decker called the Cornish Cream Tea Bus. I remember the jolt it had given me, knowing he was back in Cornwall, but I'd never considered that he'd come back for the house. 'Then, when I had already agreed with my editor that I'd write a piece on the open house, my friend showed me the article, and I realized this was yours. There was the bit about the name, and I—'

'I never forgot about you.' Ethan had gone from surprised to bleak. 'I thought you were done with me. Even after . . .' He shook his head, picked up his glass and took a long swig.

'After *what*, Ethan?'

'It was all too late. I didn't know if I'd be welcome, and the thought of knocking on your door and you closing it in my face . . .'

'Hey. Ethan.' I moved closer to him, but he shifted away from me, the movement almost too small to notice. 'It was all such a long time ago.'

He put his glass on the table and stood up. 'I'm going to check the panel again. See if I can get us out of here.'

He walked off and I flopped back on the sofa. I had imagined this moment so many times – admitting that I'd forgiven him almost immediately – and in all my daydreams, he'd been happy or relieved, wrapping his arms tightly around me. He hadn't been angry, like he was now. I rubbed my face and tried to think, but my mind was blank, so I got up, took another of the mini quiches, and went to find him.

Chapter Fifteen

April 2012

After that first time, we went on more excursions to the house. We were emboldened by our ability to make it inside, to not run screaming in terror or get caught by the local police or a curious neighbour. When it was too cold to go to the beach and we didn't want to stay in our rooms where our parents could eavesdrop, we would find sanctuary there. It wasn't a whole lot warmer, but it had solid walls that shielded us from the wind, and it was somewhere we could escape to. But it was always the five of us, never Ethan and I on our own.

We had become boyfriend and girlfriend without labelling it, but I had never felt like this before, so wholly consumed by a person, interested in everything about him – what he was thinking; what he was doing after we said goodbye. I'd told him that he made me happy, and that I could kiss him all day, but we hadn't made it much past kissing – though that was down to lack of opportunity rather than anything else.

There was one evening when he'd come to meet Mum, and while she'd been finishing the spaghetti Bolognese I'd taken him up to my room, and kissing on my bed had turned into me sitting astride him, his hands on my hips, fingers digging into my flesh as I'd writhed inexpertly on top of him. He hadn't seemed to mind my lack of sultriness, had groaned into my ear and whispered my name, his eyes bright and his cheeks flushed. When Mum had called up the stairs that dinner was ready, we'd both needed five minutes to get our breathing – and other things – under control. He'd stroked my thigh under the table, and I'd been a ball of heat and pressure, distracted from the conversation for the whole of the meal. Mum had declared, once he'd gone, that she loved him, and I was close to agreeing.

But then, one Friday in April, when the evenings were lighter, the sun had a little bit of warmth to it, and the house on the cliffs was calling to us more frequently, Mum said she was spending the evening with her friend Helen, so I told Kira I couldn't make it that night, and that Ethan wouldn't be able to either.

'Oh, OK,' she'd said blithely, then elbowed me in the ribs and pulled me in for a hug in the sixth-form corridor. 'I'm so happy for you. Make sure he treats you right, OK?'

'I will.' I wasn't confident about a whole lot of things at that point, but I knew I could rely on Ethan looking after me.

I met him after my English class at the end of the day. He was wearing jeans and a grey T-shirt that showed off his tanned arms, his eyes hidden by sunglasses, and I sucked in a breath before greeting him with a kiss. He seemed effortlessly cool, whereas I had tidied my already tidy room to within an inch of its life, taken the bus to a pharmacy three villages over to buy condoms at the weekend. I would tell him – because I already told him everything – but not until afterwards. I wanted to be his sexy, seductive girlfriend.

'Ready to go?' I asked.

He pushed his sunglasses onto his head. 'You're absolutely sure about this?'

'Absolutely,' I said, and took his hand.

When we got to mine, I had to undo both locks, which confirmed that Mum was still out. Ethan followed me in, hovering in the hall behind me. He was quiet, and I wondered if he was vibrating with tension like me, or if he felt completely calm about the whole thing. I knew that neither of us had done this before, though he'd done a little more than kissing with a girl called Bethany in York. I tried not to think about her or anyone else as I faced him, the afternoon sunlight filtering in through the glass panels in the door.

'Do you want a drink?' I asked.

'No. I just . . .' he stopped. 'But if you do, we could—'

'I don't,' I rushed out.

I took his hand and led him up the stairs, my arm twisting uncomfortably behind me but not prepared to let go – I thought this would be awkward enough anyway. But people our age were having sex – Kira and Freddy, and there were girls at school who bragged about it all the time. And the way I felt about Ethan, I wasn't doing this out of any need to catch up. I had always imagined I wouldn't sleep with anyone until after school, until I was far away from Alperwick, but he'd changed that.

I tugged him inside my room and closed the door, trying to see the space through his eyes: the lights around my mirror, the cuddly turtle on a shelf above my bed, along with some framed photos of me, Kira, Freddy and Orwell. There was a pair of jeans trapped in my wardrobe door as if they'd been trying to make a run for it.

But then Ethan closed the gap between us, cupped my face and tilted it so he could kiss me, and I realized he wasn't looking at the room, only at me. It was addictive, my blood heating as his kiss got firmer, more urgent, and I leaned into him, sliding my fingers under his shirt. He flinched, and I tried to back away, but he held me firmly.

'I'm ticklish there,' he whispered against my mouth, 'that's all.'

'Oh.' I swallowed. 'Good, I—'

'We can stop at any time.' He held my gaze, but I loved that his voice was fraying at the edges.

'I don't want to stop.' I got to work on his shirt buttons, undoing them while he fumbled with the zip on my jeans.

As our clothes came off, I shed any doubts along with them. His body was lean and toned, pale skin decorated with freckles that traced the shape of his shoulders. He seemed so unselfconscious, so wholly focused on me and the layers I was stripping in front of him. When I was down to my underwear, he reached behind me and undid my bra clasp, slid it down my arms and dropped it on the floor. He brushed his fingers over my skin, staring down at me.

'God.' He swallowed. 'George.'

He was only in his boxers, and I slid my hands inside the waistband, pushing them down. He groaned into my neck, and I felt a surge of elation.

'Let's get in bed,' I said breathlessly.

I had imagined falling onto the duvet, wild with passion and lust, but this was real and we were both nervous and it was better, this slow exploration. I pulled back the covers and slid in, Ethan following me until we were lying, facing each other, the duvet tugged up to our waists.

'You're beautiful,' Ethan said. 'Georgie, I . . . I want to do this right.'

'Me too,' I murmured, even though I didn't know exactly what that meant.

His hands explored me, smoothing over my skin, taking it slowly so my pleasure was a gentle build, and all I wanted was to get closer to him. He kept checking in with me, asking if I was OK, if what he was doing was good. The low tone of his voice sent tremors shivering through me, and when he leaned into kiss me, the tremors turned to sparks and our touches got more frantic.

He reached over to grab the box of condoms from my bedside table, and took one out. I felt dizzy, almost like I was floating, like there was this beautiful part of me that had been hidden inside all this time, and Ethan had found it.

'This OK?' he asked again.

'Yes, Ethan.'

He stroked my hair off my forehead, pressed his lips there. 'Are you sure?'

'I'm sure,' I said. 'Are you?'

'Yeah.' His eyebrows were dipped, and I knew he was trying to show me how important this was, how seriously he was taking it, but his eyes were glazed with lust and his lips were swollen from our kisses, and I couldn't help the giggle that burst out of me. 'George?' His mouth tipped up in a smile.

'I'm just . . . happy we're doing this,' I whispered. Whatever happened, whatever it felt like the first time, I knew I was safe with Ethan. I couldn't imagine doing this with anyone else.

'Me, too.' He leaned over me, kissed me again. 'Tell me if you want to stop. Any time, Georgie.'

'OK.'

And then he was there, closer, and I gasped at the new sensations, the heat and tingling, his kisses drugging me, his hands everywhere, stroking and soothing, him whispering my name against my forehead, my cheek, my ear. He was perfect, with his rumbling voice and his gentle touch, his body over mine, and I closed my eyes and gave into everything he was making me feel.

'Georgie.' His voice was rough, his eyes unfocused as he looked down at me. 'Georgie, you are perfect.' The words were exhales, dizzy and delirious, and I knew he was feeling everything I was, and it sent me closer, closer, until I was a flaring firework, limbs nothing but sensation, turning hot and sweet and satisfied.

Ethan stroked my hair, my cheeks, then kissed the places his fingers had been. I smiled at him, pressed up on a wobbling arm and kissed him, said his name into his mouth, and he followed me over the edge.

In that moment I knew that, no matter what happened in the future, I would always have this memory – me and Ethan, together like this – and nobody could take it away.

Chapter Sixteen

Now

'Any change?'

Ethan jumped, then turned to glare at me. 'Why are you silent?'

'I'm not silent. I've taken my shoes off.'

'Right.' He turned back to the wall panel just inside the front door, the screen glowing a cheerful blue while he pressed buttons. It beeped happily, while continuing to offer no possibility of releasing us any time soon.

'Panic Room Mode activated,' the Sparks voice said smoothly, in response to something he'd pressed.

'Yes, I *know* it's fucking activated!' Ethan shouted.

'Hey.' I squeezed his arm. 'Come on.'

'I mean, what the fuck? What the *fuck*, Sparks?'

'I will not tolerate that language,' Sparks said haughtily.

'How does she know you were swearing,' I asked, 'when you said Sparks *at the end?*'

Ethan rubbed the back of his neck. 'It picks up the whole sentence. Wherever the word Sparks is, it'll get the gist.'

'Which means it's recording everything we say?' A shiver ran down my spine.

'It doesn't record anything; it's just more intelligent than anything else on the market right now.'

'Of course it is.'

Ethan narrowed his eyes at me.

I didn't want us to be at odds. For however long we were trapped here, we had to get along. Then we could go our separate ways, he could continue to be mad at me for forgiving him but not tracking him down to tell him, and I could go on trying not to stalk his Instagram, and most likely failing.

'Why don't you give me a tour?' I suggested.

'What?' He folded his arms, his shirt smoothing over his deltoids and biceps.

'Don't pretend that sentence didn't make perfect sense. We're stuck here for the time being, so why don't you give me a tour? Show me all the things you love about Sterenlenn.'

'I've shown you the bedroom,' he said tightly.

'You *found* me in the bedroom,' I corrected. 'I was already there. Is that your favourite room?' I widened my eyes. 'Of course it is; I should have known.' I grinned, and some unnameable emotion flickered behind his eyes.

'George,' he said wearily.

'Come on.' I took his hand. 'Be mad at me if you like. I was mad at you: really, *really* mad. I was completely heartbroken.' I had meant it to be a rousing speech, but now I was remembering how it had felt to lose him; to sit on my bed after he'd gone, and think about all the things we'd talked about and shared, and how much I missed him. 'I was,' I went on, 'but I also got over it, and you did too. We were eighteen, when even the smallest things felt entirely momentous, and now we're not. You have created this beautiful place, and if we're going to be trapped here for the next few hours, then I want to see it all.'

Ethan tried to pull his hand out of mine, but I held on tightly.

'You must want to show it off. All those open house weirdos came here to drink champagne, be seen and think about their profit margins, but you love the house. Show it to me.'

He stared at me for a handful of seconds, as if he was trying to work out how my brain fitted together, but I knew it was a losing battle and so did he, because he sighed and said, 'OK.'

'Great.' I did a little jump. 'Where first? The separate beer and wine fridges?'

He gave me a flicker of a smile. 'No. Upstairs.'

'We did the spooky nightlights already.'

'Come and see the master bathroom.'

'You mean the en-suite disco lights are a sideshow?'

'Exactly. Follow me.'

It was alarming how much I loved hearing him say that, his low, beckoning tone more persuasive than any pipe played by a legendary child-stealer.

'It's a Jacuzzi bath, with a TV mounted on the wall and *another* drinks fridge.' I shook my head, unable to stop staring, because the bathroom at the back of Sterenlenn was bigger than an entire floor of my house. It was painted in cool sea greens and that hint of Atlantic blue, smelled overwhelmingly of vanilla and sea salt, and there was something about the ambience – maybe some subliminal messages pumped through the Sparks system – that made it infinitely soothing. I'd gone to my dentist's last week for a check-up, and had been delighted that they had a bottle of Original Source hand soap in their minuscule toilet. *These little touches*, I'd thought happily, wondering if I needed to have a rethink about my home hygiene products. Now I wanted to burn my house to the ground.

'It would be better if we could clear the windows,' Ethan said. 'We knocked the original one out here, so we could make this wall glass. When you're in the bath it's supposed to feel like you're in the ocean.'

I nodded. I could see that – when the glass wasn't dark – the view would be straight over the back garden, to the cliff edge and the wild sea beyond. Pebbles and shells in greys, creams and dusky pinks were set into the sink surround, and I could feel the lingering warmth of the underfloor heating beneath my bare feet.

'This is a light catcher, too.' Ethan gestured above us, to another crystal chandelier. It was turned on now, but I could imagine that when sunlight came in, it would snag hold of the crystal drops and cast rainbows across the tiles and the plush, upholstered bench nestled in the corner of the room. 'And in there,' he pointed to a featureless section of the wall, 'there's a massage table.'

'Show me,' I said with a grin.

Ethan pressed a discreet button, and a smooth, near-silent mechanism got to work, a padded table sliding out of the wall until it was roughly waist-height. He pressed another button and feet slowly lowered to the floor, then he unlatched the table from the wall and pulled it into the middle of the room. 'This is so the masseuse can walk all the way around it,' he explained.

'So, when I said earlier that the house doesn't give you a massage, it basically does?'

'There are no robotic arms,' he said with a smile. 'You need an actual human to get involved, but . . . I suppose so.'

'Ethan,' I said with a laugh, 'your house is insane.'

I ran my hand over the padded table. It was soft, less plasticky than the ones in Alperwick Spa, where Spence had taken me to celebrate my birthday. I always felt self-conscious in spas, being mostly naked and extremely vulnerable in front of a stranger whose job it was to put their hands on me. Spence, of course, had acted like she owned the place, but for her the massage was more than just a treat, as it helped relieve some of her pain.

'Maybe this is the way to go.' I thought of how, when the masseuse had asked me to turn from my stomach onto my back, the towel had slipped and I'd shouted, 'My boobs!' as if they were escaping and she needed to chase them down.

'You think it's a good addition?' There was something in the way Ethan said it, an inkling of hope, as if he was happy I approved.

'Yup,' I said. 'I'm going to replace my kitchen work-tops with a massage table and one of those puffy atomizer things that changes colour.'

He stared at me. 'I'm not doing this just so you can mock me.'

I glared back. 'Fine,' I said. 'Sorry.' I swallowed. 'I'm sorry, Ethan. It's just . . . this is so far beyond what's normal.'

'I know. But for this size and style of property – it's what buyers want. I put in a plan for something more traditional, something without all these bells and whis-tles, that was more in keeping with the original house and its features, but the investors didn't . . . they wanted all this.'

'Sarah wanted a massage table?'

'She wanted what the investors wanted. These days she's just . . . she's wholly focused on supporting me, and the business. And sometimes she has a much better idea of what I need than I do.'

'Right.' It was still hard for me to reconcile this new

Sarah with the one I'd known at eighteen. I examined the huge shower cubicle that was similar to the one in the en-suite. 'Disco lights here, too?'

'Of course.'

'And the special Ethan Sparks temperature setting?'

'The ambient temperature is twenty-one degrees,' the house announced, and I rolled my eyes.

'You could never live in one of your own houses,' I said. 'It would get too annoying.'

'I don't often say my surname out loud.' Ethan leaned against the shower glass and crossed his arms. I would have to stop annoying him so he didn't keep doing that, or else find a shirt that was two sizes too big for him. 'And what is the *special Ethan temperature setting*?'

'You know what it is.' I took a step towards him. 'You love showers that are so hot you're basically poaching yourself.'

'Nothing wrong with a hot, steamy shower.'

'I prefer not to boil my brain while I'm getting clean. I lose enough brain cells coming up with inane headlines for the newspaper.'

'And have you improved on your original attempt for this calamity?'

'"Sparko: the story of the house that couldn't".'

'You can do better than that.' His eyes blazed. 'If you're going to be the catalyst of my downfall, then I want something really fucking good, OK? I want to go out with a bang. And you know what . . .?'

'Please tell me.' I folded my arms, mirroring him.

'This story is so much better for you now everything's gone wrong. It's gone from a bland property piece to a juicy disaster, so I'm starting to wonder if—'

'If I had anything to do with this?' I couldn't hide my shock. 'Are you *serious*? How do you think I went about hacking into your precious house?'

'I don't know – I don't know *you* any more. I have no clue what you're capable of.'

'Ethan.' I sucked in a breath. 'I failed to charge my phone, so it's currently on less than 10 per cent. I left my spare camera battery at home. I'm – I'm not some kind of *James Bond* level technological mastermind.'

'Q is the tech wizard for James Bond – he doesn't do any of it himself – and you could just be saying that.'

'And *you* could be accusing me to take suspicion off yourself, as well as being an extreme pedant! You're the one who's supposed to know the system back to front, but suddenly it's outwitted you? Something about this is a little off, isn't it?'

'Of course it's off! We're trapped inside! You really think I planned this? That I wanted us to be stuck here together, with all that's happened between us?' He turned away from me, pushing the massage table up against the wall and pressing buttons so that the mechanism took hold and it slid back into its slot. I couldn't see his expression, and that only increased my suspicion.

'Maybe this was your way of getting to talk to me,' I hypothesized.

He tapped the wall with the side of his fist. 'I didn't know you were coming.'

'You could just be *saying* that,' I echoed.

'You have a stronger motive than me – getting to be the *star* reporter for the *North Cornwall Star*. A boost for your career. Unless you had another reason for coming today? Maybe you wanted to be trapped in here with me.'

'I didn't know anything about your precious Sparks system before I got here, and I'm not much better off now, especially as *you* seem to have lost control of it, too.'

Ethan's chest was rising and falling, anger still flushing his cheeks when he turned around, but he was a lot quieter when he said, 'You know, I am actually wondering if your article is the real reason you came here tonight. It would be a great cover for something else.'

It was my turn to look away. I wished there was a view I could pretend to gaze at instead of the blackout window. 'There's no other reason.'

'Really?' he asked lightly. 'And did you declare your personal interest in this story to your editor, or does she think you have no skin in the game?'

'We're ancient history, Ethan.' I could sense him walking towards me, stalking me slowly.

'Is that what we are?' His words shivered over my neck, and I had to swallow a gasp. 'I don't believe you.'

'Which bit?'

'Any of it. But I haven't decided if you're somehow

responsible for the house shutting down, or if you were never here to write about it in the first place. Why are you here, Georgie? What is it you're really—?'

'Can you *stop* breathing on my neck?' I hadn't meant to blurt it out, but it was so distracting, and his low, whispered words were doing funny things to me, resurrecting feelings that I'd been working so hard to supress.

'You could move,' he said, but he sounded reluctant. He put his hands on my shoulders, brushed them down my arms, his touch as light as a feather, over the sleeves of my dress and onto bare skin. 'What are you really looking for?'

Those five words sent panic shooting through me and I spun around, dislodging his hands, staring up at him. I don't know who moved first – if I stretched up, or he leaned down – but suddenly my lips were pressed firmly against his, and the sensation was so overwhelming, familiar and new all at once, that my thoughts disintegrated.

Ethan cupped the back of my head without a second's hesitation, as if he'd been desperate for us to touch this way all along. I pressed myself against him, thin dress against thin shirt, hot skin beneath. I threaded my fingers together behind his neck, clung onto him as his mouth opened and my tongue slid inside at the invitation.

It had been so long since I'd felt like this, and I was shocked by how swiftly it had happened, how wild and unhinged I had become, how much I wanted him when, moments before, we'd been accusing each other of sabotage.

'George,' he whispered against my mouth, and I said his name back between kisses.

He slid his hand over my waist, down to the back of my thigh, and brought my leg up so it was anchored to his hip. I was already melting, and this only made it worse.

'I didn't mean to—' he started.

'It's OK,' I soothed, bringing his lips back to mine, not ready for it to end.

He tightened his grip on my leg. I had the wall hard against my back, and him – strong and warm and urgent – pressed against my front. I thought if I was just a little bit higher, or him lower, or maybe we could go back to the bed, where . . . I froze. The master bedroom where the nightlights would ping on, and we'd tell the house that we needed the Sex Setting, thank you very much, with rose petals falling from the ceiling and a bucket of champagne sliding up from a secret panel in the floor.

'George?' Ethan leaned back so he could look down at me. He slid his thumb over my flushed cheek, and I had to turn my head away, because there was some-thing in his expression that made me want to devour him on the spot, and stroke his hair, and run a hundred miles in the opposite direction all at once.

'Fuck.' I slid my leg down to the floor. What were we doing? This whole scenario was beyond ridiculous.

Ethan took a step back, the fire in his eyes blinking out. 'I'm sorry,' he said roughly. 'I'm so sorry.' Somewhere along the way I'd un-popped a couple of his buttons, and his hair had turned into a sexy disaster.

'It's not your fault,' I said. 'It's mine. I should never . . . I'm sorry, Ethan.'

I couldn't run a hundred miles in any direction, but I could get myself to the other side of this huge house, give myself a few minutes to try and work out why I had thought that was a good idea, and what on earth we were supposed to do now.

'Sorry,' I said again, then I left Ethan behind with the Jacuzzi bath and the disco shower, and ran down the stairs. As I did, from outside, even though the view was still hidden and we were in our dim, locked box of a house, I heard the first rumble of what sounded like a very enthusiastic summer storm.

Dear Connor,

We don't talk about the house enough – or I don't, anyway. It has always been such a big part of my life, always been right there, but without anyone to talk to about it, it's losing its significance.

I know it's pointless, but I can't stop wondering what would have happened if things hadn't worked out the way they did, and we'd turned our pie-in-the-sky dreams into reality. The two of us living there together. Can you imagine? It was always impossible – even back then – but that didn't stop us making up scenarios as if it was within our reach.

Sometimes I walk through the rooms and remember us being there together – those few snatched times when it was possible – and I imagine that the house is ours, and we can do what we want with it.

And so, to amuse myself, I've been inventing my perfect room. I've picked one on the first floor, at the back of the house, so it looks directly over the cliffs and the churning Atlantic. The window would be bigger, so light could pour in all the time: sun, moon and starlight. I've always thought that the windows are too small: what's the point of it being right there, if you only get a peek at the magnificent view?

In my imagined room there's a desk that runs all the way along the window, so I can smooth my

*hands over the wood when I'm thinking. I'd keep
the surface mostly clear, so I was surrounded by
space and the Cornish coastline. I'd have an art
deco lamp with a shade of pink and green glass,
and bookshelves against the walls, and there's this
wallpaper I've seen – it's mad but so beautiful. It's
a mermaid print, and she looks just how I've
imagined the Alperwick Mermaid for all these years.
Her tail is made up of mauve scales, and her hair
is flowing gold, and there are starfish and minnows
picked out in silver against a blue and green background. It's ridiculously expensive because of the
foil, and I'd only want one wall – a feature wall.
That's what it's called isn't it? You would know.*

*I'd have a thick rug in the same blues and greens
as the wallpaper, but furry like the coat of a daft,
long-haired sheep, and one of those elegant
armchairs where I could curl up and read.*

*What do you think? If I told you all of this face
to face, you'd laugh, but then you'd see that, actually,
it's perfect. For the house and the space it takes up,
on the edge of the sea as if it could fall in at any
moment. I've been building this in my head for a
while now, new details coming to me at random
moments. I write it all down and a picture emerges.
Is that how it happens for you, too?*

*I wonder what you're doing now, what amazing
thing you're creating. I wish I could be as focused
as you always were, and put my heart into something besides these letters. But my heart is stuck*

with you, and I can't imagine it looking for a new home anytime soon.

I love you and I miss you.
Yours always, Amelie xx

Chapter Seventeen

April 2012

We made it back to my room whenever we could, which wasn't often because Mum didn't go out much, and when she did it was usually when I was at school. And, while Ethan's dad worked long hours, his mum was usually at home in the evenings, and Sarah was often there too. We tried to be creative, but the beach was popular all year round and I didn't relish the thought of sand getting *everywhere*, and while we continued to go to the house on the hill, Ethan and I had never been there without the others, and I didn't want rodents having a ringside seat for our intimate moments.

'How long until your mum's back?' Ethan asked one spring afternoon, my bedroom window open a crack to let in a snake of cool air while we stayed snug under the covers.

'I don't know,' I said, 'but not long, so we should—'
He moved on top of me, kissed me thoroughly, deftly
rolled the condom on.

Being able to do it so infrequently made these
moments precious. We were learning more about each
other, and I felt grown-up, having such an intense and
– I thought – adult relationship. Except right then, when
I started to lose myself to the sensations rushing up to
meet me, and something landed, *plonk,* on my face.

'Argh!' I rubbed my nose and fumbled for the
weapon. It was Connor, my cuddly turtle.

Ethan's mouth was open in surprise, then he
dissolved into laughter, burying his head in my neck.
'OK?' He leaned up on an elbow and ran his finger
gently down my nose. My eyes were watering, but with
surprise more than anything else.

'Feeling stupid,' I admitted. 'I should have moved
Connor ages ago.'

'Maybe he's jealous,' Ethan said in a low rumble.

'Shush.'

'I'll take your mind off it.'

'You'd better.' He did until, a few minutes later, I
heard the front door bang and Mum call up the stairs,
'I'm home, Georgie! I'll put the kettle on.'

Ethan and I exchanged panicked looks. 'OK! Be
down in a sec!' Ethan glanced towards the window
and I grinned. 'You don't need to sneak out like a
burglar.'

'Three teas?' Mum shouted up, and my grin turned
into laughter.

'Yes please,' I called down, and Ethan winced. I leaned up and kissed him. 'I think we have been well and truly busted.'

'Getting your homework done?' Mum asked innocently when, ten minutes later, we strolled into the kitchen, aiming for nonchalant. 'Hello Ethan, lovely to see you.'

'You too, Mrs Monroe. Have you had a good day?'

'I got some nice things at the market.' She pointed to her shopping bags, contents spilling onto the kitchen counter. 'And please call me Lisa.'

'Thanks, Lisa.'

She handed him a steaming mug of tea, then passed me one. 'I got some fish pie bits. Thought I could make that for us tonight. Ethan, there'll be enough for three, if you fancy staying?'

He raised an eyebrow at me, and I nodded. 'I'd love to,' he said, 'but only if I can help.'

Mum tucked a strand of hair behind her ear. 'You're a guest,' she said, but it was a weak protest.

'I can peel potatoes,' Ethan suggested, and when Mum accepted, he shot me a wink and then listened patiently to her instructions about where the peeler was and how many we would need to cover the filling.

The kitchen was barely big enough for two, but the three of us worked around each other. I sorted Mum's pills into their relevant organizer boxes at the table, while she and Ethan constructed a fish pie, talking through the stages together, Ethan suggesting horseradish mash

180

for the top. Mum was in a good mood, her tremors not as pronounced as they often were, and I wanted to take a snapshot: the two most important people in my life getting along.

'Georgie, I bought a box of chocolates,' Mum said. 'Can you see if I've left them in my handbag?'

'Sure.' I tidied up the pill boxes, putting the instruction leaflets in the green clip in the drawer, and went to find Mum's bag in the hallway. I rifled through it, but there were no chocolates in there – unless they were chocolates for Borrowers. My hand brushed a plastic bag, and I pulled it out, my stomach twisting as I realized what it was.

'Found them, Georgie?' Mum called.

I cleared my throat. 'Still looking!'

It wasn't a secret that some MS sufferers used weed to lessen the symptoms, and I wasn't wholly against it. But after Mum's last consultation, the doctor had made it clear that any unprescribed drugs could impact the success of the trial she was on. I felt sick, wondering why she'd got hold of some now, but not sure how to confront her. I wanted to talk to Ethan about it. He would know what to do, or – at the very least – he would make me feel better about whatever *I* decided to do. I didn't hear his phone ring, but I heard the pad of his footsteps, out of the kitchen and into our living room, ducking away before he reached me.

'Hey,' he said, his voice reaching me easily. 'What?' His tone sharpened, and the pit in my stomach gnawed. 'No. Sarah, I can't.'

There was a pause, and I slid the plastic packet back into Mum's bag, resting my head against the wall of coats.

'I'm busy right now, but . . .' A sharp inhale. 'You *broke* it? You said it was the wing mirror. A broken window doesn't happen unless you chuck a *brick* through it, Sarah! Fuck.' A shorter pause, and I could sense our perfect evening slipping away. 'No, you know what Dad will say.' Ethan's laugh was humourless. 'OK, give me ten minutes. Don't do or say anything, and don't leave. I'm serious. Yeah. Yes, I know. Bye.'

He walked out into the hall, his hair a mess of tugged strands. He was rubbing the back pocket of his jeans, where he'd kept his cigarettes until I'd asked him to quit.

'That didn't sound good,' I said tentatively.

'I have to go. Sarah's got herself in trouble, and I—'

'You're going to bail her out?'

'I'm sorry. I have to.'

'I know.' I smiled, even though I was angry that he was running straight to her. But she was clearly unhappy, and from what Ethan had told me their mum wasn't that sympathetic; too afraid of their father to stand up to him on Sarah's behalf. I just wished Ethan didn't have to take on all the responsibility.

He ran his hands down my arms and leaned in to kiss me, the gentle goodbye turning into something hotter. He groaned, low and frustrated, then went to make his apologies to Mum.

I waved him off at the door, then watched his

silhouette against the sunset, his shoulders hunched as he hurried away from me. I could hear the waves hitting the sand in the bay, the tide just reaching its highest point, and the seaside scents of slowly cooking fish enveloped me. A special treat of a dinner that we couldn't afford very often. *Especially not if Mum was buying weed*, a little voice reminded me.

I shut the door and went to join her. She was pushing mashed potato onto the steaming pie mix, an open jar of horseradish on the counter, a dollop sliding down the side of the cabinet.

'You need to watch that,' Mum said without turning around.

'I can clean it up.' I grabbed the cloth.

She looked sideways at me. 'No, I mean Ethan. He's invited to dinner and then – poof! Something more important comes up. Those little instances of unreliability will get more frequent if you're not careful.'

'His sister's in trouble.' Defensiveness made me grip the cloth too tightly. 'I've told you about Sarah. She's miserable.'

'Just make sure he doesn't take you for granted. I know what that's like, and I'm living proof that it doesn't end well. Left high and dry with a five-year-old and barely enough to pay the rent.'

'I know,' I said quietly, backing down for the second time in five minutes. That five-year-old was me, and I'd heard it so often – how hard her life had been once my dad left. I never got stories about the two of us hanging out together, Mum and daughter having fun without the need for anyone else, or about how her love for me sustained her through the difficult times. But maybe I'd been spending too much time rereading the Cornish Sands series, where everything was romanticized, with lessons learned and tragedies weathered.

'You can't have a proper relationship if you're hiding things from each other,' Mum said as she slid the pie into the oven. Before, my stomach had been rumbling with hunger, but now I didn't want anything.

'Ethan tells me everything,' I said, and then, because I couldn't hold it in, I added, 'Unlike *some* people.'

'What's that supposed to mean?' Mum turned to face me. She looked exhausted. She'd done too much, and the evening had gone to shit anyway.

'Nothing.' Neither of us had the energy for an argument. 'Don't worry about it.'

She sighed. 'I really like Ethan, love, but you're both so young, and I don't want you making the mistakes I did.'

'Ethan's not a mistake.'

'I know that, but things like this . . .' She trailed off. 'When he starts over-promising, telling you he'll make up for it, that it'll never happen again, that's when you should worry. He might believe what he's telling you, but that doesn't mean *you* should.'

'He's not like Dad. His sister's in trouble, and he's looking out for her.' The thought of my gorgeous, thoughtful boyfriend being some kind of lying womanizer was so ridiculous I wanted to laugh. 'Why don't you go and sit down? I'll make you a fresh tea, put away the last bits of shopping.'

'Thanks, love.' Mum gave me a watery smile. 'The pie needs forty minutes, and I thought we could have some broccoli with it.'

'OK.' I returned her smile, my jaw aching with tension.

She squeezed my shoulder as she passed, and I looked around the bomb-site kitchen, at everything there was still to do. It would have been fun with Ethan at my side, a room full of laughter instead of just the hum of the oven.

Dinner was quiet and stilted. I knew Mum wanted to say more about Ethan, because she was deeply paranoid when it came to untrustworthy men, and her protectiveness of me could be stifling. But she kept quiet, and I didn't mention the weed because I didn't know how to approach it.

It wasn't until I'd crawled into bed, the sheets still smelling of him, that Ethan called me.

I picked up immediately. 'Hey. Are you OK? How's Sarah?'

'Not great.' He sounded tired, and my heart squeezed. 'But I managed to convince Mr Murray that the broken window was an accident, and we gave him an account so he can claim it on the insurance.'

'Sarah did it on purpose?'

'I don't know what she was thinking, but Mum and Dad are clueless, and that's the important thing.' I didn't tell him that I thought they should know, because if she got into serious trouble she might realize how much she was hurting other people as well as herself. 'I'm sorry I had to leave. How was dinner?'

'The mash was delicious. I'm sad you missed it: we missed you, too.'

'Next time,' he said. 'I promise I won't leave again. I could cook you both something, if you like?'

'Really? You cook? What are your favourite things to make?'

As we talked I rolled onto my side, pulling the duvet up to my ear so we were in a cocoon, just me and him. Connor the turtle had a new place on my desk, and I snuggled into the pillow, listening to Ethan talk. I tried not to think about what Mum had said, tried not to let her past disappointments affect how I felt about him. Sarah was his sister, his family, and his sense of loyalty was one of the things I loved about him. He had enough room in his heart for both of us. I wouldn't be with him if I didn't believe that was the truth.

Chapter Eighteen

Now

I was still breathing hard when I reached the French windows in the living room. Our empty glasses and the plate of canapés sat on the table, a still life from a decadent afternoon, if you took a snapshot without any context.

I rubbed my sternum, trying to calm down. I had kissed Ethan, and he hadn't run in the opposite direction; he had kissed me back. Now I had renewed that thirteen-year-old memory, the sensation of his lips on mine no longer a distant pleasure point, like the brush of a petal against my skin. It had been so hot, so incredible – even better than when we were teenagers – and that realization flashed brightly, trying to override the rational side of my brain that reminded me he was a stranger, that he always had a new woman on his arm, that he wasn't the warm, committed person he'd been when we were together. It scoffed at my worry he was responsible for shutting the house down with us inside.

There was another loud rumble of thunder and I pressed my hands against the Smart glass, wishing I could see Alperwick nestled in the valley, besieged by rain. I wondered how Spence was getting on. She hated storms, something about getting stuck out in one as a child, and I hoped Denise was there, babbling about her grandchildren and taking her mind off it.

'Sparks, what is the weather doing right now?' I asked.

'Expect thunderstorms for the next hour, followed by a cloudy night with no chance of a blanket of stars. The temperature is twenty-four degrees, lowering to sixteen overnight, and humidity will remain high.'

'*No chance of a blanket of stars?*' I frowned. Ethan had incorporated it into the weather reports? There was so much about the house that felt personal to us, and I imagined for a moment that I'd decided not to come: that Spence hadn't insisted I should wangle myself a tour so we could make Connor and Amelie's reunion more realistic; that I hadn't gone to Wynn insisting that we needed to cover it for the paper. All these details would have been lost on anyone else.

I glanced at the fireplace, my thoughts tumbling over each other, then noticed a wall panel next to the French windows. The display announced that I was in the 'Lounge' and detailed its settings: temperature, air condition, lighting. At the top it said: *Panic Room Mode Activated*. A section for the windows indicated their status as: 'Dark Glass'. I pressed it, and it beeped as it scrolled through the options. *Clear*, *Frosted*, then *Tinted* at various degrees. I pressed 'Clear' and waited, but nothing happened. I pressed it again. There was a chirpy beep, followed by nothing.

'Sparks,' I said, 'please make the lounge windows clear.'

'Sterenlenn is in Panic Room Mode,' the house told me.

'Sparks, *please*. Please, *please* make the lounge windows clear.'

'Do you want to apply this to all windows in Sterenlenn?'

I stared at the panel. 'Yes! Please make all the windows clear.'

There was a series of beeps and then, before my eyes, the glass went from dark, through a series of greys, to frosted and then, finally, to clear. It was a strange effect, like watching a heavy fog dissipate in record time, but I suddenly had my view back.

Raindrops poured down the glass in skittish rivulets and fat, lingering drops, and beyond them Alperwick was a blur of indistinct buildings and lights. The dark sea writhed with foam-topped waves, and the sky was a canvas of threatening greys. A fork of lightning flashed over the scene, and I almost sobbed with relief. I hadn't realized just how claustrophobic I'd felt until I could see out of the house to the world beyond.

'All good?' the voice asked me.

'What the fuck?' I stumbled to the nearest sofa and sat down. There was no way the house should be asking me that, but I couldn't confirm it with Ethan, because he hadn't followed me. I assumed he'd needed some space from me too, but he might come and find me now I'd got the windows to work.

I remembered what I had been about to do before the panel had distracted me. I hurried to the fireplace, knelt in front of it and slid my hand up the chimney. I felt the rough bricks, their shape familiar against the pads of my fingers, and leaned up further, just a bit more, to where I almost couldn't reach and then – there. The ledge. My fingers brushed it, moved along it, unease curdling inside me as I realized there was nothing there. I pulled my hand out and slumped onto the rug in front of the hearth.

'You got the windows to work.' Ethan was standing in the doorway. He still looked dishevelled, his hair was still a mess, but the pink had faded from his lips and cheeks.

'I don't really know how,' I admitted. 'I asked the house to clear them, she said we were in Panic Room Mode, then I added another "please" and she did it. I don't . . . Ethan, your Sparks system has been saying some really weird things.'

'Like what?' He came over and sat in front of me, cross-legged on the rug like I was. His black socks had a row of brightly coloured fish around the tops, as if

190

he couldn't wholly commit to the serious architect persona. 'I assume you asked it if we could get out, too?'

I rubbed my forehead. 'I didn't think . . .'

He leaned back, his hands pressed into the rug behind him. 'Sparks, unlock the house.'

'Sterenlenn is in Panic Room Mode. The emergency services have been called.'

'Sparks, *please* unlock the house.' He raised an eyebrow at me.

'Sterenlenn is in Panic Room Mode, Ethan. The emergency services have been called.'

I stared at him. 'Did she . . . did she sound *bored?* Ethan, is this really an automated system, or have you got someone sitting in some control room somewhere, watching everything we're doing? Promise me, *promise me*, you haven't done this to us.'

He returned my gaze without a flicker. 'I promise you, Georgie, that I am not behind this. I'm as baffled – and annoyed – as you are, and I would love to know what the fuck is going on. But I can assure you that Sparks doesn't do tones, because she's not a real person.'

'We're on to you!' I shouted. 'I hope you're enjoying the show!'

'Georgie!' He laughed.

'Well,' I sighed, 'we're still trapped, but at least we can watch the storm now.'

'It's properly settled in.'

'It's been muggy for days, though.'

'Yeah.'

I looked at him through my eyelashes, at the way he was staring at the fireplace, the intricate plasterwork that his team had rescued and painstakingly restored, so the surround looked as good as new.

'Your project isn't going to be a failure just because Sparks hasn't got all its bugs squashed.'

He rubbed his eyes. 'We've spent *years* squashing Sparks's bugs. The Panic Room stuff, that's my fault because I hadn't linked up the systems, and I didn't anticipate it getting activated at the open house. But my override code failing? Some of the strange things that have been happening?' He shook his head. 'It's a complicated programme, but I thought I understood it.'

'Once she'd cleared the windows, she asked me if I was *all good*.'

Ethan's expression went from frustrated to horrified. 'That's . . . she couldn't have.'

'You know *Terminator*? I would definitely write a story for the *Star* if the house tried to kill us. As long as it didn't succeed, of course. Then we'd just be a cautionary tale about the perils of putting your faith in AI.'

'It has a huge number of incredibly useful, potentially lifesaving applications,' Ethan said.

'I'm not going to put that in my article. Nobody wants a lecture on useful, boring Artificial Intelligence. They want the horror and excitement of dishwashers firing laser guns and toasters with murderous intent.'

Ethan's mouth tugged up. 'Did you really come here for an article?'

'Is there any more champagne?' I pushed myself onto my knees. 'I'm thirsty.'

'George.' He put his hand on my arm, and I sat back down.

'My editor is expecting an article from me, but that's not the only reason I'm here.'

'So . . . what is it? Why did you come?'

I closed my eyes and heard him get up. 'Ethan?'

'Two secs,' he called, and a minute later he returned with another platter of canapés and a bottle of water with a solid stopper. He resumed his position, facing me cross-legged on the rug, and put two tumblers down, pouring us each a glass. 'Right. I've supplied you with water and nutrients, and now I want to know. What are you doing here?'

'OK.' I took a sip of water. 'So, after Mum had gone, I wasn't in a particularly good place.'

Ethan went still. 'Your mum's . . . gone? George, I'm so sorry, I had no idea—'

'She hasn't died.' I reached a placatory hand towards him. 'She's fine, a whole lot better, in fact. But she . . .' I exhaled. 'She's moved to the Lake District with one of her nurses – a guy called Dane.' I winced. 'He has a skull earring, Ethan. And a mullet that looks like it came over from Australia in the Eighties.'

'That's . . . I don't know what to say.' He was rubbing

at the pattern on the rug, his head down, and I could see that he was trying not to laugh.

'It is not funny,' I said, but my lips twitched traitorously. 'I came back from university for her, gave up everything, and then she just . . . she left.'

Ethan met my gaze, his smile gone. 'That's shit. I'm so sorry.'

'Thank you.' I sighed. 'Although, maybe that's not fair. After what happened with us, I never really settled at university, and when I look back now I'm not sure how much of it was really her, or if I was just looking for an excuse, but . . .' I faltered when he squeezed my bare calf. Just once, quickly. I took a deep breath. 'Anyway, not long after she moved away with Dane, I went to cover a story for the *Star*. That side of things hadn't been going very well, and my editor, Wynn, knew my heart wasn't in it. But, although the house was paid off, and Mum's been letting me live in it, I—'

'She's been *letting* you live in it?'

I shrugged. 'She bought it when I was little, before Cornwall was fashionable, and it's just a mid-terrace, so the mortgage is paid and she wants to sell it. It would be a good chunk of money for her and Dane, and I don't know how long I have.'

'She shouldn't be putting pressure on you.'

'This is not the point of my story,' I said, and Ethan nodded at me to continue. 'I still needed money for food, and I did *want* to do well at work, so when Wynn asked me to meet this old woman who had supposedly seen the Alperwick Mermaid – you know I love that legend – well, it felt serendipitous. I thought I could get a funny piece out of it, something I would really enjoy writing.'

'Someone actually contacted the paper to say they'd seen the mermaid?'

I smiled at the memory. 'It will make sense in a minute.'

'Go on, then.' Ethan popped a salmon blini in his mouth.

'I took my camera and notepad and walked to this address, which was one of the bungalows on the high road – you know which ones I mean?'

'With the large front gardens and gable dormers?'

'Gable dormers?'

'A little window protruding from the roof, with sloped sides.' He demonstrated with his arms, doing the universal sign for Pizza Hut.

'Right, one of those. I knocked on the door, and at first I thought nobody was coming, that the email to the paper had been kids playing a prank and they were watching me from somewhere, ready to egg me or something. But then, eventually, the door opened and there was this old woman, and I knew the *moment* I saw her: I knew exactly who she was.'

'Who was it?' He was frowning, looking wary rather than interested, and I realized his thoughts might have been going down a different route: to prom night and police cars, to the end of us.

'It was S. E. Artemis. Spence.'

Ethan leaned forward, his elbows on his knees. 'Your author? The Cornish Sands series?'

'Exactly.' The excitement from that moment filtered into my voice. 'And I did *not* play it cool. I babbled about how much I loved her books as she led me into her living room, to a table where there was a pot of tea and a perfect, bouncy Victoria sponge. She listened to me patiently, and then, when I'd finished rambling, she told me she hadn't seen the Alperwick Mermaid at all, but she wanted a PA.'

'What?' Ethan said with a laugh. 'She could have put an advert online – or in the paper if she's not tech savvy.'

'She said a journalist had the skills she needed. Good at writing, tenacity chasing things down. She didn't want to pay for an advert, so she decided she would phone the paper, get journalists to visit her house under the guise of her having a story, until she found the person she wanted.'

'You're not serious.'

'I am *so* serious. She is shameless, Ethan. She's funny and bright, and I've been working for her for two years.'

'She wanted you to come here?'

I nodded. 'Her mobility isn't great, so I've been her eyes and ears in lots of ways since I started, and this time . . .' Nobody else knew what she'd offered me; I hadn't even told Kira about it – or Mum. 'She wants to write another book in the Cornish Sands series, to give Amelie and Connor their happy ending, after all

196

these years. She said I could help her – that we could write it together.'

My heart was in my throat, because now I'd spent time with Ethan again, I was desperate for him to approve of this plan. It was a chance to be creative, to write something beyond the stories I'd started then discarded on my laptop.

'Ethan?'

He was staring at his knee, as if the blue cotton was the most fascinating thing he'd seen. After a moment, he looked up. 'Why don't you write something of your own?'

My hope dimmed. 'This is Amelie and Connor, Ethan. You know how much I wanted them to be together. I read you some of their letters.'

'I do,' he said cautiously. 'But you're their reader, not their creator. You're good enough to write something original, something that's entirely yours, and Spencer . . .?'

'Spence,' I corrected.

'Spence could help you with that. She was well known, well loved. She must still have contacts in publishing, especially if she's thinking of resurrecting her career. If she really wanted to help you, then she'd support you writing what *you* want to write, not use you for something that will help her reputation and bank balance.'

'She said we'd be equally credited.'

'But will readers notice?' He pursed his lips. 'If it gets published, then will anyone notice the name

Georgie Monroe on the cover, or will they be focused on S. E. Artemis? Are you sure she even intends to finish it, or is it this supposed prize she's enticing you with, so you'll keep working for her, keep giving into her requests?'

I sat back, surprise making me mute for a second. 'But you . . . you were always so supportive of me – of my writing. Even when you couldn't—'

'I was, and I still want to be,' he said. 'You're a great writer. I loved the stories you showed me. And I was hoping that, one day, I'd see news about you publishing your first book. But is this it, Georgie? A rehash of someone else's old characters? Is it what you want?'

'It's a great opportunity.'

'That sounds like a sentence someone else has put in your head.' He downed his water, then poured more into his glass, his movements jerky, some spilling onto the rug. 'You need to do things for *you*, not for someone else.'

'I *am* doing things—'

'It sounds like Spence is taking advantage of your good nature,' he barrelled on. 'And I know it was hard with your mum, that she didn't always give you the freedom to be fully yourself. This seems similar.'

'Ethan.'

'And isn't that why we broke up?' he said, quieter now. 'Because you accused me of prioritizing Sarah over myself? Sacrificing my future for her? You said I needed to be loyal to *myself* first, then other people

– and you were right. So what about you? What about what *you* want?'

'But this is a book!' I sounded frantic, because I didn't want him to be making sense. 'This will be a book with *my* name on the cover. It's guaranteed to get published.'

'Is it?' he asked. 'And you deserve one with *only* your name on the cover. You always have. Don't ever think you're not good enough, that you have to settle for second best.'

I swallowed, willing the lump in my throat to dissolve rather than turn into tears.

'And you're . . .' He shook his head.

'I'm what?'

'I know we've only spent a few hours together, but . . . the low phone battery, the camera – they're just small things, but you used to be so organized. The Georgie I knew would have had two spare camera batteries with her, her phone charged to one hundred per cent before she left the house. You would have had a list of questions or bullet points written down in your notebook, even if the article was a cover for something else. You didn't have as much confidence as you should have, and there was a lot standing in your way, but you were determined. This thing with Spence, it feels like you're giving up. You don't seem sorted, Georgie.'

'You don't know *anything* about me now,' I reminded him. 'And anyway, what about you?' I wanted to meet his attack with one of my own. 'You were so loyal – to me, to Sarah, everyone. Now all I see are these . . . these different women on your social media. A new model for each new mini-break; bland smiles and shitty little captions. What's happened to *you*? Are *you* sorted?'

I held my breath, waiting for his anger, his denial. Instead, he stared at me for a beat, then replied in a low, calm voice. 'You can hate me for what I've said about Spence's book, and what I've noticed about you. And you're right about me. I'm not proud of some of the things I've done, and my love life isn't worthy of a single heartfelt letter.' He gave me a quick smile, a flash of bitterness that was gone in a second. 'You can shout at me if you want to – I probably deserve it. And you can tell me I'm wrong, that I should keep my dickhead opinions to myself, but after that . . .?'

He looked worn out, like he was desperate for me to agree to just one thing.

I nodded.

'I really don't want to fight any more,' he said.

'Me either.' I didn't want to shout at him. I wanted to sort out the jumble of questions his words had turned Spence's offer into. Was he right? Was she using me?

Ethan stood up, and for a moment I thought he was going to go upstairs again, put as much space between us as possible. Instead, he stood in the middle of the room, between the sofas arranged in their companionable layout and the French windows, where the rain was still pelting against the glass, the rumbles of thunder continuous, like giant marbles let loose on a wooden floor. He held out his hand.

'Dance with me,' he said, and I was about to shake

my head when he spoke to the house. 'Sparks, play "Hey, Soul Sister" by Train.'

I laughed and said, 'Really?' but I was already getting to my feet, joining him in the middle of the room, because never mind the house with its impenetrable exits, Ethan had me completely trapped: there was no way I could resist him now.

Chapter Nineteen

May 2012

'Have you written your speech? Please can we come up with a word you have to include in it?' Kira pinched a chip off Freddy's plate then held one out to me as I stared at my untouched salad, nerves turning my insides to concrete.

'I wish I'd never entered the writing competition.' I had wanted to see if I was any good, to see if it was more than just my friends, my mum and my boyfriend telling me I could write.

'Nah, you don't wish that,' Freddy said. 'You won, didn't you? One of four winners, and it's a kick-ass story.'

'A love story about a mermaid,' Orwell chimed in. 'All a bit Disney, if you ask me.'

'That was a Hans Christian Andersen fairy tale first,' Kira said. 'Disney changed the whole thing.'

'Mine is about the Alperwick Mermaid,' I said. 'It's not as if the guy ends up with her like Prince Eric – their shared experience of seeing the mermaid brings the couple together.' I *was* proud of my story, and had been elated when I found out I'd won, coming home to an A5 envelope on the kitchen table that didn't have a plastic window or typed address, suggesting it was something worth opening.

'What's that?' Ethan had put his arms around me, his chin resting on my head.

'I don't have X-ray eyes.' I'd laughed and ripped open the seal, read through the letter then screamed. I'd turned in his arms, and he'd kissed me and spun me round, as thrilled as I was.

'You have to get a word in your speech,' Kira said again. 'Like bandana, or flibbertigibbet, or cornucopia.'

'I'll be lucky if I say anything that isn't a squeak,' I told her, but then my nerves settled because Ethan was walking towards our table with a sandwich and a coffee, and Sarah was with him.

'Hey, guys.' He sat next to me, and Sarah slumped into a chair opposite, her long, dark hair obscuring half her face.

'Hey,' I said, as Ethan kissed me.

'Don't be nervous, you'll be brilliant tonight.'

'Can I be brilliant *and* nervous?'

He pretended to think about it. 'I suppose so. But I'll be in the front row. If you get too nervous, imagine me naked.'

I laughed. 'Like that's going to help.'

'Gross,' Sarah muttered, and I flushed, embarrassed.

'How are you, Sarah?' I asked. 'Getting on OK?'

She shrugged. 'I guess.'

'Are you enjoying it here a little more now?'

She glared at her brother instead of answering.

'Georgie's my girlfriend,' Ethan said calmly, 'I tell her things. Anyway, you *are* doing better, aren't you? She got top marks in her computer science coursework.' I could hear how proud he was, how relieved.

'It wasn't that hard,' Sarah said. 'Everyone else got to go to parties while I was grounded, so I had nothing else to do. It's not a huge surprise that I did better than the people who didn't bother.' She took a sip from a pink plastic water bottle, then spun it in her hands.

I wondered where all these parties were happening, because I wasn't aware of them. But then I had always stuck to our close-knit friend group, instead of gravitating towards the popular students who threw house parties with ill-advised punch and absent parents.

Under the table, Ethan ran his palm up my thigh, rucking up the hem of my dress.

'I'm going to try and get the word cornucopia into my speech tonight,' I told Sarah. 'Kira's challenge.'

'Had we fixed on cornucopia, though?' Kira mused. 'I'm thinking it should be fucksticks, now.'

'I am not going to say fucksticks,' I said, as Sarah burst out laughing. It was the first laugh – the first smile, even – that I'd seen from her.

'Oh my God, that would be ace,' she said. 'You *have* to do it.'

204

'You do not have to do it,' Ethan assured me. 'Just say what you want to.'

'Are you coming tonight?' I was desperate for Sarah to start feeling happier, for her own sake, but also for Ethan's. I also wanted her to like me.

'I might,' she said with a shrug. 'Ethan's going to be there anyway. It's all he's talked about.'

'Really?'

His grin made me forget my nerves. 'I'm not going to bother even trying to play it cool. I can't wait to see you get your award, and I'm going to cheer louder than everyone else put together.'

Alperwick village hall was not a glamorous place, but they'd tried to jazz it up for the awards ceremony, with golden fairy lights strung up along the back of the stage, and a red carpet covering the dusty floorboards in the aisle between rows of plastic chairs.

I stood at the side of the stage, waiting to be called by Grace, the woman in charge of the *Alperwick Papers*, the local magazine that had run the competition. She was introducing the *Papers* as if she was Anna Wintour, and I pulled at the back of my dress, a new one I'd bought last week that was deep purple with blue flowers on it. I should have cut the label off, because it was itchy between my shoulder blades, and my shoes were too tight as well.

I peered around the curtain that acted as the wings, and saw Kira, Freddy and Orwell in the front row. Mum was a few rows behind them, tapping away at her tiny Nokia, and I spotted my English teacher, Mrs Elliot, beaming near the back. I looked for a head of messy, red-brown hair, in case Ethan hadn't realized the others had saved him a seat, but I couldn't find him. My fingers tingled, sweat prickling across my palms, and I glanced at the crumpled paper in my hand.

'And now,' Grace said, 'the winner of the romance category, with her mesmerizing story, "A Tail in the Bay", please give a huge hand to eighteen-year-old Georgie Monroe.' The applause filled the hall, punctuated by whoops and cheers from my friends.

On Bambi-like legs, I walked across the stage to shake Grace's hand.

'Well done, dear,' she said, 'the entire panel loved it.' She handed me the trophy, a little copper quill on a black resin stand, and turned back to the audience. 'As you know, we are compiling an anthology of our winning and shortlisted entries, with all proceeds going to the local lifeboats. You'll be able to read "A Tail in the Bay" along with all the other wonderful stories. Georgie.' She moved away from the microphone, and I stepped up to it.

I was shaking so hard I thought my voice would come out as vibrations, and I took a moment to scan the audience, looking for the one person I knew would ground me. I couldn't find him, or Sarah, and everyone's eyes were on me, eager and expectant.

'Uhm,' I started, 'I was so surprised to win this award. Thank you so – so much Grace, and all the *Alperwick*

Paper people.' Someone tittered, and I swallowed. 'I mean, Grace and the panel of judges. I just – this story was so fun to write, and I . . . just loved it.'

The resin stand was slipping in my palm. I looked at Kira, and she gave me a thumbs up. Mum was gazing out of the window. Ethan was nowhere.

I ran my free hand down my dress, and the label prickled. 'I have wanted to write stories for as long as I can remember,' I said, willing my voice to stop shaking, 'and I fell in love with the Cornish Sands series when I discovered that the writer, S. E. Artemis, used to live in the house on the cliffs.' People's eyes were back on me, the titters had died down, so I kept going. 'Her last book left me disappointed, because I'm a sucker for a happy ending, so my story, "A Tail in the Bay", was my attempt to rectify that for myself, to write a happy-ever-after for my characters, just like I thought Amelie and Connor in the last Cornish Sands book should have had – though mine, Gemma and Ewan,' I cringed at how obvious my name choices were, 'are my creations entirely.'

I glanced at Grace, and she gave me a soft smile. I said a silent apology for what I was about to do. 'I wasn't going to include the mermaid to begin with, and I know some people will frown at the fantastical element but, one, there are a *cornucopia* of books that have ghosts, mermaids and werewolves in them that do really well; two, the mermaid is a big part of Alperwick's history; and three, all love stories need something that brings the two characters together to begin with, and

I don't think it matters if it's bonkers or unlikely, so long as it makes sense to them. So in the end, I just thought fucksticks, and I did it.' Kira's whoop was so loud that everyone turned to look at her.

I could see that Grace was trying to work out if she'd heard me correctly, and I decided to wrap it up. 'Thank you again for this amazing award.' I held my copper quill high. 'It really means so much to me.' I waited a beat to soak up the applause, then I took myself and my itchy dress off the stage.

'That was immense.' Freddy flung an arm around my shoulder. 'Cornucopia *and* fucksticks. You're my hero, Georgie.'

'It was the best,' Kira said, but her response was subdued.

'Nice trophy.' Orwell touched the spike of the quill. 'Shame your oh-so-dedicated boyfriend didn't bother to turn up.'

'Shut up, Orwell.' Kira gave me an apologetic look. 'He texted me, because he wasn't sure if you'd get to look at your phone.' She held her screen towards me.

Something's come up with Sarah and I can't make it. Please tell Georgie I'm so, so sorry.

'Right.' I hadn't checked my phone yet, but I knew I'd have something similarly apologetic.

'His sister's a nightmare,' Orwell said.

'She's unhappy,' I replied, even though I was crushed

208

that whatever Sarah had done this time had kept Ethan away tonight. 'He's doing the right thing looking out for her.'

'You really believe that?' Orwell smirked at me.

'Shut *up*, Orwell,' Kira said again, and before I could come up with an answer, I felt a hand on my shoulder and spun round to find Mum. I smiled, waiting for her hug, her congratulations.

'I have to go and see a man about a cat,' she said. 'I'll see you at home, OK? You were fab.' She squeezed my shoulder and walked away.

'Are you guys getting a cat?' Freddy asked.

'Pretty sure we're not.' I knew she was still buying weed, because sometimes when I got home from school I could smell it underneath her incense, a scent that no amount of patchouli could disguise. But what could I say? She'd been told what effect it would have on the trial, and it was her choice. Confronting her would only result in an argument, so I'd buried my head in the sand and hoped she would stop by herself.

'Hey, do you want to go to the beach?' I said.

Kira looked apologetic. 'I have to get back tonight.'

'Yeah, my brother's home for a few days, so I should bounce,' Freddy added.

'I'll come,' Orwell said. But heading to the beach as the sun set, just me and Orwell, would be the rotten cherry on top of the stale cake as far as I was concerned.

'Actually, I'm pretty tired. We should do it soon, though – all of us.'

'For sure.' Kira enveloped me in a hug and whispered, 'You were gorgeous and brilliant up there, and I'm so proud of you.'

I thanked her and said goodbye to my friends, then stayed to have a chat with Mrs Elliot, who said all the things I had hoped Mum would say. Then I stepped outside, into the cool evening air, the sun a low, glowing ball, amber and peach flames settling over the water. I strode the five minutes to the beach, took off my uncomfortable shoes and walked across the sand until I reached the smooth, flat rock that locals called the Alperwick Seat. Nobody was on it right now, the beach close to being deserted, so I sat down, and felt calm for the first time that evening.

I was gutted Ethan hadn't turned up, and that Mum had been so uninterested, but I had my copper quill. It was proof that something I'd written had been noticed, and I had my writing – my characters and my worlds – and nobody could take those from me. Today was a milestone, but it also felt like possibility – that one day my writing, my escape, might lead to more.

'George.'

I jumped. I'd been daydreaming, unaware of anyone approaching, but I knew instantly who it was. I didn't turn around, but waited for Ethan to sit beside me. His warmth was irresistible, even though I was still angry. I looked at him, and saw his tired, sad expression in the final rays of the sun. I inhaled, and got a strong whiff of vodka.

'Are you drunk?' I couldn't hide my shock.

'Not me.' He ran a hand through his hair. 'Sarah just . . . I don't know, she's been drinking since lunchtime, maybe – secretly, at school. I was on my way out, and I found her at the top of the stairs. She almost fell down them, she was so drunk. I got her into her room and she threw the bottle at me.'

'Oh shit,' I whispered. 'What happened?'

'I made her drink water, eat some toast, then waited for Mum to get home.'

'You told her?'

'Yeah.' He frowned. 'I wasn't about to handle that one by myself. What if she'd passed out and been sick? Mum's looking after her, but I was already too late to get to the awards ceremony. I'm so sorry, Georgie. I wish I'd seen you.'

I flung my arms around his neck. 'I'm so glad you told your mum. You shouldn't have to deal with it by yourself.'

He pressed his hands against my back, flattening the label inside my dress. 'I don't know why we can't get her to see sense.' He puffed out a breath. 'Tell me about your speech. What did you say?'

'I got "cornucopia" and "fucksticks" into it.'

He pulled back. 'You did not.'

'I did.' He smiled, the sadness banished from his eyes for a moment. 'I wish you'd seen it.'

'You could recreate it for me?'

I shook my head. 'No.' His face fell, and I added, 'I will if you want, what I can remember, but not right now.'

211

'What do you want to do, then?'

I looked at the final, burnished streak of red on the horizon, the cliffs rising above us on either side of the bay, the silhouette of S. E. Artemis's abandoned house and the stars starting to twinkle overhead.

'Dance with me.' I pulled my iPod touch out of my bag, my eighteenth birthday present from Mum, and handed him one earphone. I put the other in my ear and scrolled through to the song I loved right then, that I'd been playing on repeat for weeks.

There were those first, perfect guitar strums, then the opening line of 'Hey, Soul Sister' by Train filled my right ear, and Ethan grinned.

He put his arms around my waist, and I snaked mine around his neck, careful to avoid the earphone wire. We swayed on the sand, Ethan taller than he usually was because he still had his shoes on and I didn't. I pressed my cheek to his chest, relishing his warmth and the cold sand slipping between my toes. We sang along, moving in time together as the final slice of sun dipped and winked out, letting the night sky take centre stage.

The song ended, and Ethan bent his head to mine and kissed me.

'Thank you for coming to find me,' I said.

'Don't thank me. You deserved more from me tonight.'

'I've got you now. You and my blanket of stars.'

His smile was sad, and I was relieved when he turned away. We looked up as an impossible number of stars shone above us, almost as if they were turning on one by one just for us, a natural glitter ball for our sandy dance floor, right there in the middle of Alperwick Bay.

Chapter Twenty

Now

'This sound-system is crazy good,' I said, as 'Hey, Soul Sister' came to an end. It was an upbeat song, but somehow, halfway through, we'd stopped with our swaying, disjointed dad dancing and gravitated towards each other, until Ethan's hand was loosely against my hip, and mine was around his waist. We'd kept our touches featherlight, as if we knew that any more pressure would turn up the heat between us, would send things back to how they'd been in the bathroom. But for me, it didn't really feel any different.

Touching Ethan took me back to being eighteen, to being completely, head-over-heels in love with him, how I'd fizzled and ached for him even when he was only holding my hand, and I'd felt like I was in physical withdrawal once it was over, university not enough of a distraction. That imprint was still there, the echo of the unrivalled satisfaction of our bodies connecting, but I was pretending to be nonchalant while we listened to a song that increased the nostalgia fix tenfold.

'We employed sound technicians,' he said. 'There are speakers in the walls, spaced throughout the house to give the best coverage.'

'It's like an auditorium, just with cosier seating,' I said, and he laughed. 'I'm sorry I didn't tell you about Spence earlier.'

'Why should you have? You don't owe me anything. I wasn't even sure I'd see you today.'

'You've managed a bit more than *seeing* me.'

He stiffened. 'That kiss, I didn't—'

'I meant being trapped with me.' Talking about the kiss felt too dangerous, and I peeled away from him. 'What's next?'

'What do you mean?' Ethan flexed his fingers at his sides, as if touching me had left them aching.

'I mean, the house still isn't prepared to release us, and we've just had the best song of the Noughties—'

'Of all time,' he corrected.

I grinned. 'Right, so what's next?' I tapped my fingers against my lips, snagged hold of another memory of dancing around my bedroom while Ethan sat on my bed, his head in his hands. 'Sparks, play "You Belong with Me" by Taylor Swift.'

'Fuck no,' was Ethan's emphatic response, but it was too late, and the first chords filled the room, drowning out the thunder and rain.

I remembered all the words and, that memory replaying in my head, I let go, dancing around the huge, opulent lounge, around the fireplace in the centre, dodging sofas and chrome tables and all the delicate touches that made the room so special.

Ethan folded his arms tightly across his chest, and I ran out of patience. I danced over to him and slid my hands along his tightly strung forearms. 'Do you realize how distracting this is?'

He frowned down at me. 'What?'

'This whole arms-crossed, aren't-my-muscles-impressive move?'

His lips tugged up. 'I can't even show my dissatisfaction at you playing Taylor Swift through my state-of-the-art sound system?'

'Be dissatisfied,' I said, 'just don't be so fucking sexy while you do it, OK?'

'Fine,' he shot back, but his smile widened. 'How's this?' He put his hands on his hips and furrowed his brow.

'Uh uh.' I danced away from him, exaggerating my movements, making my dancing extra stupid. 'Still too sexy.'

He clasped his hands under his chin coquettishly and fluttered his eyelashes. 'This?'

I laughed, my stomach flipping over. 'Better. Except I don't think you realize how funny you are.' I wove behind the sofa, in front of the fireplace. 'How hot you are when you stop being so serious.'

He changed pose, doing a classic Popeye, his arms

up and biceps flexed, his expression a stern pout. 'You think it's hot when I stop being serious?'

I guffawed and did a little twirl in front of the French windows. 'I love not-serious Ethan. I love seeing you stop giving a shit, even if it's only for five minutes.'

'And I love your ridiculous dancing.' He abandoned the pose and ran a hand through his hair. 'I love everything about you, Georgie.' The way he said it was tentative and incredulous, as if it was something he'd only just realized, but it didn't lessen my surprise and I faltered. I tripped over the edge of a rug and, as I put my hands out, thinking how lucky it was that the room was so full of large, soft things, I didn't see the corner of the chrome-edged table and my shoulder glanced off it, a sharp pain slicing along my collarbone as I hit the carpet with an 'Ooof.'

'Georgie!' Ethan sounded panicked.

I pressed my palms into the carpet and tried to push myself up to kneeling, but my shoulder protested and I dropped down again.

'Shit.' Ethan put his hand on my back. 'Are you OK?'

'I don't know,' I said into the carpet.

'Can you sit up?'

'Of course I can.' But I didn't complain when his hand slid under my waist, and he gently raised me to sitting, then tugged me towards the window. I didn't understand what was happening, my shoulder throbbing, but then I felt his firm chest behind me, and I realized he was sitting up against the French windows, his legs wide, and he'd pulled me between them so I was resting against him.

The glass was thick enough that I didn't feel a chill, but the thrum of the rain was loud, and Taylor Swift had finished singing. Mostly, I could hear Ethan breathing and feel the rise and fall of his chest against my back.

'I'm OK,' I said.

Ethan brushed his fingers along my collarbone, pushing back the neckline of my dress, and I winced. 'You haven't broken the skin,' he said softly, 'but it's going to bruise. Did you lose consciousness?'

'I didn't hit my head, just my shoulder.'

'Are you *sure* though? You seemed disoriented.'

'Because I whacked into a chrome table. It hurt.'

Ethan made a frustrated noise in his throat and ran his hands down my arms. 'Sparks,' he said, 'please unlock the fucking door. Open a window. Let us out of this house *now*.'

'Ethan, I'm fine. I honestly feel fine.'

'You are not fine, and I've had enough of this.' He shifted and held his phone out in front of him. His screen was blank, with no notifications, his screen-saver a photograph of Alperwick Bay coated in evening sunshine, the colours intense as the sun slid towards the sea. I wondered when he'd taken it. 'Fuck.' He pressed buttons, hit 999 and the green 'call' button, but nothing happened. 'I'm so sorry, George,' he murmured into my hair. 'I'm going to get us out of here.'

'I promise you I'm OK. I hit my shoulder, and it throbs a bit but that's all. I would have noticed if I'd hit my head, and anyway, I know all the symptoms of concussion, because I reported on a life-saving course at the lifeboats about six months ago, and they made me take part. I don't have any of them.'

'What are they? Tell me.'

'I hit my shoulder, Ethan.'

'Tell me what they are, and I'll stop worrying.'

'OK, so—'

'Hang on.'

'What now?'

'Sit forward a moment, if that's all right?'

'Of course.' I moved forwards on the carpet, and Ethan pushed himself up. There was a bright flash of lightning, a crackle of angry thunder that made me jump. Ethan strode across the room, and I heard him opening cupboards in the kitchen. Then he was back, carrying a bundled-up tea towel. He held his hand out to me.

'We're not staying on the floor?' I asked, but I took his hand.

He pulled me up gently, then led me over to the huge sofa that faced the front of the house, the manicured lawn and the wide stone pathway that led to the green gates, now firmly closed. He sat down, his legs wide, and patted the cushion between them.

I scooted over to him, mirroring the pose we'd been in on the carpet so I had my back to him, and he put his arm around my waist and pulled me against him.

The sofa was big enough that only our feet were hanging over the edge of the cushion, mine bare and him with his fish socks.

Ethan pressed the tea towel gently against my shoulder, and I flinched, then sighed as the ice stemmed the throbbing.

'One good thing about having champagne buckets for the open house,' he said. 'Now, what are the symptoms of concussion? I want them all.'

'You really want me to go through them?' On the cosy sofa, with Ethan behind me, I felt safe and slightly sleepy, but I knew he wouldn't put up with me drifting off.

'You have to, because if you hit your head without realizing and have got concussion, then I need to start breaking some windows.'

'I thought you said they couldn't be broken.'

I expected him to make a joke about his hidden strength, but he didn't say anything. I twisted round to look at him. His jaw was clenched, his brown eyes stormy.

'This is a disaster,' he said. 'I should never have been allowed to go ahead with any of it. You're hurt, and it could be bad, and—'

'It's not, though.'

'But what if it *was*, and there was no way I could get you out? This is so much worse than anyone being able to get in. A fatal flaw in the Sparks system.' He shook his head. 'I'll have to call Sarah, tell her the sale is off, that I've fucked it up so completely that this place is dangerous, but—'

'But you can't do any of that now,' I finished. 'So. Here are the symptoms of concussion.'

'OK.' His fingers drummed a light beat on my stomach, and I had to work very hard to remember what I was supposed to be telling him. I wasn't sure he knew he was doing it.

'One,' I said. 'Some kind of headache or pressure in the head.'

'Have you got that?' He moved the ice bundle, pressing it against a different spot.

'I didn't hit my head, Ethan. Two, being or feeling sick.'

'Either of those? I mean, you haven't been sick, but—'

'No nausea,' I said. 'Three, feeling dizzy or having balance problems.'

'What about that?' he murmured against my ear.

'I felt disoriented when I hit the table, but I'm fine now. Unless you count being close to you. What after-shave are you wearing?'

'Perspiration and regret. What about four?'

'Four, being bothered by light or noise.'

'And?'

'You were the one bothered by Taylor Swift. Five, mood swings, feeling unexpected emotions or confusion, memory problems.'

'Any of that?'

I laughed. 'Confusion and unexpected emotions? Since I walked up the hill this afternoon. They haven't got worse since I fell over.'

'And memory problems?' Ethan trailed his fingertips along my collarbone, his skin cold from holding the ice, and I licked my lips. There was a lot happening in my body and mind that I was struggling to make sense of, but none of it was to do with whacking into the table.

'My memory is surprisingly strong right now,' I told him.

'Yeah.' I heard him swallow. 'For me, too.'

He stopped talking and the silence hung between us, but I no longer felt on the verge of a nap, because I was a bundle of charged nerves, waiting for what came next.

'You know,' he murmured, 'it's a good thing that I was here, that I could get the ice for you.'

'Why's that?' I asked, but my throat tightened because I knew what was coming.

'Because something tells me you wouldn't do a very good job by yourself.'

I was transported back to the girls' bathroom in sixth form, Ethan pressing damp tissue paper into my grazed knee, a gaggle of students walking in on us. 'Maybe I wasn't that bothered because I didn't need to be,' I said.

'Right. Because smashing your shoulder open on a glass table is nothing.'

'Ethan,' I said with a laugh, 'one, I didn't smash it *open*: it's bruised, not cut. Two, it was a bump, not a smash, and that's a whole different thing.'

'What's three?' he asked, and I realized I was doing

my lists out loud again. Mum was always telling me I didn't need to number my points before I said them, and I thought I'd got out of the habit, but . . . I froze, caught in a set of imaginary headlights.

'What do you mean, *what's three?*' I whispered.

'You know. Numbering all the reasons my assessment of your accident is inaccurate. What number will you get up to?'

'Why would I get up to any particular number?'

'Georgie.' It was Ethan's turn to laugh. 'I don't know what you're talking about.'

I turned around, so I was kneeling on the sofa cushion between his legs, looking down at him. 'You know I put things into lists like that?'

'Of course.' He frowned. 'You've done it ever since I've known you. *One*, we can't go to the beach because it's been raining all day and the sand will be sludge, *Two*, we can't go to mine because Mum is home, *Three*, we can't go to yours because your whole family will be there and they'll probably be arguing, *Four*, the abandoned house is full of dust and rats. It's a Georgie thing, isn't it?'

'I suppose.' My voice was a scratch because I was all too aware of where else I'd used those numbered lists. I sank onto my haunches and trailed my finger up the front of Ethan's shirt. 'You know when you were redoing the fireplace in here?' I said it in as casual a voice as I could manage.

'Yeah?' But suddenly he couldn't look at me, his gaze set firmly on the storm beyond the window, and

223

I knew what he'd found, and I knew that he'd read them.

'Fuuuuuuuuck.' I slumped forward, my head landing in the crook between his shoulder and his neck. His arms came around me immediately.

'I wish you'd actually sent them,' he said, sounding choked.

At that moment, everything I thought I knew about where we both stood in our tentative, topsy-turvy reunion in this sumptuous prison dissolved into dust.

Dear Connor,

Why am I still calling you Connor? There's no chance you're going to find my letters now. You're not here to go snooping while I'm in the bathroom and find them under a cuddly turtle. It's how I started writing to you, and it's an important part of the ritual now, as if, by referring to us as Connor and Amelie, we'll have the same sort of epic romance they had. But it didn't work out for them, either.

If I was writing books, they would always have happy endings, however bitter I felt about my own life. You owe it to the readers, don't you, if you're a romance author? S. E. Artemis should have thought about that when she was finishing The Whispers of the Sands.

I've followed you on Instagram, but you won't recognize me from my username or photos – I'm not much more human on there than a bot. You would laugh, roll your eyes at how long it took me, my finger hovering over the 'follow' button like I was about to launch a nuclear attack instead of connect with my ex. There are lots of photos of you with beautiful women, and short, bland captions. You are the classically filtered version of yourself, but your hair is still my favourite disaster zone of all time.

But where are the life updates? I don't know if you're qualified and following your dreams of being an architect. I almost tracked down Orwell, deciding

225

that a few minutes in his company would be worth it to get some intel, but he's left Alperwick. Kira doesn't know where he's gone, but she's going to ask Freddy.

I'm still freelance, but the North Cornwall Star *are putting me on retainer, so I'll have a steady income at least. I've started writing short stories again, and I've even finished a couple. They're not good enough to share with anyone, though I would have let you read them, because I always loved you reading my stuff.*

Mum's not doing so well, and it's hard, sometimes, trying to keep her spirits up. I'm trying to get her outside as much as possible, to go for walks on the beach or to the local café. Things would be so much easier if I had you to talk to, but is that just an excuse? Maybe I need to finally let you go.

I hope you're well, Ethan, that you're thriving and happy.

I love you and I miss you
Yours always, Georgie xx

Chapter Twenty-One

June 2012

'Which part have you got to?' I rested my head on Ethan's shoulder and he lifted the notebook up high so I couldn't see where he was. 'Have you reached the bit where—'

'Shush.' He angled his head away from me so he could keep reading.

I had the urge to tickle him, but I also wanted to know what he thought of my new story. It was about two people who had met in an abandoned house, clashing because one group was drinking there, the other searching for ghosts. I suffered through two more silent minutes, then he laughed – one of those laughs that was a surprise, like I'd delighted him with one of my jokes. After that I left him to it, rearranging things pointlessly on my already immaculate desk, until he closed the notebook.

'It's really good, George,' he said. 'It's funny and romantic and spooky all at once. I know exactly who Alfie and Selina are, and I cared about them. Also, the haunting?' He laughed again. 'Those ghost hunters were looking for something profound, some hidden secret or tragedy connected to the family who'd lived there centuries ago, and all they found was the last owner's awful chihuahua.'

'Marjory the chihuahua had a lot of character.' I couldn't hide my smile. 'She didn't want to be dead.'

'Biting ankles for all eternity,' Ethan said wistfully. I joined him on the bed, and he tucked my hair behind my ear and planted a sweet kiss on my lips. 'You, Georgie Monroe, are amazing. I can't wait to celebrate your first book being published.'

My heart skipped at the implication that we would still be together when that happened. 'In a house that you've built,' I added. 'We can toast each other with champagne, look out at the sea view from the glass-fronted reception room.'

'We're going to be one of those smug couples that are really pleased with themselves, aren't we?' He kissed me again.

'It sounds perfect,' I murmured. We sat up against my pillows, and Ethan put his arm around me. 'Hey,' I said, after a moment, 'imagine if you renovated S. E. Artemis's old house.'

'What?' He turned to me with a laugh. 'How would

I ever get the chance to do that? It'll be years before I'm qualified, and whoever owns it now is bound to do something with it, either bring it up to scratch or sell it on.'

'But just *imagine*.' I wasn't ready to let go of the daydream. 'Imagine if you could buy it – or get commissioned to redo it, or whatever. What would you do?' I dragged my notebook over, turned to a fresh page, and held it out to him, along with my pen.

'George,' he said in mild protest, but he took them.

'What, Ethan?' I wanted to spend time on his dream, when he'd been so supportive of mine.

'Well, the main thing would be making the most of where it is, give all the rooms uninterrupted views of the landscape. So, larger windows, skylights maybe – a huge lounge that looks out over the bay. The room we usually sit in?'

I nodded.

'I would knock that through, so it took up the whole right side of the house.'

I went to protest, but he put a finger on my lips. 'I'd keep the fireplace,' he assured me. 'It would be the focal point of the room, open all the way around, so you could divide the space into zones.' He frowned down at the notebook. 'It would be a huge job, but I don't have any real clue *how* big yet. I've got so much to learn, but right now—'

'This is the dreaming stage,' I said. 'Don't worry about technicalities. I'm thinking a beautiful office upstairs, just in case a writer lived there, you know?'

He looked up. 'You deserve the best, Georgie.'

I brushed him off. 'It's got so much history. Do you think some of S. E. Artemis's talent has been absorbed into the walls?'

'Better that than the ghost of a bad-tempered chihuahua,' he said, and as he sketched some ideas, he was chuckling again. I thought how perfect this was, how bright our futures looked. I wouldn't listen to Mum's warnings about Ethan disappearing, even though he still dropped everything whenever there was a hint of a problem with Sarah, or her reminders that we were teenagers, that everything seemed intense right now, but we had our whole lives ahead of us. I knew she was implying that we wouldn't stay together, but I couldn't imagine wanting anyone but Ethan. We were in it for the long haul; I knew that without a shadow of a doubt.

'Banging around the kitchen is not going to make things better,' Mum said as I slammed a saucepan onto the stove, then got a tin of baked beans out of the cupboard and flung the door shut.

'It makes me *feel* better,' I said with a glare.

She was watching me from the table, where she was sorting through the bills. I had told her I would cook us something nice for dinner, then ran out of enthusiasm when Ethan messaged to tell me he couldn't join us because Sarah had had a shit time at school, and he didn't want to leave her in case she did something stupid. A few days ago we'd been sitting on my bed making plans about our future, and now this. So Mum and I were getting cheesy beans on toast, and I was fuming.

'Have you talked to him about it?' Mum asked.

'I've tried, but I sound like a bitch whenever I say I'm cross with him because he's prioritizing his sad, fucked-up sister over me.'

'Georgie,' Mum admonished, but without much heat.

'And I love how loyal he is, how he takes care of people, and he *always* makes it up to me. He takes me for chips, he reads my writing and shows a proper interest. He's so apologetic, and when we're in—' I sucked in a breath, my rant about to go too far.

'I know you're sleeping together,' Mum said. 'You think I don't know what goes on under my own roof?'

I slumped against the cooker. 'You don't mind?'

'As long as you're safe, you're fully consenting – and I mean *fully*, to everything, every time – and you're being kind to each other, then I don't mind. Better with Ethan than someone you don't care about.' She fixed me with a cool stare. 'But if he's making you unhappy, it's time to rethink.'

'Ethan makes me happy.' The thought of not being with him sent an uncomfortable shiver through me. 'And no couple is perfect.'

'You're only eighteen. Don't try to sound all sage and experienced. You need to go through a few heart-breaks before you find someone who's for keeps.'

'What if I want Ethan for keeps?' Kira and Freddy

had been together for two years and they were stronger than ever, and Grace from the *Alperwick Papers* was always going on about how she'd been married to her childhood sweetheart for thirty years. I had no interest in anyone else.

'Let's give up on the beans,' Mum said. 'How about we do homemade fish and chips? Helen gave me a new batter recipe, and the market had cod on offer today.' My stomach twisted at the thought of Mum going to the market, but the doctor leading the clinical trial was quietly optimistic, and I hadn't come home to a haze of incense covering the smell of weed for a while.

'OK. You show me how to make this new batter, and I'll peel the potatoes.'

'You're on.' Mum bounced up from the table, kissing my forehead before she dug in the cupboard for the mixing bowl. I loved spending time with her when she was like this, upbeat and in charge.

As I peeled potatoes, my mind inevitably returned to Ethan, and the niggles that sat just beneath my skin. He had seemed flustered going into the last couple of exams, which was so unlike him. His dream of becoming an architect had never wavered, but it needed hard work and dedication, and I selfishly worried what would get squeezed out if he realized he wasn't doing as much as he needed to.

'You don't keep a diary, do you?' Mum asked, as she dipped the cod into her batter mix. 'You write stories, but do you ever write your feelings down?'

'Not really. But stories are like . . . they're a way of getting feelings out, aren't they?'

'It's not the same. I've kept a journal on and off, and it helps when I need to get things off my chest and don't want to break the cupboard door off its hinges.'

'Sorry.' My guilt was instant.

'Don't be, Georgie,' Mum said with a smile. 'I remember what it was like, being in love for the first time. Your emotions are like an unruly herd of velociraptors, dangerous and impossible to bring to heel.'

I laughed. 'That's the most ridiculous analogy I've ever heard.'

'Cheered you up, though. Just think about it. I'll buy you a nice new notebook. We could go to that bistro in Truro, make a day of it and have lunch, if you fancy?'

'I'd love that, Mum. Thank you.' I hugged her, feeling lighter than I had done in a while. She smelled of her perfume, no tobacco or weed lingering underneath, and the tension left my shoulders as she returned my embrace.

'Let's get these in,' she said. 'We want to be done before Kira steals you away. The big house tonight, is it?' She winked, and I laughed again because I couldn't keep secrets from her. I wondered how I'd ever thought she was uninterested: she was just trying to be the best mum she could be.

'Just the four of us again tonight, then.' Orwell added a dusty bottle to our assortment of refreshments. It looked like cherry brandy.

'Ethan can't make it.' I shrugged, when really I wanted to wipe the smirk off his face.

'Man, his sister is a fiend.' Freddy lay his head in Kira's lap, and she took his beanie off and stroked his hair. I stared at my hands, taking the bottle of vodka when Kira passed it to me.

'She's causing lots of trouble,' I agreed. 'I just hope she doesn't get in the way of his exam focus. He's so committed to getting the grades he needs to study architecture.'

Kira waved a dismissive hand. 'He'll walk them. I'm more worried about you losing precious time with him. In a couple of months, we'll all be off to different unis.'

'We could do long distance,' I said, then amended it, because my talk with Mum had cemented how I felt about him. 'We *will* do long distance, and it'll be fine.'

'Even if you're still here, and he's off enjoying the perks of university?' Orwell asked.

'I'm not going to be here.' I chugged more vodka. 'Mum's doing better, and my grades are OK. I'm going to major in journalism and join whatever creative writing groups there are. And if we both get our first choices, Sheffield and York, we won't be that far away.' I loved the idea of being somewhere Ethan had lived for a little while. I was already looking forward to him giving me a tour of the city, showing me all his favourite parts, when he came to visit during our first term.

'You've got it all figured out,' Kira said. 'And Ethan will be all in, too. That boy adores you, straight up.'

She picked up the cherry brandy and I clinked my bottle against hers, my warm glow partly to do with the alcohol, and partly to do with Kira's faith in what we had.

I got back to my room late, and tipsier than usual, so I sent Ethan a message:

Missed you tonight. Bit drunk. I love you. G. xx

I put my phone on charge, but my head was too full to sleep, so I took a reporter's notebook off my desk. It had a plain purple cover, and was ring-bound along the top edge, but I wasn't writing a story, or a journal entry.

I had decided the best way to get my feelings out about Ethan was to write him a letter, even if I never gave it to him. I could say everything I wanted to, safe in the knowledge that nobody would see it, that he wouldn't understand how insecure I sometimes felt about us.

I lay on my back and chewed my pen. There were so many letters in the Cornish Sands series, and I loved how they made the plots tick forward, how each one was an insight into a particular character. Then I thought of the times Ethan had been in my room, under my duvet while I nipped to the toilet or had a shower; when I'd briefly let myself fall asleep in his arms. He might spy a notebook and – though he wasn't a snooper – think it was full of stories, and I'd always

235

let him read those. I imagined him opening one and seeing page after page of letters addressed to him.

I needed some kind of code, but I was only starting to learn shorthand and my feelings felt too big for that. Then I remembered the letters between my favourite couple, Amelie and Connor, how I'd savoured each one, sure of a happy ending for them that never came. Well, with me and Ethan it would be different.

I knew exactly what to do.

I rolled onto my stomach and opened my notebook to the first clean page.

Dear Connor, I wrote, then proceeded to tell Ethan everything I was thinking, everything I was worried about. My drunk brain spilled it all onto the page, and I realized, even as I scribbled those first, unsure sentences, that I could write secret letters to the man I loved, under the guise of us being my two favourite fictional characters, and nobody would ever know, least of all him.

Chapter Twenty-Two

Now

'I started doing it before we broke up.' I was still kneeling on the sofa cushion, and Ethan was trailing his hand up and down the outside of my leg, as if he was mapping the shape of me. 'Mum suggested I write a journal, so I could get my thoughts out when I was frustrated about you missing things, looking out for Sarah.' I winced. I'd always felt guilty for being annoyed with him, because I understood why he was doing it – until things went too far.

'I hated it, too,' he said quietly. 'But you know that, at the time, I didn't think I had a choice. But the letters . . .'

'I was worried you'd find them, realise how upset I was getting, so I had to come up with some way to disguise them. I thought of Amelie and Connor's letters, how I'd read some of them out to you, and thought, if you saw a letter with those names, you'd just think it was part of my Cornish Sands obsession and close the notebook. Then, later, once we broke up, the names Amelie and Connor made even more sense – I was still here, in Alperwick, and you were gone. It felt poetic, somehow, to keep calling us that.' I shrugged. 'When did you find them? During the build, I'm guessing.'

'It was one of the workmen,' he said. 'The foreman, AP, brought them to me, as he did with everything unusual we found on site. If you discover anything old, you have to stop work and establish whether it's historically important. Something like that can have a huge impact on the timeline.'

'But a bundle of love letters tied up with ribbon don't count?'

'Not when they're written in biro,' he said with a smile. 'Sarah, she—'

'Sarah didn't read them, did she?' The thought made me feel sick.

Ethan adjusted the ice pack so it was against my shoulder and neck. 'No, she didn't read them. She didn't get a chance because AP brought them straight to me, and when I saw the name at the top, Connor, and your handwriting—'

'You remember my handwriting?'

He levelled me with a look. 'How many stories did you get me to read?'

'Fair enough,' I said with a smile. 'I didn't ever plan for you to read these, though.'

I was trying to remember everything I'd said, the ones I'd written after I'd come home from university for good. I had convinced myself Mum couldn't cope without me, and the Sparks family had moved away before that first Christmas. My anger had been short-lived, replaced by desolation that all my daydreams over the last few months – bumping into him in the village, us patching things up, resurrecting our plans of a happy future together – weren't ever going to happen.

'You mean you didn't have faith that I would get my qualification and make it back here to renovate this house?' Ethan raised an eyebrow.

I laughed. 'You have to admit, a whole lot of stars had to align to make this possible. It was such a pipe dream when we were eighteen: the house could have been demolished or bought by someone else; you could have picked other projects to work on, or decided on a change of career any time over the past thirteen years. The fact that the house was still waiting, when you were ready for it, is a miracle.'

'This was always the one I wanted, though,' Ethan said. 'And when AP handed me the letters – they felt like a gift.'

'Did you ever think about coming to see me? Once you'd read them?'

'All the time. Whenever I came to the site, I made a plan to walk into the village, go to the Sailor's Rest for lunch, get a beer and work up the courage to knock on your door. I made it to the pub once, but I heard the landlord say your name, and it spooked me.'

'Rick,' I said. 'I went out with him for a few years.'

'Right.' Ethan swallowed. 'Anyway. I have nobody to blame but myself – my ego and my fear. I didn't know how long ago you'd written them, but when I read the letters, it gave me hope that you weren't still angry with me. But I wanted to wait until this place was finished, until I had something impressive to show you.' He ran a hand through his hair. 'Not that I thought . . . I did wonder if you'd come to the open house, but if you hadn't, I would have walked to yours tonight or tomorrow and knocked on the door.'

'You say that *now*.' I smiled.

He didn't return it. 'I would have. Even though I was still scared of being turned away – or discovering that, in the years since the letters, you'd got married, had a family. I'm not saying that I expected anything, but we were such a big part of each other's lives, and I've never . . .'

'Never what?'

He shook his head. 'Never mind.'

'Ethan, come on. You've read my letters now.'

'Why did you bring them here?' He put the tea towel ice-pack down and looped his arms around my waist.

'I don't know,' I admitted. 'I was a mess when I left university. I came back here and Mum was horrified I'd given up on it. Then my life turned into this treadmill of looking after her, occasionally getting out to cover stories for the *Star*, and I still missed you, so much. You'd obviously changed your number, Kira and

Freddy couldn't get hold of you, and Orwell didn't have your details either. So I just . . . it was how I'd done it while we were together: it was like a journal, but you were the only one I wanted to talk to.

'So I kept writing, kept us as Connor and Amelie, but I also wanted the letters to be special. I bought notepaper and wrote them out properly.' I chewed my lip, thinking back to the last letter I'd written, how vulnerable it had felt, even though it would never – I thought – reach him. 'I didn't want to get rid of them, but I was trying so hard to move on. This place felt right: we had spent time here when we were together, talked about it so often, and you loved the fireplace. I thought that the letters would be destroyed when the house was.'

'Are you mad that I found them?'

It seemed impossible that the dominoes had fallen this way, but also, somehow, inevitable. 'No. But I'm just . . . some of the things I said.'

'I wanted to hear it all.' Ethan brushed hair off my forehead. 'Once I realized you had written them, and I'd read the first one and understood that Amelie and Connor were you and me. I wish I could tell you that I wasn't going to read them, that I considered how much I would be invading your privacy, but I was desperate to see what you'd said. I sat in my car, in the Alperwick Bay car park, and went through them all. It was hot, my car was like a greenhouse, but I couldn't get enough of your words. It felt like having a direct line back to you, like all those times we'd

241

walked on the beach or talked in your bed, and I . . .' He stopped, his Adam's apple bobbing.

'What?' I traced a line along his cheekbone, the freckles I'd once turned into a dot-to-dot.

'I have something to show you.' He looked nervous. 'I don't think you saw it earlier.'

'Saw what?' I clambered off the sofa so he could stand up.

He held his hand out. 'I'm sure you would have mentioned it if you had.'

I put my hand in his. I no longer wanted to keep my distance. This house, the two of us trapped here, was a limbo, set apart from reality, and – like Ethan finding the letters – it felt like the universe was giving me this one night with him, a bubble where we could pretend the last thirteen years had gone differently.

He wrapped his fingers around mine and led me through the kitchen, into the foyer. The space was tinted a strange, yellowish-grey by the storm, and rain drummed against the windows as we climbed the stairs, Ethan holding onto me tightly. I paused halfway up, staring out at the raging sea, the churn of the waves, seagulls wheeling chaotically in the sky.

'What are you thinking?' Ethan asked me.

'I'm thinking that there are worse places we could be.'

He squeezed my hand but didn't say anything else. He led me up to the landing, then walked past the bathroom and turned left, where a narrow corridor led to the far side of the house, above where the French windows must be on the floor below.

He paused outside the door, then turned and leaned against it. His shoulders were up, breath and anticipation held tightly inside him. 'Don't freak out, OK?'

'Is this a . . . sex playroom, Ethan? A teddy bear shrine? Where you keep the bodies of the other architects who wanted to reimagine this house before you got your hands on it?'

'Maybe we should go back downstairs,' he murmured.

'No! No, I want to see it. I'm dying of curiosity.'

'OK. But *no* freaking out.'

'Guide's honour,' I said, even though I'd never been a guide.

Ethan turned and pushed the door open slowly, but he refused to let go of my hand, and when I caught the first glimpse of what was inside, I realized why, because I suddenly felt as if I might float away, through the ceiling and the locked-down skylights, up towards the heavens.

The carpet was a soft blue, and the walls, unlike the natural palette in the rest of the house, were a delicate, dusty mauve. My shoulder brushed Ethan's chest as he let me past, and once I was inside I could see the whole thing.

Not all the walls were mauve. There was a feature wall opposite the window that was covered in mermaid-print wallpaper: a blue and green seaweed background, the mermaid's scales purple, her hair picked out in gold and little silver fish swimming behind her. I remembered the day I'd seen it, then written down the details in a letter.

Speechless, I turned away from it, towards the huge window. Streaks of rain transformed the thunderous clouds and the sea below into a watercolour, but it was what was beneath it that held my attention.

A polished pine desk ran the length of the room, an ergonomic chair pulled up close to it. There was an art deco lamp, pinks and greens in the patterned glass shade, and a little copper quill on a resin plinth. I sucked in a breath. On the wall above the familiar statuette, there was a framed picture. I stepped forward and saw that it was a news article. One of Ethan's first achievements? I moved closer, my heart pounding, and then – I squeaked.

'I particularly liked that story,' Ethan said softly.

'I did, too. The day I covered it, anyway.'

It was one of my articles from the *Star*, from about three years ago, about a Cotswold-based mythological society that had travelled to Cornwall to investigate the Alperwick Mermaid. I'd gone to cover their investigation for the paper, because the Alperwick residents loved nothing more than finding out why interlopers were prowling their beach with strange-looking electronic devices. But they'd been fun and friendly, not paranoid conspiracy theorists, just using local legends as reasons to visit beautiful parts of the country together.

I'd ended up telling them about my short story and the award I'd won, and when the photographer was taking pictures, they'd dragged me into the group shots. Wynn had printed one of them alongside my report and my short story, which she must have dug up from a decade-old *Alperwick Papers* anthology. I'd been livid, then embarrassed, and finally I'd felt sad, reminded of how little of my own writing I'd done since then.

Now, seeing it framed on the wall in Sterenlenn, I felt a spark of hope. I picked up the copper quill. 'This isn't actually my award,' I said, turning to look at Ethan, 'unless you *have* been back to my house, to do a little breaking and entering?'

He was resting one shoulder against the wall, looking wary. 'Not guilty. This is a replica – I assume you still have yours.'

'Somewhere,' I said quietly. 'You know, the mythological society sent me a little silver mermaid not long after my piece was printed. I guess they were grateful I'd got them in the local paper, highlighted their passions. It's sort of a talisman for me, because it reminds me that people value what I do, even if it's not writing bestselling novels.'

'Of course they value you,' Ethan said, 'and I'm glad it's important to you.'

'The mermaid?' I frowned. 'But it's . . .' My words died when I saw his expression. 'There wasn't a note, so I assumed that's where it came from.' I cleared my throat. 'Ethan, did *you* send me the silver mermaid?'

He didn't reply, and I was blindsided for the second time in five minutes.

'Did you send me the mermaid?'

He held my gaze, gave a tiny shrug.

I rubbed my forehead. 'You sent me the silver mermaid, and this is . . . it's the room I described in my letter: my imaginary office in our fantasy future. The window, the art deco light, the wallpaper. And these shelves.' There was a beautiful built-in bookcase, several titles arranged elegantly, interspersed with pot plants and muted stone bookends, everything lit artfully by LEDs. I peered closer and saw a complete set of the Cornish Sands series.

'Obviously, those would be your books.'

'You mean in our make-believe life?' I shook my head. 'I can't believe you did this.'

'I wanted to show potential buyers that all the rooms could have a unique purpose, and your letter – I loved the design. I wanted it in here.'

'Don't you think it would have been easier to forget about me? We broke up over a decade ago. It's ancient history.' It was the biggest lie I'd said all night, and so hypocritical considering everything I was feeling.

'Is that really how you think of us?' He gestured to the desk, and I knew he meant the letters.

'I wrote those ages ago, when I quit university and came back here to look after Mum.'

'And you were entirely unbothered about me finding them, clearly.' He clenched his jaw. 'That's how ancient history we are to you? You came tonight because you wanted to get them back, to retrieve them before I could read them. *That's* the real reason you came, isn't it?'

'Ethan.'

'George.'

'You created my perfect writing room in your super-star Smart house, the one that's supposed to launch your career. You named the house after an in-joke we had when we were teenagers in love. It's . . .' I flung my arms wide.

'It's what?'

'It's the past.'

He shook his head. Took a step towards me. 'It's not.'

'So . . . what are you saying? I almost didn't come today.'

'But you *did*. We're here, and what if I . . .' He paused. 'What if I want you in my future?'

'I don't—'

'Or . . .' He reached out and took my hand. 'What if we ignore the past *and* the future, just for a little while. We're here, in this house, together. Can't that be enough?'

'Enough for what?' But I moved closer to him.

He trailed his finger along my hairline, down the side of my face. 'Us. Now.'

I shook my head. 'You put my fantasy office in your house.'

'It's real. All of this is real. I didn't do any of it as a joke. I did it because I wanted it here.'

'OK, and what do you want now?'

'This.' He didn't hesitate. He leant down, twisting his hand in the fabric at my waist. 'This is the only thing that makes sense.' Then he kissed me.

Dear Ethan,

I'm going to stop writing these letters. It's been nearly three years since we last saw each other, I'm standing still in so many ways, and the only thing I can think of is to try and let you go. Besides, Mum came in to my room the other day and unearthed a couple of my old notebooks, the letters I wrote to you while we were still together, and I don't want her to see these too. I don't want her to know how hard I'm finding it, being here with her. I try my best to be a good daughter, but I don't think I'm succeeding.

So, I've had an idea. I still go up to Tyller Klos by myself sometimes. I'm not brave enough to do it in the dark, but the road is part of the cliff walk, and I can still sneak over the wall and through the bushes without anyone seeing, and get in that window round the back. It looks so different in the daylight, because you can see the disrepair, all the cracks and cobwebs – and mouse poo – but you can also see the original features, the potential. There's the moulding and the brass fittings on the window frames, and in one of the rooms there's the faintest pattern of wallpaper, a hunting scene, with horses and dogs cantering across it. It made me think that my mermaid wallpaper isn't all that outlandish.

I wish we'd gone up there in the daytime together, so you could see it. It's faded, but it's still magnificent. You would have so many ideas about what to do with it, about the modern-day marvel it could become, without losing its sense of history. A Tyller Klos for the twenty-first century. Did I tell you S. E. Artemis left in the mid-Nineties? It's been empty for twenty years already – who knows how much longer it will be abandoned?

I'm still working for the Star, writing stories about sheep and lifeboats, about the new landlord at the Sailor's Rest, some guy called Rick who wants to turn it into a swanky tourist hotspot with a world-famous fish pie. Nothing that exciting or unusual, but I really like my editor, Wynn. I go for drinks with her and some of the other staff, and it feels good to be getting out, having a few tipsy evenings at the pub.

It feels good, but I wish you were here. I still miss you more than I thought possible, so that's why I've got to stop these letters. Just because Connor and Amelie didn't make it, it doesn't make their love story any less significant. And you, Ethan Sparks, will always mean so much to me. I will never forget you, but I need to let you go. I'm going to finish this, then I'm going to walk up to Tyller Klos, and I'm going to sneak inside and hide these letters in the fireplace. It's fitting that they should end up there, where we sat together on our blanket of stars.

I really thought you were it for me, but I guess we were young and I was naive, and life doesn't always play fair. Thank you for being you, for being *such a bright Spark of joy in my life – I had to get it in somewhere.* ☺ *My future might not have you in it, but nobody can take away our memories. I hope you think of me sometimes too, but more than anything, I hope you're happy. That's all I want for you: happiness and hope, living the life you always wanted.*

I love you and I miss you.
Yours always, Georgie xxx

Chapter Twenty-Three

Now

When Ethan's lips met mine, it was softer than before, but my body felt primed, as if it had known that our kiss in the bathroom was the appetizer to something a whole lot more delicious. He pushed me gently against the wall, cupping the back of my head as he kissed me, his other hand still holding mine.

I kissed him back, letting my thoughts drift away, focusing on his body pressed against mine, his lips on my lips, the storm rumbling outside, the thunder quieter, more distant. I slid my foot up his leg, hooked it around his thigh so we were even closer.

'Is your shoulder OK?' he murmured.

'Never better.' I chased his mouth so I could kiss him again, needing him to keep doing it, to keep building the pressure inside me.

'It doesn't hurt—'

'Not right now. Come here.' I slid my hand up the back of his neck, my fingers burrowing into the hair at his nape. With each kiss I fell deeper, felt hotter and softer, drugged by how good it was having Ethan this close again. His lips left mine and I made a noise of protest, but then he was trailing them down my neck, along my collarbone, light and maddeningly teasing. I tugged his hair and he groaned and bent lower, mapping a path down my body, over my dress, with his open mouth.

I closed my eyes, my head tipped back against the wall, and it took me a moment to realize he was kneeling in front of me. I opened my eyes and he looked up at me, poised, asking a silent question. I swallowed, heat slicing right to the centre of me even before he'd touched me. I nodded, and he slid the skirt of my dress up, the whisper of the fabric against my thighs adding to the sensations that, I decided, were going to drive me mad.

Ethan bent, his head and shoulders disappearing under my dress, his hands sliding up the backs of my legs, then tugging down my underwear. He placed feather-light kisses up the insides of my thighs, and I widened them, giving him better access. Then I felt his warm breath against me, and he placed a gentle kiss there.

'This OK, Georgie?'

'Yes. Please.' I squeezed my eyes closed, focusing all my attention on where he was touching me, so gently, reverently, that I had to press my palms flat into the wall behind me. He lifted my leg over his shoulder, changing the angle, and I sucked in a breath, wondering if it was the physical sensation or the emotion that was making me dizzy.

'Ethan.' I couldn't bear not seeing him, so I yanked my dress up, pushing away from the wall for a moment so I could tug it over my head, throwing it towards the polished desk that I'd dreamed about, written about in a letter I never thought anyone would read.

He paused, looking up at me. 'Hey.' His voice was rough, his eyes glazed, then he turned his attention back to me, and I watched, everything pulling tighter as I tugged at his thick hair, delirious and drunk on the feel of him. It wasn't long before I felt the growing tingles, all sensation rushing to where he was touching me.

'I'm . . . I'm—' I didn't get anything else out, but I heard him hum in approval, and he picked up his pace. 'Oh, God!' I pulled at his hair, yanked it too hard, but I wasn't in control any more. Ethan was, and he was sending me higher with every touch. He looked up, his eyes catching hold of mine, warm and brown and alive, and that sent me spiralling, gasping, pleasure igniting inside me with an intensity that felt wholly new.

Ethan held on tightly, keeping me pressed against the wall, and then, when the high slipped away, replaced by blissful contentment, he stood up, gripping my waist, and looked down at me.

'OK?' His gaze swept over my body.

'Yeah, it was OK.' I gave him a lazy smile, and his eyes danced with amusement, because he could tell from my jelly-limbs exactly how *OK* it had been.

'Right then.' He lifted me up, and I shrieked and wrapped my legs around him. The fabric of his trousers was rough against my skin, and I could feel the effect the last few minutes had had on him. He carried me into the master bedroom and lowered me gently onto the luxurious, star-silver cover.

I glanced towards the head of the bed. 'Will the nightlights get activated in Panic Room Mode, or does the house think we'll be too stressed to sleep? Will she suddenly start playing a lullaby, when we're right in the middle of—'

'Georgie.' Ethan walked on his hands and knees towards me, and I sat up to help him undo his shirt buttons.

'What about sex mode?' I whispered. 'Where will the rose petals come from?'

'Are you intent on making a joke out of this?' His pupils were ink, blown out across his irises, the only sign that he wasn't as calm as he was pretending to be. I worked on his shirt and he discarded my bra, then stopped, motionless, to look at me.

I pushed his shirt off his shoulders, saw the smattering of freckles across his collarbone, and was hit with a flash of nostalgia, of desire and tenderness so strong that the instinct to tease was gone. I traced the patterns on his skin. 'No, I—'

'We don't have to do anything.' His thumb moved my hair off my forehead. 'I just – can I hold you?'

'You can do more than that. You already have, and I . . . it's just the two of us. Right now. I want you, Ethan.'

His smile was soft, but there was heat in his gaze. I lay back on the bed and he followed me down, kissing me again, his lips sliding down my collarbone and then lower, every touch breaking through my contentment, relighting the sparks. But I'd had enough attention, so I pushed him onto his back and knelt over him. His head hit the pillow and I froze, glancing at the ceiling.

'George.' Ethan's laugh was warm and liquid.

'I just . . . don't you feel like the house is *watching* us?' I bent and kissed his throat, delighted when he groaned and squeezed my waist.

'It's not watching us,' he said. 'But if you're uncomfortable, then—'

I nipped at his earlobe as I worked on his belt. 'I'm not uncomfortable. And anyway, let it watch. It was here at the start of us, so it may as well be here—' My gaze collided with his, and for a second I saw my panic reflected in his eyes, then he pushed up on his elbows, kissing me feverishly, helping me drag his trousers and boxers off.

'George.' He kissed his way across my cheeks and nose, brushed his fingers up and down my back, and I was a confused puddle of turned on and comforted. I ran my hands up his chest, and felt his muscles tighten. He kissed my jaw as he leaned over the side of the bed, retrieving his wallet from his trouser pocket, taking out a condom.

'Let me.' I took it from him.

'Are you sure about this?' He was breathing hard, and I recognized the look in his eyes, lust and determination and restraint colliding.

'I am. Are you?'

He nodded and licked his lips, so I moved forward, over him. It felt so good, so right, and I watched as he exhaled, a sound coming from deep in his throat. But he didn't close his eyes and neither did I, and when we started moving together, the bed perfectly weighted, nothing banging against the wall, no rat-tat-tat or cuddly turtle dive-bombers, I felt as if the house had always known: as if it had been waiting for us, as if this was always meant to happen.

'God.' Ethan pressed his head into my chest, adding a muffled, 'Fuck, George,' against my skin, his words vibrating through me.

'Like this?' I felt breathless and wild, the tide rising inside me again, the reality that this was *Ethan*, that it had never been like this with anyone but him, that it never would be, making me frantic.

'Yeah, like this.'

I lifted his chin so I could kiss him, my feet and fingers fizzing, sensation blooming inside me. 'Ethan.'

He leaned back, looking into my eyes. 'This is so good, Georgie. You're – you're it. You're everything.'

His words sent me hurtling towards the spark – a spark that had only ever been this bright with Ethan.

And I knew he was close too, that his desire had caught hold of his words and run away with them, but they were a mantra, a beat in my head, as we got there together. *You're everything.*

I had never felt like I was close to enough, apart from with Ethan, and now he'd confirmed it. With him, I was all I needed to be.

He put his arms around me, and I pressed my lips to his forehead, pushing his damp hair off it. I wanted to run my fingers over every part of him.

'Georgie.' It was muffled, spoken against my neck, but I loved the way my name sounded in his low, breathless voice. I loved everything about him. I had never stopped loving him, not for a second, despite the way we'd ended things.

'Hey, Ethan?' I slid my arms out from around him, ran my thumb over his bottom lip.

'Yeah?' He looked as dazed, as satisfied, as I felt.

'It turns out we didn't need rose petals after all. Sex mode activated, without any help whatsoever.'

He tipped his head forward and laughed into my collarbone, and we fell sideways on the luxurious bedspread, just as a white, fragmented light spilled in through the rain-splattered window, and I realized that the summer storm had moved on, and that the sea outside the house, and us and the bed inside, were bathed in moonlight.

Chapter Twenty-Four

July 2012

My dress was pale blue with one dark blue seam running through it, and another that was shimmering silver. It had wide straps, a square neckline and a skirt that floated elegantly but wasn't too poofy. Kira had helped me turn my shoulder-length blonde hair into a mass of curls, and acted as makeup consultant so I wasn't too pale or remotely clownish. Her own dress was black and red, layers of lace and chiffon, but her chunky boots and cat-eye liner made her look badass rather than out of place.

'We're like the mermaid and the she-devil,' she said, slinging an arm around my shoulders as we looked at our reflections in the hall mirror.

'Mermaid and Snow White,' I suggested with a smile.

'There is nothing pure about me,' Kira said. 'You

and Ethan are coming to the house after the disco, right?'

My dress was delicate and pretty, and I fingered the soft fabric, thinking of the thorns and twigs inside the broken wall. But this was about more than a pretty dress: it was our last chance to be in the house together before the summer started. Our exams were done, our fates set – though we didn't know what they were yet – and Freddy and Kira both had family plans that would take them out of Cornwall. I would miss them, but Ethan would still be here, and I wanted to spend as much time with him as I could.

'Of course,' I said, as my phone chimed.

'Your boy on his way?'

I opened the message and my stomach fell. 'Sarah's gone AWOL.'

'What?' Kira frowned. 'Isn't she staying with friends in York?'

'She got back last weekend. Ethan said she seemed happier, ready to settle down and finish the year, but . . .'

'It can't be that unusual for her to disappear. It doesn't sound like staying at home with a book is really her thing.'

I showed Kira the message.

Sarah had a massive row with Mum and stormed out. I need to find her. I'll meet you there. I'm so sorry, I love you. Ex.

'Fuck,' Kira said. 'Fuckity fuck. I'm sorry, Georgie.'

'It's fine,' I said, even though it wasn't.

'He might still make it.'

'He might,' I echoed, even though I knew that when Sarah went off the rails, she did it in a way that consumed all of Ethan's time and energy. I replied, because despite my disappointment it was much harder for him than me.

Can I do anything? I don't care about the dance, I care about you. Love you too. xx

His reply was instant.

Go and have fun. I'll be there as soon as I can. x

Five minutes later, the limo Freddy had got his dad to hire honked outside the house, and Kira and I put our heels on. Mum gave me a hug at the door, then pinned a yellow rose corsage to the strap of my dress.

'Blue for your eyes, gold for your hair,' she said. 'Go and have fun, my precious mermaid.'

The school hall was dressed up with helium balloons hanging from the ceiling, and a projector that danced patterns of light across the floor, hiding the grime and dust that had embedded itself over decades of assemblies and parents' evenings. There was a bar consisting of Coke and lemonade, fruit juice and sparkling water, and I wondered how many of the students had brought small bottles of spirits with them to liven things up.

Crisps had been decanted into paper bowls, Hula Hoops already spilled onto the floor adding a crunch underfoot, and the DJ was the science lab tech, Lenny. We walked in as he was playing 'We Are Young' by Fun, but from the way my fellow students were clustered around the edges of the room, it was as if they were purposefully trying to contradict it.

'Fuck's sake,' Kira muttered. Freddy looked great in a blue velvet tuxedo and bow tie, and Orwell had gone for classic black and white, though he had a pair of red brogues on.

'We could go straight to the house?' I suggested. 'Ethan could meet us there.'

'Not a chance.' Kira took Freddy's hand, then mine, and I took Orwell's as she pulled us to the centre of the dance floor and started singing along at the top of her very out-of-tune voice. Soon, all four of us were shouting the words, other students looking at us with curiosity or disdain. A couple of girls from my English class started singing, and Kira pounced, dragging them out to join us. Then she did a sweep of the room, grabbing hands and shimmying in front of the bored onlookers, and the disdainful looks were replaced by grins as everyone stopped trying to play it cool.

'You're amazing, you know that?' I shouted over 'Starships' by Nicki Minaj, and Kira laughed, her head tipped back.

'It's our last night! Everything changes after this. We have to make it memorable.'

I smiled and couldn't help checking my phone.

By the time Lenny called out the last song – why was it *still* 'Angels' by Robbie Williams? – we were ragged from all the dancing, and while other students were picked up by their parents or waiting limos, some of my classmates decidedly merry, we'd been saving our booze for the house.

We walked away from the school, taking a detour onto the seafront. It was a breathtaking night, the moon fat and high, flanked by a chorus of mesmerizing stars, the sand bathed white. The tide was out, the waves a silky, distant whoosh, and the air was cool but not cold, a welcome whisper over my heated skin.

Kira slipped her hand into mine. 'Still no word from Ethan?'

I shook my head. I'd sent him a message half an hour ago: *What's happening? You OK? x* but hadn't had a reply. I wasn't surprised that he hadn't made it, but the disappointment was a cluster of rocks low in my stomach.

'He might still come.' Freddy gave me an apologetic glance. 'He's a sound dude.'

'That's part of the problem,' Kira said. 'If he wasn't such a good big brother, then Georgie wouldn't be feeling so low.'

'Hey.' I forced a smile. 'I've got you guys. We've just had an amazing night. I can see Ethan tomorrow.'

'If it really *is* Sarah he's running off to spend time with,' Orwell said, and Kira whacked him with her clutch bag.

'Of course it is. Cheating on Georgie is the last thing Ethan would ever do. He's a foundations guy, remember? Solid and dependable.'

'That's the impression he's given, anyway.' Orwell undid his bow tie and shoved it in his pocket. I'd danced with him a few times that evening, and he'd been charming and funny and taken my mind off missing Ethan for a while, which made his shit-stirring even harder to take.

'Why would he bother?' I asked, more sharply than I'd intended. 'If he liked someone else, he could go and be with them, couldn't he? Why keep me dangling too, if he's not interested any more? He could just *say* so.' I didn't want to believe Orwell, didn't want to think that there might be another reason Ethan was absent so often, but it was hard to stop the doubt creeping in, like the weeds snaking through the cracks in the walls that surrounded our abandoned house on the hill.

It felt different with us all in our party gear, the weight of the next few months hanging over us, full of possibility but also the dread of things changing, our neat little sixth-form bubble popping and letting us out into the real world.

We sat in our favourite room, next to the fireplace, the windows letting in swathes of moonlight. We'd left rucksacks on the house side of the wall earlier, so we didn't have to take them to the disco, and I had my blanket of stars. I spread it on the floor and Orwell immediately sat next to me, crossing his legs without a glance in my direction.

Kira caught my eye and gave me an exasperated look, and I discreetly rolled my eyes at her.

'What do you think will happen to this place if we don't visit any more?' Freddy rested his elbows on his knees.

'You mean, will it be sad without us?' Kira asked. 'Of course it will be. Who wouldn't want the pleasure of our sparkling company?'

'Either the guy who owns it will get around to developing it, or he'll sell it to someone else.' Orwell grabbed a handful of Pringles. 'A plot of land like this is prime for a hotel or an old people's home.'

'Fuck that,' Freddy said. 'Old folk with glaucoma won't appreciate the view.'

'Freddy.' Kira leaned against him and he put his arm around her. 'Don't be so cruel.'

'Nah, maybe you're right. I can't be jealous of whoever ends up getting this place. It's not like any of us have a chance.'

'It needs someone with a great imagination, a confident vision, and a whole lot of love in their heart,' Kira said dreamily. 'Ethan's rambled on about it enough. Maybe when he's a high-flying architect, he'll come back and transform it?'

Orwell shook his head. 'Someone else will make a decision long before he gets the chance. This place isn't going to be abandoned for much longer, I bet.'

I shuffled away from him, reaching for the bag of

Haribo. It felt all kinds of wrong that Ethan wasn't here on our last night, with Freddy off to Spain in two days.

'I hope it gets the future it deserves.' I slid my hand over the moulding around the fireplace, the swags of plasterwork leaves and flowers.

'We haven't checked if anything's been hidden up there.' Freddy sounded sombre, as if – even though we were sitting right next to it – we'd somehow lost the opportunity to look.

I took my phone out, not expecting to see anything from Ethan, but he'd sent me a message. My heart leapt, and I opened the screen to read the whole thing in one go, but all it said was:

I'm so sorry, Georgie. I'll explain everything as soon as I can. Ex

My insides clenched with worry, but when I tried to call him, it rang and rang then clicked through to voicemail. Kira gave me a puzzled look and I shook my head, not wanting to say anything in front of Orwell, who would pounce on Ethan's ambiguous words with malicious glee.

As Freddy launched into a story about Dagger Dave climbing up to the school roof with his maths teacher's satchel on our last day, my ears tuned into the sound of sirens, somewhere not too far off. I didn't think anything of it, because it was a common enough sound, especially in the summer months when spirits were higher, beer gardens were open late, and the fields on the outskirts of Alperwick were dry as tinder when the rain had stayed away, and susceptible to the smallest, most innocuous spark.

Chapter Twenty-Five

Now

'What's it like working with the great S. E. Artemis?' Ethan stroked his hand up and down my arm, and I tried not to think about how good it felt to lie here, my head on his chest, like we used to. We'd pulled back the covers, got in under the silky eiderdown and plump duvet, the moonlight lying across us fragmented by the raindrops on the window.

'It's exhausting,' I told him, 'but not always in a bad way. She's feisty and confident, not at all introverted. Did you know that she ended the Cornish Sands series the way she did because her husband left her?'

'She decided she couldn't write a romance because she didn't believe in it any more?'

'She didn't put it like that. She said she'd had enough, that the Rosevar family had run out of steam, but I think you're right – she was heartbroken. Now she's found some new inspiration, and she's ready to give her readers the happy-ever-after they always deserved.'

His laugh was a low rumble. 'You like working with her, then?'

'I'm really working *for* her. Part of the reason I came here – aside from the letters – is that she said if we were bringing Amelie and Connor back, we needed to have a good idea of what the house was like inside.'

'Couldn't you just have created that, though? I know it was an important part of the series, but it's still fiction. And Sterenlenn's been in magazines,' he added, a little sheepishly. 'You told me you saw the pictures.'

'Nothing beats being here, experiencing the view and how the light floods in; all the little touches like the disco shower. I do get what you mean, though.' It had seemed strange at first, her insistence that I come to the open house. 'I think she was desperate to see what it was like herself, because it used to be hers, and she can't because of her limited mobility, so she's using me instead.'

'And you'll give her a few more photos and a report of your visit?'

'I'm a great storyteller, Ethan.' I poked him in the ribs. 'Hasn't anyone told you that?'

'Which is why you should be writing your own book, not going on missions for someone else, helping them write *theirs*. You're good enough, Georgie. More than.'

'It's so hard,' I mumbled into his warm skin. It was hard when I was trying to get a journalism degree, trying to put my heartbreak over Ethan into a box, fielding calls from Mum. Then I abandoned university and came back here, looking after her and getting reporting gigs at the same time. I'd put any thoughts of writing fiction on the backburner.

'The worthwhile things often are,' Ethan said, 'but you have to do them anyway.'

'What's been the hardest thing about Sterenlenn?' I danced my fingertips over his chest. 'Was it like an episode of *Grand Designs*?'

He laughed. 'Nothing this big or complex goes smoothly, and everyone said I was making things extra difficult for myself, starting with a renovation rather than a new-build. I thought having the original house here would be easier, but it wasn't. Every plan, blueprint, formula – when it came to it, we needed so many workarounds. Sparks was the thing I was most confident about, because we'd been developing it for years – it's such a dedicated team. It felt like the final flourish once all the hard stuff was done.'

'You have a team of computer whizzes? Are you thinking about sacking them after this?'

'No, I . . . You know, that is very distracting, what you're doing.' I could hear the restraint in his voice, which only encouraged me. I trailed my hand lower.

'You have faith in your team, despite what's happened?'

'It's a teething problem. And OK, it's pretty fucking

serious, but we've worked so hard – there must be a way to fix it.'

'Good. You should be confident. You've got this, Ethan Sp . . .' I stopped in case the house tried to do something else unexpected.

'I'll have to go back to the office as soon as we're out,' he said. 'Take the house off the market while we fix it.'

My heart sank at the thought of him leaving immediately, and I wondered how much of this would have happened if we'd been free to leave. Would I have walked out when I planned to, right after the event ended, and never seen him again? 'You could say it comes with an escape room feature?' I suggested. 'One of the hardest in the country. Home and entertainment centre, rolled into one.'

Ethan turned onto his side, facing me. 'Great idea. Maybe you should have written the marketing material for me.'

'You didn't offer me the job,' I said, looking into his brown eyes. They seemed warmer, now; he'd lost the impassive, detached look he'd had on the front path a few hours ago. He'd kindled back to life, and I liked to think I'd had a lot to do with that. 'Did you have to give a presentation about this place in front of a whole load of investors?'

'Yes.' He grimaced. 'It ranks up there with the least fun days of my life.'

'You didn't imagine them all naked?'

His gaze trailed from my face to my neck, then lower. 'No,' he said eventually. 'I pictured you naked instead.'

'You did not.'

'I did.' He nodded, decisive. 'Thinking about the house came hand in hand with thinking about you, and that whole stage – pitching to investors, getting my proposal approved, developing then rehashing the blueprints, getting them locked down so they passed the endless surveys and checks – it was so stressful, because if it failed at any point, I would have lost the house and all those years of work. So I thought about what you would say to me. You always believed in me, encouraged me, even at the end. It was your faith in me that made you so angry.'

I chose to ignore that last point. 'So you imagined me giving you a pep talk, naked?'

His lips tipped up. 'Maybe. Sometimes.'

'What memories did you go back to?' I had meant it to sound challenging, but it came out far too sincere, like I was hanging on every word.

'The first time we were together,' he said. 'I don't know – a whole slideshow of memories. That time on the beach.' He grinned, and I groaned.

'Anyone who says they like having sex on a beach is lying. A Cornish beach, anyway. I bet they don't have seaweed in the Seychelles.'

'They get deadly box jellyfish in the Seychelles.'

'Well then, all beaches are out.'

'It was fun though. I laughed a lot.'

I returned his grin. 'Yeah, me too.'

'You always made me laugh. I've sort of . . . forgotten how. Everything's seemed so serious, lately.'

271

'That might be the saddest thing I've ever heard. Ethan S., young architect on the cusp of a brilliant career, has forgotten how to laugh.'

'That's a very long-winded headline,' he murmured, as he traced the line of my collarbone.

I closed my eyes, distracted by his touch, and by his warm body so close to mine. '"The Spark has gone",' I said in a deep voice. '"When success comes at the cost of happiness".'

'Ouch,' Ethan said quietly. 'Maybe I don't want you making up headlines about me, after all.'

'Sterenlenn is in Panic Room Mode,' the house said at the same time.

'Yes, thank you, Captain Obvious.' I rolled my eyes, then ran my fingers over Ethan's freckle constellation, realizing I knew the shape of it by heart. 'Has it been worth it?'

'The house?'

I nodded, held my breath.

He glanced towards the window, where the moonlight was drifting in, reaching across the room to dust our skin, then brought his gaze back to mine. 'It has,' he said eventually. 'But I'm not sure it would have been if the Smart system hadn't broken down.'

'Right.' It took me a second to work out what that meant: that he was happier we'd ended up trapped together than he would have been if his showcase had gone perfectly. He was prepared to face all the hassle just to get time with me. And we only had right now

– until the bug fixed itself and the house released us, or Sarah realized what had happened.

'I think we should try out the shower.'

Ethan frowned. 'Why?'

'The disco shower,' I explained. 'I don't know if you've noticed, but I've been obsessed with it since I saw it. We've tried out the bed, the sofas. We should try out the shower next. Maybe I'll write a piece about what it's like to live in a Smart house for a night: I could do it without mentioning that I didn't have a choice.'

'That's how you're going to frame your article?' But he sounded distracted, and his gaze was hazy. Perhaps he was remembering, like I was, that we were quite good at showering together.

'It'll be like Goldilocks and the Three Bears,' I said. 'The sofa was too big, the beer fridge was way too small. The bed, however, was just right. The villain in my fairy tale will be the house itself, because that voice has said some strange things, and it's just plain creepy.'

'It's not . . .' he started, then stopped. The look he gave me was intense, calculating, and before I realized what was happening, he'd scooped me up, holding me against him as he clambered off the bed and walked us both towards the en-suite.

'Have you been in here?' I asked, holding onto him tightly.

'No.' He opened the door and put me down gently. 'There's no body wash.'

'I'm not interested in body wash.'

'No, all you care about are the lights.' He pressed buttons on the panel and it beeped a few times, the lights around the bottom of the shower flickering on, pulsing between red, blue and white.

'The lights are OK,' I said.

'Just OK?' He pressed another button and the pulsing sped up, the colours changing to an out-of-sync rainbow: green and crimson, violet and lemon, orange and sky blue. 'You know you can have them flash in time to music?'

'Let's do that, then. Do I have to ask the creepy voice?'

Ethan rolled his eyes. 'What shall we . . .' He hesitated, his finger inches from the screen. I looked at him, standing there naked, unselfconscious because I'd given him a task and he was entirely focused on it. His body was gorgeous, strong and firm and freckled. 'This,' he said, triumphantly. He pressed a series of buttons then stepped into the shower with me, walking me backwards until he could reach behind me and turn it on. The water came out of the rainfall shower head perfectly warm, heating to hot in a couple of seconds.

'What song did you pick?' I asked, as Ethan bent his head towards mine.

'Patience, Georgie,' he whispered against my lips, and a moment later the song started, lights flickering in time with the opening chords, and I smiled up at him, hoping my emotions weren't showing on my face, and that he couldn't see inside to my racing heart. My love for him had crashed right over me, a new, confounding wave, even more intense than it had been when I was eighteen.

'Whatever it Takes' by Lifehouse filled the shower cubicle.

'Oh my God,' I said. 'The cheese.'

'Everyone loves cheese. Nobody can live without it, whatever they say.'

A laugh spilled out of me. 'A staple part of every diet. What would you say this is? Camembert?'

I stretched up to kiss him as the hot water rained down on us, washing away everything except the reality of this moment: disco lights dancing and a song I hadn't heard in years, but was now branded onto my heart for ever, along with the taste of Ethan's kiss and what it felt like to have him back in my arms, even if it was only for a night.

Chapter Twenty-Six

July 2012

Because it was prom night and our parents had given us a bit of leeway, we stayed at the house until two a.m., even though my heart wasn't in it. I drank the vodka and didn't feel remotely drunk; I offered up my own stories about sixth form, about my overly passionate media studies teacher and how easily distracted he was; we laughed and joked and Kira and Freddy were drunkenly affectionate, knowing they would be apart for the summer at the very least.

When we finally left Tyller Klos behind, I imagined the Rosevar family watching us from the windows, their brows pinched as we made slow work of the undergrowth in our finery. The sky was a rich, royal blue dusted with stars, as if it hadn't wanted to get completely dark, as if it was enjoying the summer too much.

I'd heard nothing more from Ethan since that one message, and I'd given up playing it cool. I'd sent him a handful of replies, and I'd called him, but it had gone to voicemail every time.

Kira slid her arm through mine as we walked down the hill. 'He'll be OK,' she slurred, giving me a wide grin.

'Of course he will be.' I aimed for confident. 'He's had to stay at home because Sarah's managed to ground them both, that's all. I bet he's annoyed he missed the prom.'

'You in that mermaid dress most of all.'

We said goodbye at my front door, the gentle rasp of the sea our early morning soundtrack, and I crept up to my room, wondering if Mum was listening to me get home, confused at why there weren't two sets of footsteps climbing the stairs.

My sleep was light and disturbed, so I sat bolt upright the moment my phone pinged. I looked at the clock on my bedside table: it was just after six a.m.

Are you awake? Can I come round?

I replied immediately: Yes and yes.

I'll be there in 15.

I put a thin cardigan on over my sleep shorts and T-shirt, and went downstairs to put the kettle on.

Twenty minutes later Ethan messaged that he was outside, and I hurried down the hall, relief shooting through me when I could see his tall silhouette in the wavy glass of our front door. I pulled it open, not sure what I wanted to say to him, but every opening line was knocked out of me when I saw him.

He was in his white shirt, black jacket and trousers, the bare bones of the tux I had expected to see him in last night, but his tie was long gone, and what remained was in tatters, the shirt stained with something dark and ripped at the hem. Ethan's eyes were red-rimmed, his cheeks hollowed out with exhaustion, and his thick hair was a disaster. The way he looked at me sent a shiver running over my skin.

I pulled him inside and wrapped my arms around him. He was rigid to begin with, and only softened slightly when I tightened my hold. 'What happened?' I leaned back and looked up at him.

'Can we go to your room?' His voice was rough, unused.

'Of course. You go up, I'm going to make us tea.'

He nodded and trudged up the stairs, using the handrail to haul himself up. My mind was racing as I re-boiled the kettle, got the teabags and milk ready.

I took the tea up to my room and found Ethan sitting on my bed, his elbows on his knees. He was right on the edge, as if he was already preparing to leave.

'Hey.' I held the mug out to him.

'Thanks.' He stared at it for a moment, then put it

278

on the floor, turning to face me when I sat on the bed, leaning against the pillows.

'You can come up here, you know.'

He rubbed a hand over his face, then crawled over the duvet to sit beside me, angling his body towards mine.

'What happened?' I asked again.

He held my gaze for a moment, then looked down at the covers. 'Sarah stole Mum's car.'

My mind went blank. Sarah, Ethan's little sister, who was only just sixteen. I knew she was reckless, but this sounded crazy. 'What?'

'She got in a huge fight with Mum after school – I don't know what about – and she stormed out, which wasn't unusual, so I just . . . I thought she would blow off steam, then come home. She called me just as I was about to leave to meet you.'

'Is she OK?' It had taken me too long to ask, I realized.

'She's OK,' Ethan said, and my shoulders slumped with relief.

'Why did she call you?'

'Because she didn't know what to do. She's too young to drive, but she'd taken Mum's car, swiped the keys and driven off into the countryside, and then she crashed it.'

'Shit.' I put my hand on Ethan's arm, but wasn't sure he noticed. 'But she's OK?'

'She was shaken up, she sounded frantic when she called me. She asked me to come and meet her, to not tell Mum and Dad.'

'You didn't tell them?'

He looked up at me. 'She's been in so much trouble. She got a caution in York for criminal damage, and—'

'She's been in trouble with the *police*? Oh my God.'

'I went to meet her. I had to walk, because I didn't have any other way of getting there, and . . .' He leaned back against the pillows, covered his eyes with a hand. 'Mum's car was on fire.'

'She'd set it on *fire*?' It came out as a squeak.

'She hadn't, but she spun the car when she crashed, and the back end hit a rock in the verge. She damaged the fuel tank, and . . . she wanted me to fix it.'

Anger hardened inside me. 'Ethan.'

He shrugged, looking defeated, and I tried to squash it down. 'She didn't know what to do, but the car was on fire and there was a farm building, some kind of barn, so I didn't have a choice. We couldn't just pretend it hadn't happened or drive the car away from the scene.'

I felt cold all over. 'What did you do?'

'I called the police, the fire brigade. I said that I'd been driving the car, that I'd crashed it.'

The chill shivered through my body. 'You told them *you'd* stolen it?'

He nodded.

I got off the bed, walked the three paces to the door, then came back. 'Why would you do that?'

'Because it isn't as bad if I've taken Mum's car without her permission. I can drive, I'm on the insurance. And Sarah's been in enough trouble.'

'And she keeps getting away with it, because you keep bailing her out.'

'That's not fair. Mum and Dad come down so hard on her.'

'Because she's being an idiot,' I said. 'Though I didn't realize it was a *criminal* idiot. Ethan, you cannot cover for her.'

'She's my little sister.'

'Yes, and she makes her own choices.' I flung my arms wide. 'She makes her choices, and you make yours. You've got such big plans – you're going to be an architect. You need a degree and credentials and a good reputation and for *people to trust you with their stuff*. You can't be convicted of stealing and destroying a car.' My throat thickened, the reality of what he was risking seeping into my bones. 'You just can't.'

'But it's a first offence,' he said. 'Mum and Dad won't press charges, so it's mostly that I caused the crash, started the fire. Dad has a good lawyer, so—'

I slumped onto the bed. 'So you actually did it? You've been interviewed and cautioned and . . .'

Ethan nodded. He was looking at me warily, but there was something closed-off about his expression, too. He felt far away from me. 'They just released me. They think I'll get off with a caution – or a fine – for careless driving. It's a first offence, a mistake.'

I shook my head, my tears falling freely. 'You can't do this. You'll have a criminal record, and you think it'll make Sarah change her behaviour?'

'It's done now. I can't go back.' Agitation crept into his voice when he added, 'It was the right thing to do.'

'It wasn't.' I got up again, not knowing where to put myself. 'What about your future? You have worked so hard, and you're such a *good* person. You're messing up your whole life for her.'

'I'm not. It'll be fine.'

'And if they work out you covered for her, you'll get done for that . . . that perverting the course of justice thing. That's serious! I can't believe your dad agreed to this!'

'By the time he knew about it, it was too late. Georgie, please don't cry.' I wiped frantically at my eyes, and saw that he was holding his arms out. I wanted to crawl into them, to comfort him, but I couldn't believe he would risk everything like this.

'You know we only have one chance at this, right?'

'I'll be fine,' Ethan said again.

'But you're not fine right now. And it's not just that you've been up all night and interviewed under caution and been in a cell when you should have been with us. You're putting on a brave face for me, and I don't want you to do that. I don't want any of this to have happened.'

'You think *I* do? You think I want to have missed our last night at the house? A chance to celebrate everything? You think I wanted to end up at the police station in Truro? I couldn't just leave her there, could I?'

'You should have got your mum and dad involved!

282

Got them to take responsibility for once. I hate that they leave it to you, that you don't stand up to them!'

'Oh, and you do?' Ethan's eyes were blazing. 'You stand up to your mum when she stops you going out, makes you get her pills, or take her to her trial appointments while she's smoking weed and ruining it for herself? I don't see you standing up to her, Georgie. What if, when it comes to it, she stops you from going to university?'

'She's ill!'

'And Sarah's miserable. She's ill too, basically, and she's my family. I'm not just leaving her.' He hung his head, the fight going out of him. He picked Connor the cuddly turtle off my desk and squeezed him.

My tears were falling faster, Ethan's accusations and mine swirling in my head. He was right about Mum, but I loved her, and I knew that he loved Sarah too, but it felt so different to me. 'You need to put yourself first, or you'll never get to do what you want. All your dreams will just be gone.'

'Yeah, well.' He let Connor drop to the bed. 'Some things matter more than a stupid dream that isn't going to happen anyway.'

'What?' I swallowed. 'You're going to achieve yours. Out of all of us, you're the one who's going to do it. You're going to qualify as an architect and then you're going to come back here and turn Tyller Klos into something magnificent. You're going to give it a new life.'

'That was always a fantasy. It's never going to happen.'

'Don't say that.'

'I need to go home.' He stood up. 'Dad's expecting me.'

'Is he proud of you for doing this? For taking the blame?'

'I need to go, Georgie.'

'And what about us?'

He stopped in the doorway, turning to look at me. 'What *about* us?'

I didn't know how to say all the things I was feeling. It had been bad enough when he'd abandoned me to cover for Sarah, but the thought that he was prepared to abandon his principles, his own future, for someone who probably wouldn't even be grateful – who might not change her destructive ways – was crushing. 'I just never thought you would do something like this,' I told him. 'I didn't . . . I don't know if you're who I thought you were.'

I wasn't sure how I'd meant it to come out, but the moment I said it I knew I couldn't take it back. I saw it hit: how he suddenly looked even more devastated. I took a step towards him, but he folded his arms, putting a barrier between us. 'Probably better you realise that now,' he said. 'Better that I let go of that dream as well, do it all in one night.' He turned away from me, and I saw him swallow. 'Bye, Georgie.'

I could have said something. I could have called him back, told him we could survive it all, but I didn't. It was as much an answer as if I'd spoken. He hovered for a second in the hallway outside my room, waiting for me to give him another chance, but I kept quiet. I didn't even say goodbye, and he ducked his head in understanding.

Ethan walked down the stairs and out of my front door, just as the sun was peeking above the hills, dusting Alperwick with the golden promise of another perfect summer's day.

Chapter Twenty-Seven

Now

The bed was far too comfortable. After my and Ethan's intense disco shower (where I discovered that one, the speakers worked in the shower cubicle, pumping our Lifehouse song to us clearly over the spray, two, he had got even better at working the angles that made us fit perfectly together – perhaps because this shower was so much bigger than mine – and three, he still loved them scalding hot), we wrapped ourselves in the oversized fluffy bath sheets, supposedly only for display purposes and getting a lot more than they bargained for, and fell back on the bed. At some point, we replaced the towels for the duvet and bedspread, and I snuggled into him again.

Just before we'd drifted off, he'd looked down at me, eyelids already fluttering, voice thick, and said, 'I've missed you so much, George. I didn't realize how empty my life was without you. How pointless.' But then he was asleep, and I didn't have the chance to respond, even if I'd known what to say.

At first, I wasn't sure what had woken me.

The room was cast in a blue tinge, and I looked for the source of the ethereal light. It was coming from the window, where the moon had slid out of view, but it seemed to surround me, too. I glanced up, and through the last wisps of sleep, I realized I was looking at the stars, the sky surrounding them a breathtaking, pre-dawn blue. The skylight was open, and the effect was more magical than I could have imagined: take the glow-in-the-dark stars from childhood ceilings, turn the wow factor all the way up, and you might be halfway to understanding what I was lying beneath. For several seconds I just stared, trying and failing to pick out constellations, and then, slowly, it sank in. If the skylights were open, did that mean the rest of the house was, too?

I looked at Ethan. He was lying on his stomach, his head turned towards me, resting on his bent arm. His eyelashes were inky feathers, his hair tousled, his breaths soft and relaxed. He looked peaceful, and I was reluctant to wake him. Part of me wanted to stay in this bubble, just the two of us, but I reminded myself that it wasn't real, it had been forced on us, and the longer we were trapped here, the more the worry and irritation would fester between us.

I heard a buzz, something familiar but quiet, and

saw that Ethan's phone was vibrating on the bedside table. I picked it up, because if it was making noises, then surely there was a signal now, and Panic Room Mode really was over.

His display told me that it was almost four a.m., and that he had a message from Sarah. I couldn't help reading the snippet – it was right there on the screen – and my brain stuttered, the uncertainty over what had caused our predicament blooming bright again. I needed to see the whole conversation to make sense of it, but when I tried to unlock the phone, it said my face wasn't recognised, then asked for a passcode. Gingerly, feeling guilty but determined because now I was sure he had been keeping things from me, I held the phone in front of Ethan's face. He had always been a deep sleeper, and I hoped this wouldn't wake him.

At first, nothing happened, so I held my breath and moved the phone closer. There was a quiet snicking sound as the screen unlocked.

Turning away from him, I opened WhatsApp and scrolled back through the message chain between him and his sister, to the one Sarah had sent him just after she left Sterenlenn, before the house had shut down:

18:45 Sarah: Take your time, boss man. It's gone brilliantly, so just enjoy it now. Amazing that Georgie turned up, huh?

18:50 Ethan: Thanks for everything you've done. Safe trip back – I'll call you when I'm on the train.

19:01 Sarah: 🖋 (don't think I didn't notice you avoiding the whole Georgie thing)

There was a gap, then a message from him much later in the evening, after we'd been stuck here for several hours.

23:15 Ethan: If this gets through, can you tell me what's happening? Sparks is having a meltdown, we're trapped inside. Me and Georgie. Can you check it for me urgently?

I didn't know when he'd written it, but I assumed 23:15 was the time it had got through to her, and I tried to remember what we'd been doing then: if we'd been too distracted to notice some kind of signal returning; if he'd written the message hours earlier, and it had been sitting, waiting for Wi-Fi or 5G to finally release it. Her reply came soon afterwards.

23:20 Sarah: Don't sweat it, bro. Just a little something I've been trying in Beta. I hope I didn't scare Georgie with the impromptu Sparks responses. 😩

Impromptu Sparks responses? I felt a wave of something close to nausea as I remembered how polished and grown-up Sarah had been that afternoon; how I'd been stunned that she was there, and surprised by how different she'd seemed. I kept reading. Ethan's reply was much later, and I realized he must have found Sarah's message after our shower. I thought he'd fallen asleep before me, but he must have woken up after I'd dropped off. Had he taken his phone out, had one last try to reconnect everything and get us out, or had this been something else altogether?

1:57 Ethan: What the fuck? What are you talking about? You did this?

1:58 Sarah: Where you been, E? I had a little fun, that's all. It was this whole thing, but it's for your own good, I promise. You'll thank me later. ☺

1:58 Ethan: Unlock the house now. Georgie was hurt! We needed to get out. You've been in control the whole time? I don't believe this. Could you hear us?

1:59 Sarah: Chill big bro. You were never in danger. I left it in Beta, set the wake words to Sparks and Sterenlenn, so I could only hear those prompts. You know how strong the security protocol is. I wasn't listening to you.

2:00 Ethan: Unlock it, set Sparks back to auto. I mean it.

2:01 Sarah: ☹ Spoilsport.

2:02 Ethan: Now.

2:15 Sarah: OK I've unlocked it. You can get out now.

2:16 Ethan: I can't believe you did this.

2:20 Sarah: You and Georgie though. Did it work?

2:21 Ethan: She was scared. You might have ruined everything.

2:23 Sarah: I doubt it. And I had a lot to make up for.

2:25 Ethan: Don't go there. This is beyond fucked up. I'm getting the first train back to Bristol in the morning and we're going to sort this.

2:27 Sarah: Nothing to sort. Sparks is working fine.

2:35 Sarah: You there? You out now, or are you saying a proper goodbye? I'll leave you and Georgie to it. My work here is done. 😉

My skin prickled, my disbelief and horror rising with every message. It made a sickening sort of sense that Sarah was embroiled in our reunion, that things had come full circle. The house wasn't turning into *The Terminator*, it had been manipulated by Ethan's clever but disruptive little sister, and he was planning on leaving as soon as there was a train so he could deal with her, rather than stay and talk about our night together. Had he really not known? He sounded furious in his messages, but what did he mean when he said: *you might have ruined everything?* Did he mean the house sale, his reputation, or something else?

I had never considered an alternative scenario – Ethan being trapped here with Sarah, or even on his own. But it looked like, if we hadn't been in our orchestrated places – together in the house – then none of this would have happened at all.

I slid out of bed and picked up my bra, tiptoed through the silent corridors to the beautiful office Ethan had created for me, gathering my clothes and putting them back on. I thought my sandals were in the living room, and I flushed, embarrassed at how I'd left little bits of me all over the house, as if I owned it. I paused, looking out of the huge window, the silver-blue of the ocean just before dawn, the sky that seemed cracked because the stars were so bright, light spilling through it. In place of the storm there was an eerie calmness, the water as still as it ever got, the waves rippling instead of raging.

I realized I was trailing a finger over everything, the art deco lampshade and the fake quill award, the frame with the story Ethan had carefully picked out. How had he even got hold of copies of the *Star?* Had he seen the stories online, or set up a Google alert for my byline? I had so many questions, so many things I wanted to say to him now that I'd had a few minutes space, but I couldn't ignore the messages. Sarah had been the driving force between us, just like before. It had only been one night, and I couldn't do it again. I needed to walk away.

I picked up my rucksack from the bedroom floor, heard a rustle from the bed and paused in the doorway, able to make out Ethan still lying there, his head resting on his arm. I wished I could slide back under the covers, tuck myself against him and forget that this wasn't the real world, where there was a multimillion-pound house to sell and Ethan's life was in Bristol, not here, and I had a chance to help Spence write her new book. I waited for the familiar flash of excitement, but it didn't come.

I tiptoed quietly down the stairs and walked through the kitchen, into the living room. There was the fireplace I'd hidden my letters in, the table my shoulder had connected with when I was dancing, the sofa we'd sat on together. I slipped my sandals back on and turned in a slow circle, taking everything in. I didn't have any photos of this room, but somehow that was better. Did I really need any more reminders of what had happened here, when my brain would force me to relive it far too often anyway?

I walked back through the gleaming kitchen, past its various fridges, and into the hall, with its blossoming bouquets and elegant staircase and those long windows bringing the outside in. I paused next to the panel Ethan had pressed so frantically when we first got trapped. I didn't know if Sarah had done what she'd said and reset the system, and I didn't want to risk saying something and making the voice echo through the house, waking Ethan prematurely, if I didn't need to. But then I noticed something on the digital display that hadn't been there before, when the house had been in Panic Room Mode. 'Unlock front door' it read, and I pressed the button next to it and heard the thick, heavy clunk of the locks releasing – the work of only a moment.

I reached out and pulled the handle, and the door slid easily towards me. The fresh, rain-scented air washed over me, filling my nose and throat, the contrast to the locked, air-filtered box I'd been stuck in stark and overwhelming. I stepped onto the door-step, then looked back.

I thought of Ethan, lying in the bed upstairs, and how completely he'd overtaken my senses, reminding me that nobody else had ever compared to him; that knowing him, sleeping with him a decade later was just torture, really, because he was even better – warmer and smarter and sexier – than he had been when I'd first fallen in love with him. I didn't have a hope of forgetting about him now, but I knew I had to try, for nobody's sake but my own.

'Goodbye,' I whispered. And then, because I couldn't help wondering if Sarah was still there, listening to the commands we were giving the house, manipulating everything, I said, 'Sparks, please look after Ethan for me.'

'I'm sorry,' the voice said blandly, 'I don't know who's speaking.'

Sarah had done what Ethan had asked. She'd reset

the system, and Sterenlenn didn't recognize me any more. Tears filled my eyes and I swiped at them, brushing them away before they could fall. Then I stumbled down the front path, away from the house and into the slowly emerging day.

Chapter Twenty-Eight

March 2013

It was a testament to how little I'd settled into university life that when I decided to quit halfway through the second term, I could get all my possessions in a large holdall and a slightly battered cardboard box. The journey from York to Alperwick was doable on the train, but it was extra-long, with delays and cramped carriages, wailing toddlers and an atmosphere of unbridled disgruntlement, and I ended up sweaty and frustrated long before the final connection that would take me into Cornwall.

I had made a couple of friends in my halls of residence, and when I told them what I was doing, they tried to talk me out of it, to give it until the end of the year at least. But I had already made up my mind, and I hadn't connected with them deeply enough to stay in touch once I was gone. I'd only met my assigned tutor three times, because I'd been flying under the radar since I got to York, so nothing felt like too much of a wrench as I filled in forms confirming the severing of my course and accommodation, stating blandly that my home situation had changed, and finalizing the return of most of my loan.

The spring sun was watery but determined as I got on the last train and leaned my forehead against the cool glass of the window, wishing I could block out the squabbling family sitting in the seats across the aisle. I tried to work out if I was feeling dread, resignation or relief at returning to my life in Alperwick, to Mum and our little terrace, but there was nothing but a bleak sort of flatness. It had been there since Ethan had walked away from me the morning after the prom, and had only intensified when I'd come home for my first Christmas break to discovered that the Sparks family had left Cornwall altogether.

I had sent emails to the *North Cornwall Star,* the *Western Tribune* and the *Alperwick Papers* when I'd decided to quit my course, hoping that they would see my decision as a sign of my dedication to Cornwall, a need to be back here, rather than a lack of sticking power. I needed to do something more than look after Mum, prove I could be productive and make something of myself, even if a journalism degree wasn't it – at least not right now. I knew from Freddy that Ethan was in Sheffield, that he'd got the grades he needed, but I hadn't heard from him at all.

I still hadn't got my head around how it had ended so suddenly between us.

After Ethan's visit the morning after prom night, my anger had faded almost instantly. I'd been sad, sorry for him and everything he'd been through, and even sadder that I hadn't been able to put my frustrations aside and support him when he'd needed me. I'd expected to hear from him, to at least get a message once the shock had faded and he'd had a chance to process what had happened. But it was Kira and Freddy who had filled me in, a couple of days later when I'd met them on the beach. Freddy was off to Spain the following day, and I hadn't planned to hang around long, wanting them to have some time to themselves, but Kira's sympathetic expression when I greeted them at the edge of the sand told me she knew what had happened.

'What a clusterfuck, eh?' she said, after we'd had a suncream-scented hug. 'I'm so sorry, Georgie.'

'I can't believe he did it,' I said. 'Although, actually, I can. He's always put Sarah first.'

'Yeah.' Freddy wrinkled his nose. 'Not easy for you, though. Especially now he's gone for the whole summer.'

'Did you get to say goodbye before he left?' Kira asked.

My mouth had gone dry. 'What do you mean?'

Kira and Freddy exchanged a glance. 'Oh babe,' she said quietly. 'Didn't he tell you?'

'Tell me what?' The day had blurred around me, seagulls and the crash of waves, the bustling and laughter of the busy, summertime bay fading as Kira and Freddy took turns to update me on the news that, apparently, they'd found out from Orwell. Ethan had told him and not me, and it felt like one more betrayal; proof that it was over between us.

The Sparks family were going to a remote part of Scotland for a *much-needed break*, according to Ethan's father. They would be there for the whole summer, a place where phone signal was almost non-existent, then Ethan would go straight to Sheffield University, if he got in – and I knew he would because, despite all the distractions, he had worked hard. It was looking like he'd escape the careless driving charge with a caution, everything neatly swept under the rug by his dad's lawyer because he'd taken the blame, and it had been his mum's car that had been taken.

So that was it.

I'd dismissed him after the prom, told him he wasn't who I thought he was, and there was no second chance, no opportunity to see him in person, apologize or take any of our angry words back. He was hundreds of miles away, and I hadn't even got a final hug.

I'd listened to my friends, trying to take it all in, then I'd made my excuses and hurried home, getting to my bedroom before I burst into tears.

After that, my summer was hollow. Kira went to London and Freddy was in Spain; as the days passed, I ignored the sunshine and the beach minutes from my house – something people waited all year to experience – and wrote in my room. I wrote letters to Connor from

Amelie, and bits of stories that had been crowding my thoughts. I wrote a whole notebook's worth of a love story about two people torn apart by the heroine's conniving cousin, and I didn't bother to change a whole lot because nobody else was going to read it.

Then I went to university and drifted through the first term. It was as if I was experiencing everything from behind a frosted screen, and when I came home at Christmas, it seemed as if Mum was getting worse again, and the Sparks family had moved away permanently. I should have kept going. I should have returned to my course and my boxy student room with renewed enthusiasm, but instead I'd limped on for a couple more months and now here I was, with all my stuff on the seat beside me, and Alperwick the only future I'd allowed myself.

The sun was a glowing red streak along a swiftly darkening horizon when I finally made it home, trudging from the station with my bag and my box, and the air was icy and bitter. The familiar landscape seemed worn, as if I was already tired of being back here, but the front room light was glowing around the edges of the curtains when I stopped outside our house, and I ferreted in my rucksack for my key. Before I found it, the door swung open, Mum standing on the other side.

She looked better than I had expected her to, in a red jumper that highlighted the pink tinge in her cheeks, her hair longer than it had been at Christmas, falling in light brown waves to her shoulders.

'Georgie!' It was a surprised bark. 'What are you doing here?'

'Hi, Mum.' She stared at me like I was a mirage of the Alperwick Mermaid instead of her daughter, so I clarified. 'I'm back.'

'For how long?' She reached out for my box but, even though my arm muscles were aching, I held onto it. She stepped back to let me in, and I dumped the box and holdall on the floor under the coat rack. I stood up straight and massaged my spine, letting a groan escape.

'Georgie, for *how long*?'

Our eyes caught in the hall mirror. 'My course wasn't working out,' I said, and watched as her shock morphed into something else. 'You need me here, Mum, and I—'

'I don't. I have never asked you to give up university to look after me. Not once.'

'You didn't need to ask.' I thought of all the times I'd skipped classes to go to her hospital appointments with her, or when she'd phoned the school office to check up on me because I hadn't replied to her messages soon enough. She might not have said the words, but I knew she needed me.

'So . . . what?' She folded her arms, not taking her eyes off me as I hung up my jacket. 'You've just quit everything? You're not going back at all?'

'I can reapply in a couple of years, or find a new course when things are more settled.'

'What does that mean?' Her laugh was incredulous. 'My MS isn't going away, but I'm managing it. I'm doing all I can, and what made me happy, what made me feel content and, if I'm honest, relieved, was that you were in York, getting on with your life. We've talked about this *so* often. I don't want you to be my full-time carer.'

'I'm not going to be. I'm going to get a job, and . . .' I glanced towards the living room, where a soap opera was playing on the TV. 'I just think it's better if my life is here right now.'

'I told you not to do this.'

I shrugged past her into the kitchen, taking a glass off the draining board and running the cold tap. 'I know you *said*—'

'I meant it, too. I don't want you here.'

'Thanks very much.' I gulped down the water, felt relief as it cooled my overheated body.

'You know what I mean.' Mum perched on the edge of the table. 'I know that, in the past, I've depended on you more than a mum should, and that I haven't always been there for you when you've needed me.'

'You've been there,' I said quietly.

'But I am fine,' she went on. 'I have a routine, and regular appointments. Helen helps out whenever I need it, and I have other friends I can rely on. The last thing I wanted was to clip your wings just as you'd started to spread them.' There was a pause, and I used it to study my scuffed trainers. 'Can you go back?'

I looked up. 'What? I . . . no.'

'You've cancelled your course, your accommodation – everything? Without talking to me first?'

'It's done, Mum.'

'Jesus Christ, Georgie! This is your *future*.'

'Exactly. I have to do what *I* think is right.'

Mum glared at me, and I thought that would be it, that I'd be able to slink off to my room and unpack slowly, thinking about my next move. But she wasn't finished. 'This is about Ethan, isn't it?'

'No, I . . .' I stalled. 'No, Mum.'

'Oh, love.' All the anger seeped out of her, and she got up and wrapped me in a hug. I resisted for a moment, but then I let her, surprised by how reassuring it was. Her tight arms around me felt fierce and dependable. 'You can't give up your whole life because you're sad about a boy.'

'I'm not.' I hugged her back. 'Things just weren't working out at uni, and there were . . . more reasons for me to be here right now.'

'OK,' she said calmly, and I braced myself, because that neutral tone was never a good sign. 'We can talk about this some more once you're settled.'

'There's no need, because—'

'But I want you to know that I think it's a mistake.' Mum planted a swift kiss on my cheek, then turned to the cupboards, taking out a saucepan and a tin of baked beans, flashing me a smile as she got out the grater. 'Beans on toast for tea?' she asked, as if I hadn't upended both our lives with this decision, by not telling her until it was a done deal and I was back on the doorstep. 'We can do something fancier tomorrow, now I know you'll be here.'

303

'Great,' I managed past the lump in my throat.

It was this: sliding back into our old ways, almost as if I had never gone to university in the first place, that made me really question what I was doing for the first time. But I'd done it, and there was no point crying about it. I was back in Alperwick, and I would just have to make the most of it, do whatever I could to make this part of my life count.

Chapter Twenty-Nine

Now

Alperwick was preening after the thunderstorm had washed it clean the night before. The sky was a deep, mesmerizing blue, and the biscuity slabs of Sterenlenn's front path glittered in the glow from the low-slung moon. The fresh scents of newly washed vegetation and the salty clean of the sea filled my nose as I tiptoed away from the entrance, and a couple of birds – robins or blackbirds – had begun to sing in anticipation of the dawn, their jaunty chorus soothing when I felt so defeated.

At the gates, I turned to look back. The house was magnificent, standing proudly against the sky. The windows were in darkness, but the porch light and spotlights along the path glowed gently, as if pointing the way to a magical kingdom. In some ways, it had been, and I had been fully caught up in the fairy tale.

I turned away, and for a horrible second thought the gates wouldn't let me out, but as I pulled on a green rung, the gate swung easily inwards, creating a gap that was big enough for me to slip through.

I took my time walking down the hill, my rucksack slung over one shoulder. I got my phone out and checked it, but it was completely out of battery, and wouldn't have helped me when the Wi-Fi came back on in the middle of the night. As I passed Barry Mulligan's house, I wondered if he ever peered through his telescope at this time of day; if he looked for cheese on the moon. But his windows were dark and still, and only a few lights shone further down in the village.

I walked past the turning to Spence's road, and wondered how I could possibly tell her about the night I'd just had, and which bits I was prepared to share with her. She would delight in all the drama, but right now I didn't have the energy for it. Something flickered in the back of my mind, a weak flare of connection, but I was too exhausted to grab hold of it. I kept going, reaching my quiet road, then let myself into my house, dumped my bag in the hall and went to make a cup of tea.

I leant against the counter while the kettle boiled, and couldn't help appraising the kitchen, trying to imagine what Ethan would have thought if he had knocked on my door. It was mostly the same as when I was growing up; I'd made hardly any changes since

Mum had left, unable to think of it as permanent when I knew she would be selling it. I was stuck between the past with her and the prospect of moving on, finding my own place.

I let out a long, slow breath. I'd been living in the same house I'd grown up in, using the same chipped crockery, and Ethan had reimagined, redesigned and then got a whole team to create Sterenlenn. He hadn't given up on his dream, despite what he'd had to sacrifice for Sarah. He'd done the courses and the training, he'd forgiven and then hired his sister, and he'd come back and transformed Tyller Klos into something remarkable. He hadn't let setbacks stop him, and he hadn't settled for second-best.

I had quit my degree before the end of the first year and returned home on the pretence of looking after Mum. I'd worked for the local paper, written stories and letters, but never tried to get any of my fiction published – or even shown it to anyone – since the competition at school. I'd gladly accepted Spence's offer of a job because it was easy, while telling myself I was closer to my dreams because she was the author I'd loved growing up. Now she was giving me the chance to write something with her, and I should have felt triumphant, but I thought of what Ethan had said, and wondered how much of it would really be mine: the publicity, the credit – the story itself.

I poured water on top of a teabag and added milk, then took it into the living room and sat on the edge of the sofa, remembering when Mum had found me the morning after prom night, after Ethan had walked out in the face of my silence.

She'd been sympathetic, rubbing my back while I cried, making me tea and a cheese toastie. When I'd finally run out of tears, she'd waited until I'd wiped my streaked face, and said, 'You don't always have to take the path of least resistance, you know.'

'What do you mean?' I'd asked, my voice thick.

'You don't have to accept things as they are, go with the flow. You can *make things happen*, Georgie. You're bright and kind and you know your own mind, and you don't always have to accept it when someone else tells you how it's going to be.'

I'd nodded and told her I understood, but then I'd waited for Ethan to contact me. A couple of days later he was in Scotland, far away, and the fact that he didn't try and get in touch told me he'd already started to move on.

It wasn't until I was in York, trying and failing to embrace everything that was so unfamiliar, that I found out through Freddy that Ethan had got the grades he needed – of course – and was in Sheffield. I sent him a congratulatory text, but it bounced back and I realized he must have got a new phone: a new number for a new start. He didn't use Facebook much but he had a profile, and I could have got in touch with him that way, but I was stung that he hadn't contacted me at all, so instead I set my sights on that first Christmas holiday. I would go home and see Ethan in person, not try and repair all the damage I'd done with a DM.

I'd driven myself mad thinking about the girls he would be meeting in Sheffield, aspiring architects like him, engineers and mathematicians who didn't write stories about mermaids. But I'd held out hope, and felt almost as if Santa was still real, I was so giddy with anticipation that December. I bought Ethan a beautiful stone model of one of the old, higgledy-piggledy buildings along the Shambles in York, wrapped it carefully and nestled it inside a gift box, tied with a crimson bow. I wanted to apologize for my reaction the morning after prom night, for dismissing him so quickly, and ask him to give me a second chance. I had realized that he was the most important thing in my life.

I sipped my rapidly cooling tea, remembering the day I'd lugged my bag off the train at Alperwick station that December, and – before I'd even made it home to Mum – bumped into Orwell, who'd told me the Sparks family were gone for good. I had been devastated, furious at the gleam in his eye, his obvious satisfaction at knowing something I didn't, and when he'd tried to comfort me, I'd pushed him away and hurried home, my bag bouncing painfully against my hip, all my Christmas spirit gone.

Ethan and I had fizzled out, and I knew it was a lack of bravery on my part, not telling him how much I loved him and wanted to make it work. But, even then, I hadn't messaged him on Facebook, had accepted it when Orwell told me he didn't have Ethan's new number, even though that was probably a lie. I'd been

309

resigned to my heartbreak, and then, only a couple of months later, I'd told myself that Mum couldn't cope without me and so had come home for good, deciding that university wasn't for me.

'The path of least resistance,' I whispered, the mug cool between my palms.

It was, I realized, what I'd always done. I'd accepted things, hadn't fought for them, and yet I'd been mad at Ethan when he'd walked away from me the morning after prom instead of staying to try and fix us. At least he'd gone on to do what he'd always intended. And what was I doing? Feeling grateful that an author in her eighties who hadn't published anything for thirty years was offering me the chance to write a new book with her? The truth was, I would still be her PA. I would do the leg work and the research, and maybe she would ask what I thought of her chapters, but it wouldn't ever be *my* book.

I finished my cold tea and went upstairs to get changed. My gaze was drawn to the neat row of Cornish Sands paperbacks on the shelf above my cluttered desk. They weren't fancy editions, and the spines were cracked where I'd read them over and over.

I picked up *The Whispers of the Sands*, thinking how much the names Connor and Amelie had come to mean to me. I remembered something Ethan had said last night, when I'd told him about Spence, and her insistence that I see inside Sterenlenn for the new book. *Couldn't you just have created that, though? I know it was an important part of the series, but it's still fiction.*

Why had she needed me to see it? If it was just curiosity about what her old house had become, she could have got a car, a driver, someone to give her a proper tour, while she waxed lyrical about accessibility, making enough fuss that everyone, Ethan included, would have done whatever she asked. But she hadn't wanted to go herself: she had wanted *me* to go. She'd said we needed to recreate the modern house in the new book. But we didn't – we could have turned Tyller Klos into anything we'd wanted, because it was fiction. And, as Ethan had said, there were already shiny, professional photographs for her to pore over.

There was something else to all this, something Spence had been keeping from me from the beginning.

I threw on a pair of jeans and a clean T-shirt, tied my hair up into a messy ponytail since I'd slept on it wet, and shoved my feet into trainers. I had a whole lot of thinking to do, but I couldn't start doing it until I knew what was really going on.

Chapter Thirty

Now

I had a key to Spence's house, but it was still only early, and for a few moments I hovered on the doorstep wondering what to do, trying to ignore the fact that if I turned around I would be able to see up to the top of the cliff, to Sterenlenn bathed in the golden light of dawn. It was still too early for the trains to be running, and I wondered if Ethan had found some other way of getting home, or if he was still lying peacefully asleep in the huge bed, or if he'd discovered I'd left. I tried to ignore the niggling internal voice that said walking away from him after I'd discovered his messages with Sarah was yet again the path of least resistance. It felt like history was repeating itself, and I couldn't cope with that. What I needed to do was find out exactly what had been going on with Spence.

I took her house key out of my rucksack and unlocked the door.

'Hello?' I called softly as it swung inwards. Spence was usually an early riser, but this might be *too* early even for her. The corridor was thick with the vanilla scent of her air diffusers, and I called out again as I rounded the corner into the living room. 'Jesus!' I jumped. It had felt so quiet, so still, that I hadn't expected her to be here. 'Hey.'

'Georgie.' She was sitting in her chair, a cup of coffee resting in her lap. 'You're back.'

'Of course I am. The open house was last night.'

She sipped her drink and I scrutinized her, wondering if my slowly developing hypothesis could be close to the truth, or if it was just the madness of having everything turned on its head in less than a day.

'There's coffee in the pot.' She gestured to the kitchen, and I poured myself a cup, adding a generous slug of milk because she always made it strong enough to stand the spoon up in. She hadn't bombarded me with questions the moment I walked in, which was what I had expected after sending me on a mission like that. I was sure, now, that there was something more going on than the simple plan we'd hatched.

I sat on the sofa opposite her. Outside, the sea was the colour of forget-me-nots, the early morning sun dancing across it. There was little evidence of the previous night's storm, apart from the raindrops clinging to Spence's immaculate front lawn and making it shimmer.

313

'The event finished on time, did it?' Spence asked.

'For most people.'

She raised an eyebrow.

I took a deep breath. 'For other people it turned into the world's most ridiculous escape room, because Ethan's Smart system malfunctioned and we got trapped inside.'

'Goodness! I hope you weren't stuck for too long.'

I briefly closed my eyes at her less than Oscar-worthy performance. 'Only about half an hour,' I said, and caught her quick-as-lightning frown. I put my coffee on the floor. 'You knew about it. You knew the house was going to go wrong, and that Ethan and I would be trapped. How did you know?'

Spence smoothed down the skirt of her bottle-green dress. 'You do remember that I was famous for creating love stories? And unlikely ones at that.'

'Of course,' I snapped. 'We've spent hours talking about your books, about how we're going to reunite the characters you let escape.'

Spence nodded. 'But what if I found a more deserving couple? Another pair of lovers destined for each other, who had been torn apart at the worst possible moment?'

I stared at her. 'But . . .'

'It was obvious as soon as you started working for me, as soon as you mentioned his name, that Ethan was the love of your life. Never mind Rick in the Sailor's Rest – Ethan was the man you were supposed to be with.'

'We weren't *torn apart*.'

'No? From what you've told me, your families made it impossible for you to be together. His, mostly.'

I thought of the Sparkses' trip to Scotland, how his dad had put Ethan beyond my reach for the whole of that summer. 'Mum loved him.'

'But she was over-protective of you. She'd been hurt, abandoned by a man when she was young, and she didn't want the same to happen to you.'

'Right, but with Ethan, we could have made more of an effort – we could have stayed in touch; used Facebook or email – I could have messaged and asked for his new number. But I was banking on him being here that first Christmas, then, when he wasn't, contacting him when he hadn't reached out to me felt like . . .' *the path of least resistance*, the voice in my head finished for me.

'You thought you didn't deserve him?' Spence said.

'No! That wasn't it at all.' I wasn't sure how convincing I sounded. 'Anyway, never mind why we broke up. I want to know what you had to do with last night, because not all of it was fun, and I need to know exactly how many people conspired to put me in that situation. Was it just Sarah? You and Sarah? All *three* of you?'

'Oh tosh.' Spence waved a hand. 'Ethan had nothing to do with it. Sarah and I simply altered the system to suit our purposes.'

I reached down to pick up my mug, and realized my hand was shaking. 'So it was you, too? It wasn't just Sarah?' On some level I had already known that, and my hurt mingled with the relief that, according to Spence, Ethan hadn't been involved.

'I saw a golden opportunity, but I needed a little help to turn my plot into reality.'

I rubbed my forehead. 'I'm fairly certain I'm about to be incredibly angry with you, but could you explain exactly what happened, and I can decide just how angry I'm going to be?'

Spence laughed, and I already knew "incredibly angry" might not cut it.

'Of course.' Her eyes were bright. 'But I hope you understand that this wouldn't have happened if you'd questioned my plan. You agreed that we needed intimate knowledge of the new house for Amelie and Connor's resurrection. You didn't bat an eyelid.'

'I had my own reasons for going last night,' I said, a slow shame creeping over me that I hadn't thought more about her motivation. I'd said two words to Ethan and he'd challenged it, but me? I'd just nodded along, as usual. Spence was looking at me curiously. 'That's not important now,' I said. 'Tell me what happened.'

'Certainly.' She cleared her throat, as if she was preparing to give an after-dinner speech at a grand gala somewhere. 'A couple of years ago, I got the planning notice through the letterbox for Alperwick House – Tyller Klos, as you insist on calling it.'

Not any more, I thought but didn't say. 'The whole village did,' I said instead. 'We've known about the renovation for a long time.'

'Yes, but I was particularly curious. It was a house I'd lived in for years, and I wanted to know what they were proposing for its new chapter. I called someone at the firm to talk through the details of the application and find out who would be transforming it.'

'The planning team at the council?'

'I called them first and asked them to put me in touch with the build team: the firm that was going to be responsible. They were reluctant to begin with, but I can be persuasive as you know, and eventually they gave me the details. I phoned, and spoke to a lovely young woman called Sarah.'

I pressed my lips together, gesturing for her to go on.

'I explained who I was and why I was interested, and she was very receptive. She told me that she'd known about the house, had lived in Alperwick for six months, and that her brother had even spent some nights there with his friends, during the time it had been abandoned. I listened to a sad story about how unhappy she'd been, how she'd turned into a teenage tearaway. Her older brother had always looked out for her, kept her on course when she was so close to veering off into the weeds. How, without his sacrifices, she wouldn't have had the chance to turn things around. She told me that, once he'd established his architectural practice, he'd brought her on board to work with him, using her skills in digital security and monitoring systems to create a new Smart system.'

I gulped my coffee for something to do. 'Ethan's sister.'

'Of course,' Spence said smugly. 'And it wasn't that long into her story that I realized I'd heard echoes of something similar, but from a different perspective. You'd recently started working for me, and it honestly felt like this was fate, destiny – whatever you want to call it. I had my own admission for Sarah, about my dedicated PA and what she'd been through.'

'Oh my God.'

'And you know,' Spence continued gleefully, ignoring my horror, 'Sarah is a spirited thing, and she still clearly has an adventurous streak, despite her dedication to her job. We stayed in touch during the build, she gave me titbits of information – though of course she didn't want to betray her brother's trust by telling me *too* much. Then, when it was close to completion, I asked about the Sparks system and what it was capable of, and she said there were ways it could be manipulated – not wholesale, but as a one-off while it was still in Beta mode, because she'd had a hand in engineering it. She told me she could personally tap into the mainframe, hear and respond to any Sparks requests, overriding the automatic process.'

'You set the whole thing up?' My voice was a scratch.

'I asked her about Ethan, and about you. Sarah said that he'd never got over you, and that she felt partly responsible for you splitting up. I offered her a chance to redeem herself.'

'All those little asides,' I murmured. 'The things the house said that made no sense, that seemed more human than algorithm. She *was* listening.'

'She could only respond to requests,' Spence said firmly. 'She assured me she couldn't listen to everything – that the system doesn't work like that – and, considering this involved her brother, I'm confident she was telling the truth.'

'I played right into her hands. I was the one who said it was an emergency, but she would have found some other way to lock us inside, to activate Panic Room Mode. She was always going to do that.'

'Forced proximity romances are very popular these days,' Spence said, and I couldn't get over how she didn't seem to have even a glimmer of remorse.

'You thought you could trap us in the house together, and it would turn into some kind of magical love story for the ages?'

'It didn't?'

'Do you see Ethan anywhere? Is he here right now, holding my hand and staring adoringly into my eyes?' I flung my arms wide. I felt exhausted all of a sudden.

'So what happened? Sarah and I were sure that you only needed to see each other again, that the love was still there, for both of you.'

'You were *that* certain?' I sat up straight. 'Even though all you know is what I've told you, and you've never even met him? You were sure we'd perform the way you wanted us to? We're not your characters, Spence.'

'Georgie, come on.' Her tone was mollifying. 'A beautiful clifftop house he'd created, partly with you in mind. A secret you've been keeping that made convincing you to go back there easier than I'd expected – though I still don't know what that is – and a chance for the two of you to be together, with absolutely no distractions. It's the perfect plot.'

Spence had always followed her own path, but I still couldn't believe her audacity or the assumptions she'd made, and that she'd thought it was perfectly OK to ask Sarah to mess with the Sparks system for Ethan's crucial event. I felt a twinge of guilt, because when I'd seen the messages on Ethan's phone, I'd thought that it was all her – or her and Ethan, conspiring against me. But Spence was the driving force, and I knew all too well how persuasive she could be. Sarah *had* changed, she'd got her shit together – I'd seen the results at the open house – but she had still been lured by Spence into breaking the rules.

'You didn't bank on a whole lot of messy emotions,' I said quietly. 'On people not being quite as predictable as you expected. On you not being the only one making assumptions.'

For the first time, she looked unsure. 'You really can't work it out?'

I shrugged. I didn't want to feed her any more information. 'I need to go.'

'You've only just got here.'

'Yes, to discover that the crazy night I just spent with my ex and a psycho Smart system was all down to you. It's not exactly the matchmaking approach I'd expect from a friend.'

'You're lucky you have a creative friend, then.'

I stood up. 'You don't get it, do you? I'm not a damsel in distress for you to manipulate. I'm a real person and this is my real life – these are *our* lives, mine and Ethan's. You think it's fine to toy with us, to move us where you want us, but you never stop to think, do you? You don't think about what it feels like to be trapped in a place—'

'I very much do,' she said firmly, but I kept going.

'And you can't imagine how it feels to be offered something *so* great, something potentially life-changing, like writing a book with your favourite author, only to realize it's her way of keeping you in check.'

Spence's gaze sharpened. 'That's a genuine offer. We were always going to write it together. My motives for getting you to the house might have been a little more complicated, but—'

'And what else will be complicated? When there's a discussion about the payment, or my name on the cover, or any kind of genuine recognition? What compromises will I have to make? What will be just a little *too* unorthodox for a publisher once I've put in all the hard work and the book is written?'

'I would never hurt you.'

'Not intentionally, but you're blinkered as to how I might get hurt inadvertently. Like putting me in a house with Ethan, making me realize what I've lost, and that . . .' I took a gulping breath, surprised by how close my tears were to the surface. 'I thought I'd moved on, but now I'm right back where I was, and it's all still out of my reach.'

Spence's expression softened. 'Oh, my dear.'

'I need to go. I can't do this now.'

She was frozen for just a second, caught in imaginary headlights, but then she smiled. 'I understand that this has been a shock, but I do have some correspondence to get done today, so I really don't think you can shoot off just yet.'

'I'm sorry.' I took our mugs to the kitchen, rinsed mine in the sink and topped hers up, then returned it to her side table because I couldn't completely abandon my duties. 'I've got other things to do this morning.'

'Other things like what?' Spence sounded curious rather than irritated.

'I need to follow up on some letters of my own,' I told her. 'And these ones are really urgent, because they've stayed unanswered for a very long time.'

I left her sitting in her chair with her fresh cup of coffee, and walked down her vanilla-scented hallway to the front door, where Alperwick and its bright summer sunshine were waiting for me.

Chapter Thirty-One

Now

I realized, once I'd flounced out of Spence's house, being overdramatic in a way I knew she would appreciate, that I only had a vague plan. I was about to do something daunting, something that meant ignoring the clamouring voice that was demanding I go back up to Sterenlenn and see if Ethan was still there. I was sure Spence was telling the truth, that he had nothing to do with us getting locked in together, but I also realized that seeing him again now would be the path of least resistance. I was treading water, and so many of the things I needed to sort out didn't involve him at all.

In the messages to Sarah, he'd said that he was getting the first train back to Bristol, but would he still do that when he discovered I was gone? I was split down the middle, desperate to see him again but also to have space from him, to work through everything and consider what I wanted. I imagined getting home and finding him waiting outside for me. I knew I would invite him in without thinking about it, without stopping to remind myself that it couldn't work for us long-term if we were flinging ourselves at each other and pretending the last decade hadn't happened.

So I didn't go home. I went to my branch of the *North Cornwall Star* office, which was actually a little café I had adopted, because the view was much more inspiring than the one from the limited workspace the *Star* had. The café was tucked away on the opposite side of Alperwick Bay to Sterenlenn, located in an old Victorian house, and was run by Nick and his sister Molly. They had converted the ground floor into a cosy tearoom, where they did the biggest, stickiest cinnamon buns.

'All right, Georgie?' Nick asked, giving me a warm smile. He already had flour dusted down his canvas apron, even though he had only just opened for the morning.

'I'm good thanks, how are you?'

'Can't complain, especially not with this weather. But this is a bit early for you, isn't it?' He had a stack of laminated menus and was putting them on the tables, giving each one a quick wipe down.

'I've got a lot on my mind.' I tapped my temple, then felt ridiculous. 'Thought I'd get ahead while it's quiet.'

'Coffee and a cinnamon bun to help you work?'

'Yes please.'

Nick saluted me and disappeared, and I sat at my favourite table in the window. It had views over two roads-worth of rooftops and then the sea, which was azure and glittering as the June sun rose up to shine on it. I hadn't gone home after seeing Spence, so I didn't have my laptop, but I got out my notebook and opened it to the next clean page. The previous one had scribbled notes about the plan to visit the house, which I'd written days before I knew it was Ethan's. My handwriting was messy, because I'd been eager to please Spence, to go after the carrot she was dangling in front of me. Now, as I looked out of the window at a couple of men in shiny wetsuits jogging along the sand, brightly coloured surfboards under their arms, I saw it all differently.

I hesitated, wondering what my title should be, then I just wrote *List*.

One, speak to Mum about the house. Pay rent, decorate, make it my own.

Two, speak to Wynn at the Star. What do I want to write? Go to her with ideas, don't just wait for the next cow disaster.

Three, Spence's book. What shall I do?

Four, <u>MY BOOK</u>. Gather up scribbles, turn them into a plot.

Five, Ethan??

I sat back, chewing the end of my biro. Walking away from the house, I had realized that the letters I'd written, back when I'd given up on university and returned to the village, were a catalogue of everything I didn't like about my life: work; living with Mum; the fact that I wasn't writing; some of the decisions I'd made. I'd focused all my sadness on not being with Ethan, but he wasn't the problem. I needed to understand all the ways I'd been stalling, everything I'd failed to do that I'd blamed on my doomed teenage love story.

'New article idea?' Nick put my coffee and bun down, the scent of cinnamon sugar making my stomach rumble. I hadn't had anything to eat since yesterday lunchtime, apart from a few style-over-substance canapés, and I was ravenous.

'New life idea,' I said with a smile, and Nick laughed and went back to the kitchen, where a local radio station was playing Noughties hits.

I pulled at the doughy, delicious pastry of my cinnamon bun, unravelling the curl. There was a flash outside and I looked up, realizing it was the sun hitting Sterenlenn's glass on the other side of the bay. From here it was a gleaming toy house, shimmering and impossible, and my breath hitched as I thought about Ethan waking up in that huge bed, discovering he was alone. Was he already on his way back to Sarah? I turned my gaze to the surfers, and then, when I'd finished eating, to my list.

The least daunting task was number two. Speaking to Wynn would be easy, because she always wanted me to push myself, and as much as the paper was being squeezed out by online news sites and social media, she cared about providing the residents of North Cornwall with high-quality information and entertainment.

I chewed my pen, icing sugar transferring from my lips to the tip, and felt the crack of the casing vibrate through my teeth. 'Fuck.' I reached into my rucksack for a new pen and my fingers found something weighty and familiar, wrapped in a soft velvet bag. I took out my silver mermaid and put her on the table, on a tile coaster with a painting of a robin on it.

All these years I had been sure she'd been sent to me by the Mythological Society, when really it was Ethan. He'd seen my piece, how Wynn had published my short story alongside it, and he'd wanted to mark the occasion, albeit anonymously. Now, with distance from him and the house, all his revelations were sinking in: how often he'd been thinking about me in the years we were apart.

I smoothed my hand down the mermaid's back, along her shimmering scales. He was worried about my article, what I would say about the open house, and the impact it would have on his career. It was a good story, great gossip for the village: the clifftop house, shiny and fresh, ready to be sold to new owners who could gaze down on Alperwick like royalty. Did they need to know about the lock-in? There were so many details I didn't want to share, but I was a writer. I could be creative.

I turned to a new page and wrote: *A Night in Sterenlenn*. I started scribbling, the words flowing out of my brain and onto the paper through my cracked biro. Occasionally I remembered to have a sip of coffee.

If you were invited to the lifestyle event of the year, the grand launch of an architectural masterpiece and the transformation of Alperwick's most notorious house from abandoned relic to gleaming modern mansion, would you go? The answer, I was quick to realize when I got such an invitation, was yes. (It was good that this was partly a work of fiction, because I hadn't been invited, I'd gone because Spence had told me to. I thought of lovely Aldo's warm, guileless welcome, and smiled.) *I was lucky enough to be one of the first people to see what had become of S. E. Artemis's old house. Transformed into Tyller Klos in her bestselling Cornish Sands series, now it is Sterenlenn, with a brand-new façade, interior, and future, as well as a new name.*

It has been reimagined by up-and-coming architect Ethan Sparks and, as a beautifully appointed luxury house, it hits all the right notes. It is spacious and welcoming, shimmering and soft. He's made the most of the house's enviable position on the cliffs above Alperwick, the views of the sea and sky, the twinkling lights of the village. It's as if he's giving the house to its surroundings, rather than focusing on seclusion and exclusivity. I was enthralled by it, and I'll never forget the few hours I got to spend there.

But Sterenlenn has a hidden magic too: the Sparks system, a comprehensive, ambitious application that turned it into the smartest of Smart homes. Everything can be controlled by wall panels, voice activation and the elegant app: the heating and lights, the sound system and security; the massage table; the tint-level of the windows. Fall sleepily onto the beds and your bedside lamp comes on automatically; ask for a specific song to be played and the music washes over you, the bass rumbling in your bones as you walk into the sleek study. There are, I'm sure, other tricks I didn't have time to discover, but this is just the first building with Sparks installed, and the possibilities are endless. (An old man who had been flicking through *The Times* at the next table was giving me a curious look, and I realized I was grinning.)

As I took in each exquisite space, trailing my fingertips across the textured wallpaper and velvet cushions, gleaming handrails and cool tiles; as I discovered the greens and blues of the coastline had been threaded throughout the design, and heard the clunk of a door locked securely into place by someone saying a few words, I let my imagination run away with me.

The Sparks system has been tested for thousands of hours by the hard-working team who conceived it, and on my visit nothing was left to chance, but

– in my writer's mind – I conjured up a scenario where, instead of being trapped outside (something we can all identify with because, let's face it, this house is a one-off), what if you were trapped inside? What if you got to luxuriate in Sterenlenn for a night, enjoy everything it had to offer, because the Smart system you were relying on malfunctioned and you physically couldn't leave? We all know AI is going to take over soon, so let's indulge in some positive repercussions of that before Arnie comes to seal our fate.

So. This is my fantasy: what it would be like to spend a night trapped in Sterenlenn.

By the time I'd finished my draft, my hand was aching and lunchtime had been and gone. Nick had kept me fuelled with coffee, and I ordered a chicken and bacon sandwich and ate it slowly, looking out over Alperwick Bay, now teeming with locals and holidaymakers in the summer sunshine. I felt strangely satisfied, getting out a version of the previous night that was at least close to the truth, though in my imagined piece the two captors hadn't had inside knowledge of the Sparks system, and they certainly hadn't ended up testing out the master bed together.

I didn't know if Wynn would want my hybrid of fact and fiction, but I thought it spoke to everyone's desire to see how the other half lived, and if someone had told me that I'd get trapped in a dream house with a man I loved, it would have sounded pretty amazing.

The reality had been a lot more complicated, but that wasn't what readers of the *Star* wanted to hear.

My ten-minute walk home felt like a trudge through wet sand, my lack of sleep catching up with me. My house looked the same, with no gorgeously dishevelled architect leaning against the front door, disgruntled that I'd made him wait but elated that I was finally here. I sighed. Walking away from him had been the right thing to do, but it didn't feel great right now.

I unlocked the door, intent on charging my phone because it had been dead for hours now, when my foot skidded on something on the mat. I pulled the folded piece of paper out from under my trainer and opened it, reading the few words that were written there in handwriting I recognized:

Georgie. I woke up and you were gone, and now you're not here. Please call me. E x.

He'd put his mobile number at the end, giving me a direct line to him, and it took all my willpower not to stand over my phone until it had a hint of juice and then do as he'd asked. Instead, I made a cup of tea and took his note to my room, then stripped and got in the shower, pushing away the memories of a cubicle that was five times the size of this one, a rainfall spray that was hot in seconds, disco lights and speakers, and Ethan walking towards me, joining me under the water, bending his head to meet mine.

Chapter Thirty-Two

Now

The next couple of days were ceaselessly bright, the sun refusing to break its hold even as the humidity rose again, and I used it to keep me on course: if the sun could keep shining, then I could keep going, too.

I redrafted my article and sent it to Wynn, and she said she would publish it in Saturday's edition – a week after I'd emerged from the open house event. She used words like *inspired* and *hilarious* and asked me what was next, and I felt validated and hopeful. I prayed that Ethan, if he was still keeping tabs on me, wouldn't mind that I'd twisted the facts to protect him. I kept his number inside a notebook on my desk, and was astounded that I'd had enough willpower not to tap the numbers into my phone, even though I was painfully aware that it was there. My resolve was always at its lowest when I was talking to my best friend.

'You have to call him,' Kira screeched when I finally phoned and told her everything, two days after Sterenlenn. I could hear her son, Barnaby, cooing in the background, Freddie chattering to him and then trying to get in on our conversation when Kira over-excitedly gave him the highlights.

'I have too much to sort out first,' I said firmly.

'What, though?' Kira sounded indignant. She had always loved me and Ethan together, had perhaps seen him as my saviour in the same way I had until recently. But I needed to be my own saviour, and I told her that.

'I've got to speak to Mum about the house, so I actually feel like I can live here; that I'm not just squatting until she decides to sell it. I have to work out what to do about Spence's book, and—'

'Ethan's right about that,' Kira cut in. 'You're good enough to write something original. I know Spence makes you go all starry-eyed, but she's only in it for herself.'

'I think she's in it for Amelie and Connor,' I said carefully. 'She wants to bring them back together.'

'Does she, or does she know that's what *you* want? Is it her way of keeping you interested?'

'Interested in what, though?' I laughed. 'She wouldn't be asking me to write a book with her if she didn't care about it.'

'Or she knows you're destined for greater things than

sorting out her fan letters, and doesn't want to lose you. She set you up to get trapped in a house with your ex because she thought it would be a fun thing to do. And *we* both know Ethan's the best guy, but she didn't know anything about him other than what you and Sarah told her. She could have been trapping you in there with a monster, not to mention all the things you and Ethan were worried about – one of you getting hurt, a fire starting. It was a shit, *dangerous* thing to do, and she did it because she sees you as her plaything.' Kira took a deep breath. 'Sorry. I get worked up.'

'No, that's OK.' I rubbed my stomach, which was tight with anxiety, because what she said made a lot of sense. I didn't think Spence was malicious, but it wasn't hard to imagine her conjuring up schemes because they entertained her, and telling herself there were no risks simply because she didn't want there to be. 'It was a shitty thing to do.'

'And Sarah.' Kira clucked. 'Who would have thought?'

'Yeah.' I picked at a thread on my shorts. 'It was one of the biggest surprises. But Spence got her claws into her, and she's going to get enough of a bollocking from Ethan because of what she did.' I swallowed. 'She will have had it by now.'

'So next, you're going to call him.' Kira said it like we'd already agreed to it.

I closed my eyes. 'I'm not ready.'

When Ethan told me he'd found my letters, I asked

him if he'd ever thought of coming to see me. He'd admitted that he'd wanted to, but as well as fearing the reaction he might get, he wanted to have achieved something that mattered – to have something to show me. I felt the same way. I couldn't call him yet.

Kira's growl was low and exasperated, and I heard Barnaby trying to copy it in the background, then he and Freddy descending into fits of giggles. 'I'm going to nudge you every day,' Kira said, ignoring them. 'I'll be like one of those annoying motivational apps, only my sayings will all be about reconnecting with the man you love. You . . .' she lowered her voice, and I could hear her breathing up against the microphone, '. . . you slept with him, and it was better than all your rose-tinted memories. Understandable, because you're both adults now, and eighteen-year-olds think they know everything when they know nothing, but it wasn't like tinned ravioli, was it?'

'What?' I said with a laugh.

'I used to love tinned ravioli when I was little, and somehow it came up in conversation, so we got a tin last week, and it was disgusting. The meat was like cat food. All those memories, destroyed.' She made a shuddering sound. 'Ethan was the opposite of that, you said.'

'I made no references to tinned ravioli *or* cat food, but . . . yeah.' My whole body heated just thinking about it. 'It was . . .' I swallowed. 'It was the best sex I've ever had.'

'There you go, then.' Kira sounded smug, as if that

335

was her closing argument. 'It's because you still love each other. You *have* to call him. I will pester you until you do. End of.'

'Understood,' I said, and we changed the subject, spoke for an hour about other things and then said goodbye. I didn't call Ethan.

I hadn't intended to fix items one and three on my list on the same day, but – after nearly a week of not seeing Spence, telling her I needed time to myself (which she could hardly quibble with after what she'd done) – I relented, agreeing to help her with the fan mail replies that had built up in my absence. I couldn't put off the conversation for ever, and I would feel better once I'd done it.

Mum called me as I was walking to her bungalow, my dress sticking to my back even though it was only nine in the morning.

'Hey, Mum,' I puffed. 'How are you and Dane?'

'We're dandy,' she said. 'We're going on a steamer trip on Ullswater in a bit. Taking a picnic.'

'That's . . . so great.' It *was* great that she was generally so much better, that the clinical trial she'd started while I was doing my A-levels, fretting about her smoking weed, had eventually reduced some of her symptoms, and that her quality of life had improved. I thought it was partly to do with her being happy, finding Dane, though I wasn't about to tell her that because, one, she would accuse me of going all woo-woo, and two, as much as she loved Dane, she wouldn't want to give credit to a man for turning her life around. 'It sounds like a lovely day.'

'What about you, love? How are you getting on?' I hadn't told her about Sterenlenn or Ethan, and I didn't know if I wanted her take on it while it was still so fresh in my mind.

I leaned against a garden wall. 'Things are picking up at the *Star*. I've got a chance to be a bit more creative, which is good, and . . . Mum?'

'Yes, Georgie?'

'About the house.' I pushed my shoulders back which, according to a podcast I'd listened to, would make me sound more confident. 'I want to stay in it.'

'You can, love, until I'm ready to sell.'

I huffed out a breath. 'I'd really like to stay in it for the next year. That'll give me a deadline I can work towards, for getting my own place. I feel like a short-term tenant, waiting for you to boot me out, so I'd like to stay there and pay you rent, make it official. I need it to be my home, and right now it isn't.'

My words were met with silence, and I winced, pushing off the wall when an old lady glared at me from the window of her house.

'Mum?' I said eventually.

'I didn't realize you felt like that.' I heard her exhale, long and slow. 'I had never . . . of course you can stay. I'd like to sell up eventually, but I wouldn't kick you out. I only mentioned it because I thought you wanted your own place anyway: you don't want to live in our tatty old terrace for ever. I'm sorry, love. It's yours, and there's no need to pay rent. Use the money to save up for somewhere new, wherever you want to go.'

I gazed at the deep blue of the water in the bay and the seagulls circling, the golden sand and the owner of the ice-cream hut raising his lime green awning, getting ready for another busy day. I'd been so desperate to leave Alperwick, but I was beginning to wonder why I'd ever wanted to. 'Thanks, Mum. That means a lot. I'm . . . going to make some changes, if that's OK?'

'You haven't done that already? You're still in the back bedroom?' She sounded incredulous. 'Take the front room, get yourself a new mattress, put a desk under the window. Christ, Georgie. I'll put some money in your account.'

'No, Mum, you don't—'

'I have to go or we'll miss our boat. Love you lots, G. Have fun.' She hung up and I was left staring at my phone, delighted, but also angry with myself for not speaking to her sooner. My mind whirred with all the possibilities; how it would feel to wake up to sunlight coming in through the bay window, the slice of sea visible above the rooftops. Or maybe I'd stay in the back bedroom and turn the master into an office. I couldn't stretch to mermaid wallpaper or tinted Smart glass, but that didn't mean I couldn't make more affordable changes. I could do it, even without Ethan's expertise to guide me.

'I don't want to write your book with you,' I said an hour later, while I diligently folded up Spence's handwritten letters and slid them into thick, cream envelopes. Despite how things had gone with Mum, my confidence had wavered as soon as I'd seen Spence, because she was acting like nothing had happened; like she hadn't executed a plan that had left me trapped in her old house with Ethan, and still didn't realize the emotional upheaval it had caused. But my irritation had been steadily growing in the face of her breezy attitude, so as I sealed envelope fifteen I blurted it out.

'What do you mean?' Spence signed her name with a flourish at the bottom of another letter.

'I mean that I don't want to resurrect Amelie and Connor with you.'

She looked up, shocked. 'But it's all we've talked about. What about all the preparation we've put in – your jaunt to the open house?'

'Jaunt?' I shook my head. 'We need to get it out in the open that my *jaunt* had nothing to do with Amelie and Connor. You wanted to see what would happen if I was locked in there with Ethan, and I . . . had my own reasons.'

'Which I'm still none the wiser about.'

'Good.' I went back to folding and sliding and sticking.

Spence laughed. 'You don't want to write a new Cornish Sands book with me, then?'

I swallowed. Those two words did something to me: my adoration of her series had created some kind of Pavlovian response. 'I'm going to write something of my own,' I said, my voice only wavering slightly. 'Something that's entirely my idea.'

Spence didn't say anything for a long time, and eventually I looked over at her, sitting in her armchair, her portable leather writing desk perched across the armrests. 'You're certainly good enough, Georgie,' she said.

I scoffed. 'How do you know that?'

'You think I wanted any old journalist to be my PA? That I didn't read your articles, do my research first? Your editor published your short story about the mermaid.'

'I wrote that when I was eighteen.'

'Yes, but all your pieces have energy, a narrative, even if it's only an account of the Alperwick Flower Festival. A writer can spot another talented writer a mile off, and you've got it.' She tapped her fountain pen against the leather surface. 'You really don't want to help me with Amelie and Connor?'

I thought of all the letters I'd written under the guise of her star-crossed lovers. 'I've spent enough time with other people's characters. I need to focus on my own.'

She nodded, though her eyes were bright with something that wasn't mischief, and she looked her age, suddenly; frail and small. I wavered, but I knew I had to do this.

'I'm so touched by your offer, Spence, and I'll still be your PA if you want me. I'll help you bring Connor and Amelie the happy ending they deserve in any way I can – research and emails; whatever other support you need – but I don't want to write it with you. It's time I wrote something that is wholly mine.'

Spence took out another piece of notepaper, lying it precisely on the board in front of her, and I held my breath. She looked up at me, her lips twitching in that familiar way. 'That, Georgie, is a perfect solution. Because I can't do without you, you know. I pretend I can, but I rely on you.'

I rolled my eyes. 'No you don't. You have Denise.'

'Denise can't fold a letter like you can: she has fat fingers.'

'Spence!'

'I'm serious. You can't walk out of my life now.'

'OK.' I turned properly to face her, folding my arms. 'I won't walk out, but you can't do *anything* else to me. You can't manipulate me or trick me or plan anything behind my back, and you have to leave me to do what I need to do.'

She raised an eyebrow. 'With Ethan?'

Warmth rushed over me. 'With everything.'

'Sarah says he's distr—'

'Stop!' I held my hand up. 'This is what I'm talking about. No tricks or hints or . . . anything. If you're still in touch with Sarah, that's none of my business.' But it was so hard not asking her to finish that sentence. *What* was Ethan? Distraught? Distressed? Distracted?

'Understood.' Spence nodded, all business. 'No more funny stuff. And if you support me with my book, then I'll support you with yours. Whatever you need, though I promise not to interfere.'

'Really?'

'Of course.' She sounded surprised. 'You mean a lot

to me. I might not always show it in the best way, but it's true. I want you to succeed, but I selfishly want you to do it while still spending time with me.'

I nodded, my nose prickling unexpectedly. 'Course. You are my favourite author, after all. That counts for a lot. Now, do you want another coffee? How many more of these letters are there to do today?'

'We're about quarter of the way through,' she said, then tutted when my mouth fell open. 'I'm lots of other people's favourite author, too. Think yourself lucky you get more access to me than most. It's not something you should be taking for granted. Now, don't forget, I want cream in my coffee because it's Friday. Not plain old milk like you gave me last time.'

I hid my smile as I went into the kitchen. Order was restored, but I felt better equipped to deal with Spence now, my slowly growing confidence like heavy metal beams supporting a splintering wooden foundation, shoring me up and making me stronger.

Chapter Thirty-Three

Now

On Saturday, a week since I'd walked home in the blissful dawn after one of the strangest nights of my life, I woke up before the alarm, immediately alert. I rolled over and saw that it was a little after five a.m., and told myself it was just because I'd moved into Mum's old room at the front of the house – my new mattress would arrive in the next few days – and that I'd taken the heavy green curtains down, so the sun was streaming in. But it was also the day my piece about Sterenlenn was being published in the *Star*, and I was anxious about how it would be received.

I kept myself busy, carrying on with the purging of Old Life I'd started earlier in the week. I got crockery out of cupboards, burrowed through drawers where Mum seemed to have kept every tea towel she'd ever bought, however threadbare. The day was bright with pearly sunshine, and it picked out the dust motes all my reorganizing had kicked up. As I worked, I kept my phone on silent on the other side of the room.

It wasn't until I was wiping the sweat out of my eyes, a whole chest of drawers empty and bags ready for the charity shop and textiles recycling, that I let myself look at it. I had a message from Wynn telling me they were getting good engagement online, and another from Kira saying it was excellent, and that she could read between the lines to the moments when *shenanigans* had gone on. She ended by telling me, again, that I should call Ethan. I even had a separate message from Freddy, promising that this was the start of something big for me. I wondered if Kira had put him up to it.

I hauled the bags into the village, deposited them in their assigned places and then treated myself to an ice cream, scoops of clotted cream and pistachio, and sat on the low wall that separated the bay's car park from the sand. The sky was clear of clouds and the beach was a riot of people, walking and swimming, surfing and sunbathing. Someone walked past holding a copy of the *North Cornwall Star*, rolled up like a makeshift rounders bat. I could hear the waves, a constant in the background, overlaid with the thrum of talking and excited shrieks, and I enjoyed the feeling of being anonymous in such a busy place.

I went through the afternoon on autopilot, and only thought of Ethan about once every two minutes.

Would he see my article as a betrayal, or would he be amused by it? I could find out if I used the number he'd left me, but I didn't.

My life settled into a new kind of normal. I was actively living in the house I'd grown up in, brightening the rooms with pictures I loved and getting rid of clutter I'd only held onto because I thought Mum would want me to keep it. I bought some paint samples and tested them out on the living-room walls. I was thinking of feature walls – of the way Ethan had brought the landscape into Sterenlenn – and tried shades called Boat Shed Blue and Sea Spume Green (actually a nice colour, despite the name).

Wynn asked me to come up with new ideas for the paper, saying that as long as I stuck to the facts where news stories were concerned, I could write more imaginative pieces too. I was flattered, until she told me she was prepared to try anything to get circulation figures up. I decided that she was at least partly joking, and set about making a list of the subjects I wanted to write about.

I was walking back from the local eight-'til-late one July evening when I saw Grace, who had presented me with my quill trophy all those years ago, and who still ran the *Alperwick Papers*.

'Georgie!' She stepped swiftly off the kerb, crossing the road to join me. 'How are you?' She was still slender and statuesque, only the lines fanning out from her eyes and bracketing her mouth giving her age away.

'I'm good, thanks, Grace.' I put my bag on the floor. It had a bottle of wine in it, and the handle was biting into my palm. 'What about you?'

'Oh, chugging on as usual. I read your piece in the paper.' She paused, as if she was waiting for a thank you. I just nodded. 'Did you really get to go inside Alperwick House after all this time?'

'I did.' I didn't add that I'd been inside when I was a teenager, too. 'It was magnificent.'

'It sounds it. And I loved the way you wrote about being trapped. It felt so real.' She laughed.

'It was a bit of whimsy,' I said with a smile, then wondered what Ethan would think if I described our night together like that.

'Well, if you'd like to direct any of your whimsy my way, the *Alperwick Papers* is always looking for stories.'

'You are?'

'Of course.' She sounded slightly disgruntled, as if she hadn't ignored the pitch emails I'd sent her over the last decade. 'You'll find my contact details on the back of the latest edition.' She gave me a brusque nod and stepped past me, her kindness quota exhausted.

'Bye, Grace,' I called, picking up my bag. She was a fierce gatekeeper, so my article must have impressed her. I walked home with a spring in my step, and when I got in, all I wanted to do was open my laptop, where the ideas for my own novel had sprawled into a document over twenty pages long.

That was the other thing that felt entirely new: the sense I had that, if I committed time and energy to my writing, then it had the potential to become something. I had put it off for so long, giving myself a catalogue of plausible excuses, but it had always been about fear – the very real possibility of failure – and I was starting to appreciate that nothing terrible would happen if I tried and it didn't work out. I could just try again.

Now I opened my laptop with a flourish instead of a sense of dread, desperate to spend time with my messy ideas and my half-formed characters, chip away at the sprawl and make it more coherent. I thought about my heroine and hero while I strode across the beach or along the cliff path, when I was sealing and posting Spence's correspondence, or helping her with research for Amelie and Connor's return. I was energised by the thought that I could create something too, and that it might, one day, be as cherished as the Cornish Sands series, or as Sterenlenn would be by its new owners.

I hadn't sought out news about the fate of the house, how quickly it had been snapped up, because those searches would inevitably lead me to Ethan. But, knowing that Sarah and Spence had been behind the Sparks anomalies, I didn't think there would be any problems with the sale. In fact, I expected to hear about removal vans and new arrivals on the village grapevine any day, Barry Mulligan starting off the ripple from his I-spy position on the hill.

I was busy living my new Georgie Monroe life, and while it had felt like I was trying on an uncomfortable dress to start with, as the weeks passed it felt more like it was meant for me, as if this was what I should have been doing all along. I was *living*, in the house and at the paper, working on my own projects, helping Spence, but keeping boundaries between us. I was no longer taking the path of least resistance, and it felt as exhilarating as climbing the steepest part of the cliffs, up to where you got the best views of the bay and village. I had started doing that, too: enjoying all that Cornwall had to offer outside my front door.

I was standing there one afternoon, a couple of days from August, my chest heaving from the walk and Alperwick busy with holidaying families, when I realized I had done all the plotting and procrastinating I could. I had two articles to write for the *Star* the following day, and then on Saturday I would open a new document, type *Chapter One* and begin writing my own book. I raised my arms to the sky, the fresh, clear breeze caressing me, and closed my eyes. Sterenlenn was perched on the cliffs on the opposite side of the bay, and I offered it a silent thank you, and tried not to think about the phone number on a scrap of paper tucked inside my notebook.

When I opened my eyes, it looked like there were people standing in the manicured gardens of the beautiful house. From where I was, they were no bigger than tiny smudges, and they could have been anyone – gardeners trimming the lawn, prospective buyers, a group of teenagers more adventurous than we'd ever been who had scaled the six-foot wall. They wouldn't make it inside now, but the thought of a new generation of friends being drawn to the house made me smile as I started for home, the late afternoon sun heating the back of my neck.

I pushed open my front door, tugged my walking boots off and put them neatly under the coat hooks where a number of jackets now hung, neat and uncrumpled, ready for me to use in a variety of different weathers. I was standing there admiring them, feeling like I might actually be an adult now, when I noticed something gleaming out of the corner of my eye. There was a white envelope on the doormat; I must have kicked it out of the way when I came in.

I picked it up and turned it over, and my brain stuttered. There was my address, in a neat, straight script, but not my name. The letter was addressed to *Amelie Rosevar*, and our lovely postman Alf had covered the rest of the envelope in his biro scrawl: *This you? Been round the houses a bit but it's the right addy! I'll pick it up and return to sender if not!*

But I didn't want him to return it to the sender, because my heart rate was already speeding up and, even though I'd got home sweaty and parched from my walk, a shower and a glass of water were suddenly low on my priority list. I went into the living room, sat on the sofa and slid my fingernail under the flap of the envelope, opening the letter that was addressed to my favourite Cornish Sands heroine, the one I had masqueraded as in my secret letters to Ethan. I took out the sheet of notepaper, unfolded it and laid it on my lap, smoothing my palm over it to flatten it down.

My pulse pounding in my ears and a lump in my throat, I started reading.

Dear Amelie,

I miss you, that's the first thing. I know I already posted my number through your letterbox, and I am certain *that was your house, because I spent time in it when we were together – though part of me hopes I've got it wrong, that I've misremembered it after all this time, and you never got it. Whatever the reason, sending this letter to the same place is the biggest example of hope over experience, but I had to do something.*

I could have emailed you at the Star, *I could have worked out which of my bot-type Instagram followers is you and sent you a DM (why don't you have a proper account? You live in such a beautiful place, and you have a lot to say, and if I could have opened the app and seen a photo of you, it would have made all this easier. Or would it have been harder? I don't know any more). But I didn't think DMs or emails to your work address would cut it, so here I am trying to write you something that will, at the very least, make sense.*

I know why you left. You saw the messages between me and Sarah, and I can understand why you felt like I'd betrayed you. I promise I didn't know that she'd delayed the final update of Sparks – that she was even able to control it manually. She says it wasn't her idea to lock the house down, but she won't tell me who asked her

351

to do it. I think I have a good idea, but it's not something I'm going to pursue on my own.

This is what I want to say to you George. (I can't keep calling you Amelie.)

One, I miss you. I know I've already said that, but I really want to <u>emphasize</u> it. There. I don't think I ever stopped missing you, not after I was forced up to Scotland that summer, not during university or anytime afterwards. I have always had a voice in my head that whispers, 'What would Georgie think of this?' I told you about the panel of investors? That was all true; thinking about you naked, using you to calm me down. We haven't been together, but you've never been far from my thoughts. Now, though, as the house sale goes through (Sparks is working seamlessly, would you believe?) and Sterenlenn is getting a future, it's harder than ever to carry on without you. Our night brought us together again, so then I had to start over, at day one without you, and it's worse than I imagined it would be.

Two, I never meant to hurt you. Not then, when Sarah was in trouble, and not now. I didn't know we were supposed to end up stuck there together. It could easily not have happened, if you'd left before the end of the event, when other guests were still there. I'm guessing Sarah had a plan B if you did, but she didn't have to put it into action. Perhaps she knew you'd be reluctant *to leave, or guessed – correctly – that I'd want you to stay after everyone else had gone. But I'm sorry for not waking you the moment the house was unlocked. You looked peaceful, sleeping next to me, and I selfishly wanted you to myself for a bit longer.*

Three, I don't want this to be it. Everyone says that your first love, especially if you're a teenager, is intense and unrealistic, that it's all hormones and heightened emotions, that it's not meant to last. I don't agree. I didn't before that Friday night, and I'm even less convinced now. What do you think? The fact that you've not been in touch should tell me something, but the truth is: I am not over you, George.

Four, We have a buyer for Sterenlenn, so I'm coming back to Alperwick sometime in the next couple of weeks. I've got new projects and ideas, but nothing is pinned down, and I'm still focused on a perfect corner of the north Cornwall coast. I would love to see you. You have my number, and if you'd like to meet, call or text me, and I'll let you know what date I'm coming.

Five, if I don't see you again, then know that I meant it – what I said in the house. You are everything. Regardless of what happens next – if this really is it for us – I want you to know that.

I love you, Georgie Monroe.

Ethan xx

Chapter Thirty-Four

Now

I was still sitting there, with tears running down my cheeks, when my phone started ringing from the hallway. I wiped my face as I went to get it, and saw that it was Spence. My mind was on Ethan's number, waiting for me in my notebook upstairs, but like he'd said about DMs in his letter, would a phone call be enough right now? It was a two-and-a-half hour drive to Bristol, and if I left now, I could be there before eight. Should I call and ask for his address? Could I—? My phone stopped ringing then started up again immediately. I answered it, only part of my mind on the conversation.

'Hello?'

'Georgie, I – are you crying?'

I sniffed loudly. 'I'm fine. What is it?'

There was a pause, as if she was debating whether to push, then she said, 'There's activity at Sterenlenn.'

I thought of the people-shaped smudges I'd seen from the clifftop. 'Prospective buyers being shown around?'

'I think it's more than that,' she said. 'Actually, Barry Mulligan thinks it's more than that. He says several shiny cars have turned up with tinted windows, the works.'

'Prospective billionaires being shown around?' I went to find a tissue. 'They love all that stuff.'

'*Barry* thinks this might be the new owners.' Spence sounded smug. 'And don't you think, with a property like Sterenlenn, something that costs upwards of seven figures, they would want a personal welcome from the genius behind it?'

I blinked, then ran from the kitchen to the living room, dropped to my knees and picked up Ethan's letter from where I'd left it on the sofa.

'Georgie?' Spence prompted, but I was too busy reading.

We have a buyer for Sterenlenn, so I'm coming back to Alperwick sometime in the next couple of weeks.

'I know you're focusing on other things right now,' Spence was saying, 'but if you *did* want to see Ethan again, to clear the air, then it might be worth a walk up the hill.'

'I've just walked up a big hill,' I murmured, but now I was rereading Alf's scrawl on the envelope: *This you? Been round the houses a bit but it's the right addy.*

'Georgie!' Spence sounded exasperated. 'Are you going to miss out on seeing Ethan because you've hit your step count for the day?'

'I have to go,' I told her, and hung up.

I looked at myself in the mirror. A lot of my hair had been tugged out of its ponytail by the wind, and I was wearing a faded black T-shirt and denim shorts, and definitely looked like I had been up and down a cliff in the hot sun, but I didn't know how much time I had. I also didn't know if either Spence or Barry's information was trustworthy, but I couldn't risk the possibility of missing him.

I was back outside within five minutes. The late afternoon sun was blistering, the sea and sky both breathtakingly blue, and at sea level the wind was almost non-existent. I could hear the rhythmic shush of the waves, the shouts and laughter from families and friends enjoying the bay. Alperwick was at its best, and I felt a squeeze of fondness for the place I hadn't wanted to stay in, but which had comforted me in so many ways.

I strode through the village, retracing the journey I'd taken just over a month ago. Barry Mulligan's house was quiet, and I wondered if he was in his spare bedroom, telescope trained on Sterenlenn, phone open to the village WhatsApp groups. Would I be the only one going up there, or would the rumours encourage other people to come and see what was going on? Would there be security blocking my way?

I cursed, because I had forgotten to take Ethan's number out of my notebook or give him any kind of warning, and now I was over halfway there I couldn't face turning around. I kept going up the hill, jumping when a football thumped in front of me on the pavement, then bounced off down the road.

'Sorry!' a small boy called as he chased after it, and I stood, frozen for a second, as I realized how close it had come to hitting me. I set off again, picking up my pace, a fresh trickle of sweat running down my spine. My breaths puffed out in time with my strides as I ate up the distance, my bare legs brushing the wildflowers that were escaping from the verge.

There was no Aldo waiting for me this time, and the sage green gates were closed. I stopped in front of them, wrapped my hands around the rungs, and looked up the path. There were no cars or people milling about, and the house looked quiet and stately, a shimmering statue, with the first pink-hued clouds of the approaching sunset behind it. The buyers must have already left, or else Barry and Spence had been wrong, and it was gardeners tending to the lawns, like I'd first thought. But Ethan's letter was real, and so was his mobile number, tucked snugly inside my notebook at home.

I took my hands off the gate, already thinking about what I would say when I called him, but my breath hitched because the wide front door was sliding open, a man stepping out into the late afternoon sun. He had on a white shirt, ink blue trousers and a tie the colour of the Atlantic in summer, and his auburn hair was exceptionally, beautifully dishevelled.

I pushed on the gate and it swung inwards, admitting me, as Ethan strode across the wide front step and onto the path, closing the gap between us.

I walked towards him, drinking in the sight: the turquoise sea matched by the endless sky; the gleaming glass framed by soft grey stone; the gabled roof with its built-in skylights, and the glowing LEDs leading up to the wide, inviting entrance. And, just in front of it all was the man who had created it; who, out of everything I could see, had always impressed me the most.

'Hello,' he said, when we were only a few feet apart. He sounded wary, but his brown eyes were warm, and looking directly at me.

'Hi.' I was still slightly breathless from the walk, and now, from being so close to him again. 'You're here.'

'I'm here. You got my letter?'

'Today. Just now.'

He frowned. 'But . . .'

'Alf the postman was confused that it wasn't addressed to me.' I couldn't help smiling. 'He went searching for an Amelie Rosevar in the village before giving up and posting it through my door.'

Ethan stared at me in consternation, then he groaned, his head tipping back. 'I thought the postcode was all that mattered. I checked I'd got the right address so many times.'

I shrugged. 'Alf knows me.'

'Fuck.' He looked at me again, his gaze intense. 'But you came. I thought, after I'd left you my number and I didn't hear from you . . .'

I ran my hands down the front of my shorts. I had so much to say, I didn't know where to start. 'Can we sit?' I gestured to the step. 'Unless – are the new owners in there?'

'No, they left a while ago. They're moving in after the summer, but they wanted another look, to measure up the spaces, plan some changes to the layout.'

'They're not keeping it all as it is?' I couldn't see how the house could be improved on, and was disappointed on Ethan's behalf.

'Everyone has different tastes,' he said easily. 'It's going to be theirs, so they want it to be perfect for them. They're keeping the sofas in the lounge, and the beer and wine fridges – of course.'

'Of course.' We exchanged a smile. 'Do you like them? The new owners?'

He nodded. 'The woman is CEO of a multinational company, and from what I can gather her husband is a stay-at-home dad, and a keen fisherman. I can't tell you their names, but they have five children. It's a big, sprawling family.'

'Like the Rosevars.'

'Like the Rosevars. We can go inside, if you like?'

I eyed the front door, and my throat tightened. 'It's a lovely evening. How about we sit on the step?'

'Sure.' He held out his hand, as if guiding me. I

didn't think he intended to touch me, but his fingertips brushed the cotton of my T-shirt, and I had to resist the urge to lean into him.

We sat down, our bodies angled towards each other. Beyond Ethan I could see the manicured lawn, the redbrick wall and the cliffs on the opposite side of the bay. I couldn't believe I'd been standing there only a couple of hours earlier. I focused on Ethan, who was staring at where his hands were clasped tightly in his lap.

'I'm sorry I didn't call you when you left me your number,' I said, and he looked up. 'That night was so . . . it changed everything for me. I was angry with you, and Sarah, but only at first. I know you had nothing to do with what happened, and that she wasn't really behind it, either.'

'Spence?' Ethan asked.

I nodded. 'We were her new love story, apparently. She wanted to get us back together.'

'Shit. I thought that was it, from what little Sarah told me, but there was no way I could prove it.'

'She admitted it,' I said. 'She was proud of it, even. But I've told her she needs to focus on her fictional characters, not turn her friends into puppets. And I was wrong, about Sarah. Especially back then.'

Ethan let out a slow breath, but he didn't interrupt me.

'Looking after her was the right thing to do, and I guess I was just . . .' I tried to think of the best way to put it. I had done a lot of thinking over the last few weeks. 'I was angry because you were *doing* something. You were trying to help her, and I wasn't.'

'What do you mean?'

'I wasn't helping Mum. I was afraid to confront her, because I didn't want to upset our relationship or make my escape to university less likely. I should have told her what I was worried about, not buried my head in the sand.'

'Georgie.' He put his hand on my knee, and my skin tingled at the contact.

'Sarah got enough tough love from your parents, and you knew that she needed affection and encouragement, not the opposite. I didn't get that until recently. And I know that what Sarah and Spence did was wrong, especially because it made you think Sterenlenn was compromised, but—'

'Sarah's shown me exactly how she did it, and now it's out of Beta it can't be operated manually. She's too clever for her own good, but she's assured me everything with Sparks will be above board from now on.'

'I'm glad,' I said. 'But it wasn't just Sarah or the messages that stopped me from calling you. It was because I needed to sort myself out. I realized that I'd pinned all my dissatisfactions – my lack of ambition and progress – on losing you, which is a big enough burden for anyone to have.'

'You know I would have—'

'I know,' I cut in softly, and covered his hand with mine. 'But I wanted to be certain that I could do it all without you, first. I wanted to know you again, but I didn't want to rely on you.'

Ethan turned his hand over under mine and wrapped his thumb around my little finger. 'So, your book?'

It wasn't the first thing I'd expected him to ask about. 'I've planned it all out,' I said, the smile bunching my cheeks. 'I know what I'm writing, and I'm ready to start.'

'That's the best news I've heard in weeks.' He reached out to touch the tendrils of hair straggling on either side of my face.

'They're sweaty,' I warned him. 'I was on the cliff path before I got home and found your letter.'

'I don't care.' He slid his fingers into my hair.

'Ethan!' I leant away from him, but he moved his hand to the back of my head and held it there, so I had no option but to look into his eyes.

'You're writing your book,' he said. 'What else?'

'I'm not writing Spence's. I've said I'll help with research and my usual admin, but nothing else. And she's promised me that when I've finished mine, she'll give me some contacts and help with what comes next, if I want to get it published.'

'Good,' Ethan murmured. 'That's the least she can do. What else?'

'Mum's house is mine for as long as I want it. And I do want my own place, but it's good to know the pressure's off, and I can think of it as home for now.'

His expression softened, his little finger rubbing circles at my nape. 'What else?'

362

I chewed my lip. 'You know what else,' I said softly.

He frowned, and I realized he was teasing me. 'Oh, you mean your piece on Sterenlenn? Where you *imagined* being trapped inside?'

'Did you mind?'

His eyes kindled: Ethan Sparks firing back to life. 'Did I mind reading it on the verge of a heart attack, wondering how much detail you'd go into about what your characters got up to in the writing room?' He raised an eyebrow and I laughed, my cheeks heating at the memory. 'Did I mind that your article led to Sterenlenn's eventual new owners getting in touch with Sarah, asking for a tour?'

'They did *not*.'

He nodded. 'I didn't mind *entirely* when I was contacted by three escape room companies who wanted to know if entertainment spaces were part of my portfolio.'

'Ethan!' I laughed.

'I'm serious. About all of it. I loved every word, but I've been living on the edge of sanity ever since, jumping whenever my phone made a noise, wondering if it would be you.'

'I'm sorry.' I looked at my knees. 'I just had to do those things, for me.'

'I understand,' he said, though he was sounding less certain. 'And now?'

I looked up. 'Now, I'm ready.'

'Ready?' He toyed with the hair falling down my back, his gaze fixed on me. The space between us was a bubble holding our past, all the things we'd left unsaid.

'I've missed you, Ethan,' I whispered, and the bubble broke.

He leaned in, cupping my face, his thumb brushing my cheek. 'I regret every single thing I have done and said that has stopped me from being with you.' Every touch was a tiny tremor, as if my pores and nerve endings were rejoicing at having his skin against mine.

'You can't,' I said. 'Look at the house – look what you've achieved.'

He stared at me with a sort of wonder, as if he couldn't quite believe I was there. 'I would have done this regardless,' he said. 'I would have loved more of it, let myself enjoy it more if I'd had you with me.'

I nodded, unable to speak, because that was how I felt about every day of my life since he'd walked out of it. 'The writing room wouldn't have been a surprise if I'd been on site with you.'

He gave a brief shake of his head, but he was smiling now. 'You wouldn't have been on site with me every day. You've seen *Grand Designs* – the way those couples argue. Sterenlenn wasn't ever mine, but I was still completely invested in it, and I know you would have been too. The pressure's intense.'

'I can only imagine,' I said, as he brushed his lips across my forehead. 'I have so many feelings about this place, and it belongs to someone else.'

'We had a memorable twelve hours in it, though.'

'Christened it, in a way, for the new Rosevar family.'

'Made sure the disco shower really delivers.'

'"Whatever It Takes,"' I said, and he groaned and pressed his head into my neck, his hot breath puffing against my collarbone as he laughed. I decided there was nothing I loved more than Ethan's laugh, than him finding refuge in me. 'So what *does* it take?' I asked, knowing we couldn't stay like this, wondering how the suspended time of being locked in Sterenlenn together could translate to a future for us.

He pulled back to look at me. 'There's nothing tying me or Sparks to Bristol, and I've always loved Cornwall more than anywhere else.'

My heart missed a beat. 'Seriously? Just like that?'

'I've been working through a few things over the last month, too. You remember that abandoned shop on the corner of the seafront parade?'

'The old watchmaker's. The glass is like—'

'Picture glass,' he finished. 'It's got all the original features, and a good-sized flat upstairs.'

'You know this because . . .?'

'I'm buying it,' he finished. 'I'm moving the firm here – part of it, anyway. Sarah and the technical team can stay in Bristol, but it doesn't hurt to expand, and I won't be that far away. The watchmaker's needs a lot of work, but at the end I'll have a new office with living space above.'

'Ethan.' My throat was fully clogged up. 'When you say you're buying it . . .'

'My offer has been accepted, I just need to sign the paperwork. But I didn't want to come back here, be

365

minutes away from you if you didn't want to see me; if it would feel like unwanted pressure when you were trying to move on. If that's the case, George, then I will stay in Bristol, but—'

I leaned in and kissed the words off his lips. Our knees knocked together, the position awkward but the kiss perfect, because it was Ethan, and there was nobody else.

'You're moving here,' I said, when I'd forced myself to put a couple of inches of space between us.

'I can run my business from anywhere. There's a whole lot of real estate being bought up in Cornwall because people want secluded seaside mansions, so it's ideal, really – there'll be so many new projects. And most importantly . . .'

'What?' I frowned.

'That was a lot of talking. Can I kiss you again?'

'What's *most importantly*?' But I let him kiss me again, and by the end of it I was quite proud that I hadn't crawled onto his lap. I glanced at the empty house, thinking of all the furniture being shipped out to make way for the owners' new things, that huge bed that we already knew was so comfortable.

'Most importantly,' he said breathlessly, 'if you *do* want me here—'

'I think I've just proved that I do. Do you need me to tell you that I love you? That I've never, ever stopped loving you, and that of course I want you here?'

'I . . .' He swallowed. 'Right. Then, *most importantly*, I'll also need to be here for my other role.'

'There's something *else* you're doing?'

'*Going* to be doing.' He ran his thumb along my jawline, as if he couldn't stop touching me. My hands were at his waist, itching to get under his shirt and feel his warm stomach, so I was in much the same predicament.

'What's that, then?'

He smiled at me. 'Supporting my girlfriend while she writes her first book – a future bestseller – reminding her constantly how talented she is, and occasionally bringing her breakfast in bed after I've shown her, thoroughly, how completely in love with her I am, that I always have been and always will be.'

My heart skittered. '*Occasionally* bringing me breakfast in bed?'

Ethan grinned. 'That's the part you're taking from my heartfelt speech? Are you, Georgie Monroe, determined to make a joke out of this?'

'I don't know,' I murmured. 'It depends how long I have to wait for another kiss.'

Our noses were inches apart, and I knew I had the same look of delirious elation on my face that he did. He'd waited for me, he'd never stopped loving me, and now he was uprooting his whole life to be with me. I already knew I would do as much as I could to match his commitment: whatever it took.

'Not very long,' he said, 'but you have to give me a couple of seconds.'

'Why?' I asked, joy bubbling up inside me.

'Because it's going to take a while to get used to this

future. One filled with – what was it? – happiness and hope, living the life I always wanted?'

'You memorized my letters,' I said, as he wrapped his arms around me, scooping me onto his lap. Sterenlenn watched on silently – for once – and I hoped it approved of the decisions we'd finally got around to making.

'Of course I memorized them,' he said. 'They were you, George. They were my way back to you.'

I kissed Ethan on the front step where, only a few weeks ago, I'd been standing, preparing myself for one of the most difficult nights of my life.

But I had got into the house, I'd done what Spence had asked me to do, and I had found what I was looking for – though it hadn't been some divine inspiration to help her write her book, or a bundle of letters written using her characters' names. I'd found something much more important than either of those.

As Ethan and I kissed until neither of us had any breath left, and his hand found its way under my T-shirt, his warm palm pressing into my lower back so he could get me even closer, and the sun dropped lazily towards the horizon, content at having provided Alperwick with another perfect day, I sent a silent thank you to Tyller Klos – Sterenlenn – for being there, and for knowing that this was always how it was supposed to go: Georgie Monroe and Ethan Sparks, and our very own Cornish love story.

The End

Acknowledgements

A *Cornish Love Story* was a book of two halves. I wrote the first draft in a giddy, frantic four-week sprint, obsessed with my characters and the story and so excited about what it could become. And then, when it got to the editing stage, my real life got tough and this book was an escape but also a challenge when my focus was limited, and so . . .

I say this every time, but this book really couldn't have happened without all the help and dedication of so many people.

Thank you to Kate Bradley, who has not just been the kindest, most insightful editor, but such a good friend, giving me so much support and encouragement, and space when I needed it.

Thank you to my wonderful agent Alice Lutyens, who has been a rock for me, as well as a sharp and brilliant agent who I feel endlessly lucky to have. Thank you to the whole Curtis Brown team, for all their support of me and my books, including Rakhi Kholi and rights agent Emma Jamison.

The HarperFiction team are the absolute best, and I am so grateful for everything they do to get my books out to readers. Thank you especially to Lynne Drew, Frankie Gray, Susanna Peden, Sian Richefond, Jo Kite, Holly Martin and Katelyn Wood.

Thank you to Penelope Isaac, my copy editor, and Kati Nicholl for proof reading. My books are so much sharper and shinier because of their invaluable input, and I am always amazed by their ability to spot the tiniest mistake amongst so many words.

Thank you to designer Emily Langford and illustrator Camila Gray for the actual cover of dreams. I don't think I could love it more, and I get a thrill every time I look at it. Who wouldn't want to stroll along that path by the sea, under such a beautiful sky?

I have had so much support from wonderful writing friends over the last few months, for book and life related things, and I don't know what I would have done without them. The biggest thanks to Kirsty Greenwood, Sarra Manning, Jane Casey, Pernille Hughes, Sam Holland, Katie Marsh and Rachel Burton.

I feel like I'm running out of ways to thank David for being the best, kindest and most supportive husband. David, THANK YOU. You know how lucky I am to have you.

I have had so much encouragement and insight from my mum and dad over the years. They always responded to my book news – story ideas, new covers, sales figures – with enthusiasm, and they were so keen to talk to me about Georgie and Ethan while I was planning and writing this book. Thank you to my incredible, irreplaceable Mum and Dad. I know you're not here anymore, but I'm still going to tell you about future books, and I know I'll always have your love, all the things you taught me, and your belief in me, to keep me going. Thank you also to my brother Lee, for all the hugs and support.

I have to reserve my final thank you to you – readers, bloggers, booksellers and librarians – who pick up my books and shout about them, share reviews and love for them online, and with friends and customers. My books would be nothing without readers, and I know this one is a little different to some of my others, so I really hope you love Georgie and Ethan and their complicated love story as much as I do.

Fern Britton Picks
Exclusively for
TESCO

EXCLUSIVE ADDITIONAL CONTENT
Includes an author Q&A and details
of how to get involved in *Fern's Picks*

Dear lovely readers,

This month, prepare to be whisked away to sunny Cornwall in Cressida McLaughlin's heartwarming romance, *A Cornish Love Story*. Full of Cornish charm and characters you'll fall in love with, it's the perfect book to take with you on holiday this summer.

Georgie Monroe dreams of writing a novel, following in her favourite author's footsteps, and in the meantime, works as a journalist covering local events. But when a story she's writing about a newly renovated Cornish home leads to an encounter with an old flame, Ethan Sparks, Georgie realises that not all is as it seems. As they spend time with each other, their complex past starts to unravel. Like the transformed home, can Georgie and Ethan strengthen their fragile foundation – and write the next chapter of their love story in the process?

Set in a gorgeous seaside location, with characters who will stay in your heart, *A Cornish Love Story* is the perfect escapist summer read! It's uplifting and romantic, and I can't wait to hear what you think.

With love
Femi x

Look out for more books, coming soon!

For more information on the book club,
exclusive Q&As with the authors and
reading group questions, visit Fern's website
www.fern-britton.com/ferns-picks

We'd love you to join in the conversation,
so don't forget to share your thoughts using
#FernsPicks

A Q&A with
Cressida McLaughlin

Warning: contains spoilers

A Cornish Love Story is your seventeenth novel, and in total, your books have sold over a million copies worldwide! How did your writing journey start?

I have always loved books and reading, but I didn't want to be a writer until my mid-twenties. I was working for Norfolk Adult Education and was given the opportunity to do a term of a course for free and, because I loved reading, I chose creative writing. After only a few sessions of writing poems and short stories, and sharing them with the group, I was hooked. I went on to do a whole year of the course, and at the end I decided, very naively, that I was going to write a novel and get it published. It took roughly six years, and hundreds of rejection letters, before I got my first book deal, but all the hard work and perseverance has paid off because I can't imagine loving anything as much as I love being a writer.

How do you decide which stories are the ones you want to tell? Do your fans ever send you any ideas for your plotlines?

The stories I want to tell come to me in different ways. Sometimes a character pops into my head and won't leave me alone, sometimes I'm inspired by a location, and sometimes it's a situation I'm desperate to explore – what if two people who loved each other as teenagers but parted acrimoniously got trapped in a misbehaving Smart House for a night? Fans do send me ideas, especially for my series books, because they love certain characters or couples and want something specific to happen to them. Sometimes they're great ideas!

Millions of people have read and fallen in love with your novels. How do you connect with your readers?

Aside from connecting with them through my stories, I love being in touch with readers via social media. Instagram is where I'm happiest, and I don't want to spread myself too thinly (and am bamboozled by TikTok) so I focus on that and Facebook. It's great because it means I can connect with readers anywhere in the world, but also, I love in-person events. I've been lucky enough to do a lot of those over the last few years, in places as varied as Cornwall, London, Wales and Leeds, and I've done panels and solo events and quizzes. There's nothing better than meeting readers and talking to them about my stories and our mutual love of books.

Alongside great characters, the locations of your novels lay a gorgeous foundation for your storytelling. Do you prefer writing about Cornwall or other places? Do you spend a lot of time thinking about the next destination(s) in your upcoming novels?

Settings are so important in my books, I spend a lot of time thinking about the perfect location for the story I want to tell. Often, the place feels like a character in its own right. I love writing about Cornwall, and also Norfolk, which is where I've lived for the last twenty-five years. Sweeping coastlines, beautiful countryside and quaint villages are perfect settings for the stories I want to tell. But I've really enjoyed setting books in London too, specifically the areas I grew up in. I love that I can charm readers with a fictional village that they wish was real, or put my characters into a setting they recognise, that they've visited or that holds happy memories for them.

You've written many different books over the years. What do you like about writing series versus standalones?

There is something so comforting about returning to a familiar setting and characters I already know. I love that with my series books, I can introduce people who might play a small role in one book, then get to be the star in the next. I can explore more of the village or town, and get to see what happens to couples over a longer period – and I know that readers love that too. With a standalone, it's a different kind of excitement – I just have one book to tell this couple's story, and I can be bold and experiment with new things. I'm so glad I get to write both, to constantly challenge myself as a writer and bring my readers new delights.

Will you ever go back to the Cornish Cream Tea series?

I would never say never! I loved writing that series. I have a huge fondness for all the characters and the beautiful location, and often wonder how everyone is getting on. I've moved onto other things now, but I can't imagine *never* going back and, if you loved Charlie and Daniel and their beautiful café bus, you might notice a little Cornish Cream Tea Easter egg in *A Cornish Love Story*.

Who have been your favourite characters from your books, and why?

This is one of the hardest questions! I love all my characters, and am usually obsessed with the ones I'm spending time with, but there are some who stand out. There's Charlie and Daniel, from *The Cornish Cream Tea Bus*, because I had such fun writing their love story, and because they've appeared in quite a few of my books now. I also really love Sophie and Harry from *The Secret Christmas Bookshop*. They're slightly older than a lot of my couples, and I felt like there was something really special about them. And Felix, my cuddly tearaway goat. He holds a very special place in my heart, and in lots of my readers' hearts too, judging by all the messages I've had about him.

Which love stories have inspired you as an author?

Oh, so many! I am constantly inspired by other love stories, and have so many romance authors on my auto-buy list. There are two specific stories that inspired me to want to write romance books when, in my early twenties, I was mostly reading crime. The first is *A Hopeless Romantic* by Harriet Evans, which is set between Norfolk and London, has the most loveable heroine and hero, and a love story that felt so real and messy, and was achingly romantic. The second is *Twenties Girl* by Sophie Kinsella, which made me laugh out loud and sob uncontrollably. It has a mystery at its centre and a ghost, as well as a hot American hero. Both those books made me want to write love stories – I wanted to make people feel the way those books made me feel; I wanted to make readers *that* happy.

Do you ever feel like writing something completely different to what you've done before?

I would love to write a ghost story. I'm fascinated by all things paranormal, and readers might notice that I often slip a few spooky things into my books. I would really love to write a sinister, terrifying ghost story one day, though I have realised there would also have to be a romance in it – but not a ghostly romance! A spine-tingling haunting with a real-world romance in it. I can't ever see myself writing a book that doesn't have a happy ending for my main characters.

What can we expect next from Cressida McLaughlin?

I'm just about to go back to Mistingham in North Norfolk and write another Christmassy, magical story for the Secret Bookshop series. I'm looking forward to revisiting those characters, the windswept beach and the fish and chip shop, and giving two new people their happy every after. After that's done, well . . . I have so many ideas, and I can't wait to turn them into uplifting, romantic love stories.

Questions for your Book Club

Warning: contains spoilers

- *A Cornish Love Story* takes place in stunning Cornwall. How important was the setting of the novel to the storyline? Did it influence the characters and/or the plot in any ways?

- A beautiful old Cornish home's transformation sets the stage for Georgie and Ethan's present-day story. Would you rather live in a classic older house, like Tyller Klos, or in a modern, high-tech one? Why?

- What was your initial impression of both Georgie and Ethan? Did this change as the story went on, especially in light of the novel's flashbacks?

- Which part(s) of Georgie and Ethan's story did you find the most moving, and why?

- Which character's actions had the most significant impact on the storyline? How so?

- Connor and Amelie's letters are scattered throughout the novel. What do you think these add to the storyline, and to the emotion behind Georgie and Ethan's own love story?

- Which character did you relate to the most, and why?

- What was your favourite quote or scene from the story? What feelings did it spark in you as you read?

An exclusive extract from Fern's new novel

A Cornish Legacy

CHAPTER ONE

North Cornwall, April, present day

Delia squinted through the windscreen, the sun ahead dazzling her. 'You'll see the turning on the right in a minute,' she said. 'Keep an eye out. I might miss it.'

Sammi tipped the last of the crisps into his mouth and sat up a little straighter. 'My eyes are peeled.' He pulled the sunglasses down from his head. 'Will there be some kind of landmark?'

'There's a big metal sign swinging on a post above the gates. Remember? You said it looked like a gibbet.'

Sammi chuckled. 'The gibbet! Yes, of course! Such a welcome.' He sat up straighter, alert. 'There!'

Delia saw the emerging gap amongst the tangled hedge of rhododendrons, with the rusted sign hanging from the post.

'Is that it?' asked Sammi. 'Can't read the name.'

Delia slowed, changing down through the gears. She wasn't smiling. 'Yep. This is it. Wilder Hoo.' The sight of the tatty sign that she had never wanted or expected to see again forced her stomach into a tight knot. Turning, she slowed the car and braked to a halt. 'I really don't want to be here.'

Sammi reached over for her knee and tapped it briskly. 'You're not on your own. I'm here, and those horrible people are gone. Come on.'

Delia put a hand to her chest and took a deep breath to control the old anxiety welling within. 'It's quite late. Let's go and find somewhere to stay tonight and come back tomorrow.'

'It's only half past four!'

'But it'll be getting dark soon.'

'Darling, it's April, not December.' Sammi's voice became soft and sympathetic. 'I know this is hard. But you can do it, and you will do it.'

'I don't want to do it.'

'The past is past. Dead and buried.'

Sighing heavily, Delia put the car in gear and slowly drove the winding tarmacked drive. 'Dead people can still haunt us.'

Stiff clumps of grass and dandelions had forced themselves between the cracked pitch, and in other places, huge potholes housed red, muddied puddles.

'It'll cost thousands just to repair the drive,' she said. 'Look at it.'

She knew that Sammi saw through different eyes. For him, this was an adventure. When Delia had first told him that the house had been gifted to her, he had been ready to celebrate, despite her horror of the whole thing. He seemed to feel only the thrill of an escapade.

Looking out of his side window at the ancient, rolling parkland with great oaks dotted across the scene he said, 'Delia, this is utterly captivating. Please tell me there's a lake. I'm expecting Colin Firth to stride forth in his wet breeches and shirt.'

Delia was scornful. 'If only. No lake, I'm afraid. Just a beach and all these acres of parkland. Do you know, it takes four men with a tractor each an entire week to cut all that grass? When they get to the end, they have to start again. It's a bloody money pit.' Her eyes flicked to the avenue of ivy-clad beech trees ahead, the bare branches forming a tunnel over sodden leaves. 'That ivy needs cutting back too. Argh. Who can afford all this, I ask you!'

Sammi was not listening. 'How long is this drive again?'

'It's 1.2 miles.'

'Very specific.'

Delia sighed. 'My father-in-law preferred to tell everyone it was two kilometres because that sounded longer.'

'And all this land belongs to the house?'

'Yup.'

Sammi was grinning. 'I'd love to jump on a tractor and spend a whole summer mowing all this.'

'You really wouldn't. Back in the day, there were sheep and deer to crop it.'

'Sheep and deer! Delia.' Sammi laughed. 'And all this is actually yours!'

She shrugged. She was weary and wretched. 'Not for long, I hope.'

They rattled over a cattle grid and onto a sparsely gravelled drive.

'OK. Here we go.' Delia swallowed hard. 'Round this bend, you'll see the house.' She took a nervous breath and added, 'I couldn't do this without you.'

Sammi tutted, 'I wouldn't let you come on your own, would I?'

Delia steered the last curve – and there, suddenly, was Wilder Hoo.

Available now!

The No.1 Sunday Times bestselling author returns

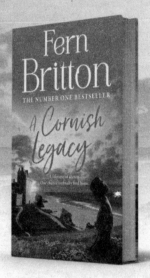

A lifetime of secrets. One chance to finally find home.

Cordelia Jago has lost everything. All she has left is a legacy she never expected – and would never have wanted.

Wilder Hoo – The Wild House – is a crumbling Cornish Manor House which she hates, full of unhappy memories. It is falling down to the brink of ruin.

Determined to sell-up and forget the past, Cordelia begins to spruce up its echoing rooms – but the house seems to exert a pull on her and awakens a connection she thought she had buried forever.

With the help of the locals, Cordelia breathes new life into the home, but will she find a way to heal her heart too?

Cosy up with more delightful stories

rom Cressida McLaughlin

All available now.

Discover Cressida's brand-new seasonal series set in the beautiful seaside village of Mistingham. *The Secret Christmas Bookshop* is out now, and *The Secret Mistletoe Promise* is coming in November 2025 . . .